TREY

A REBELS HAVOC

BOOK THREE

USA TODAY BESTSELLING AUTHOR

BROOKE O'BRIEN

TREY

***USA Today* Bestselling author Brooke O'Brien delivers a whirlwind rock star romance about the newest bad boy of A Rebels Havoc and the good girl virgin who brings him to his knees.**

Trey Whitt is no stranger to the rock 'n' roll life.

New city every night, and a new fling in his bed. He could have any woman he wanted, but he set his sights on me.

After joining A Rebels Havoc, Trey's not ready for what comes along with his sudden rise to fame. He certainly never could've prepared for all his dirty secrets and sex life to be dragged through the headlines.

For all my life, I've never been the one who gets chosen, the one all the men desired. I've spent the past twenty-two years holding on to my innocence. So when I catch Trey watching me from across the nightclub, I decide he's the one I want to claim it.

I know better than to think anything more could come from hooking up with a rock star. During my walk of shame the following morning, I'm forced to face reality when he calls me by the wrong name.

No matter how hard it is to forget our night together, I'm determined to put him and his dirty mouth behind me. Only neither of us is ready for the turn our life takes, bringing us back together again.

Secrets, lies, and rumors—each of them could destroy his career and tear us apart.

Yet there's one secret from our past neither of us saw coming, and when Trey finds out, it could ruin everything we have between us.

Forever.

Thank you for reading **TREY**! I hope you love Trey and Layken's story as much as I do.

You can join my Facebook group, Brooke O'Brien's Rebel Readers Group, to discuss the series and get sneak peeks on future releases. Sign up for my newsletter to find out more about my new releases. To join, visit: www.authorbrookeobrien.com/followbrooke

Happy reading!

A REBELS HAVOC SERIES
READING ORDER

BRIX

a stepbrother, enemies to lovers, rock star romance

SINS OF A REBEL

a summer fling, brother's best friend, rock star romance

TYSIN

a brother's best friend, forced proximity, rock star romance

TREY

a surprise pregnancy, virgin heroine, rock star romance

MADDEN

a frenemies to lovers, journalist/rock star romance

DEDICATION

To anyone holding out on love, waiting for the one who makes you feel chosen.

Always remember your worth.

PROLOGUE

TREY
FOURTEEN YEARS OLD

"Where have you been? I've been waiting up all night for you. Can't you have the decency to call?"

The familiar sound of cabinets slamming jerk me awake. I force myself to breathe slowly, my ears straining for any other subtle sound.

This isn't the first time my parents have woken me up this week. My mom is convinced my dad is messing around on her, and it's become an endless cycle of arguing over his comings and goings.

I fist my sheets and pull them away, taking a deep breath, attempting to slow my racing heart.

"I didn't tell you to wait up for me. Dammit, woman, give me some fuckin' space and go to bed," he grunts.

"I'm sick of this, Tim. You get home at all hours of the night. You've been sneakin' off, actin' like I don't know what you're doin' or where you're at. I know, Tim." Her voice breaks. "I know it's her, okay? You think I don't know you've been slinking around with Jo? A woman always knows when there's someone else. It's her, isn't it?"

A knot twists in my gut, and I curl my lip into a snarl, shaking my head. She's not wrong. Even if he won't admit it, I've suspected it for a long time myself.

It all started when her cocky fucker of a son started making jokes at school about him seeing my dad around his place.

The fucker knows my dad's married, yet he gets off on digging under my skin about it. He struts around in his name-brand clothes and perfectly gelled hair with girls hanging off his arm. He thinks his shit doesn't stink, and I do everything I can to stay away from the likes of him.

I keep my earbuds in, my head down, and go through the motions of every day until I can escape this hellhole of a town.

There's another loud slam, and I picture him walking away from her, like he always does. He does this to her. He disappears, then gets her upset and refuses to give her any answers.

He's driving her crazy and doesn't seem to give a shit how she feels.

"Well, I went snoopin' through your stuff and—"

"YOU DID WHAT?" he roars.

I swing my legs over the side of my bed and tiptoe down the hall toward the staircase, peeking over the balcony into our living area. Their shadows move around the dining room as my father's boot-covered feet pace back and forth, intermixed with her low sobs.

My anxiety is getting the best of me lately. Their constant fighting only seems to get worse each day, and I can hardly manage to get to sleep before I'm woken up by another round of chaos.

I'm constantly on high alert, waiting for when shit hits the fan and I need to race downstairs to protect my mom.

How sad is it that I'm protecting her from my own father?

Tomorrow, she'll go back to pretending everything is okay and it's all a big misunderstanding as if I don't see through her fake reassuring voice.

I'm not stupid.

Nothing about our home life is okay, and it hasn't been for a long time.

"Tim," she sobs.

Her voice cracks through the pain. There's a loud squeal followed by a subsequent bang, jolting me where I stand. I clench my hand into a fist, waiting for any sign she may need me, trying to inhale slowly through each strangled breath.

"Please. I'll let it go," she begs. "I don't want Trey to wake up again."

Too late.

"You should've thought about that before you started in on me the second I walked through the fuckin' door."

Some days, I wish he'd admit to the affair so they could go their separate ways. They haven't been happy in a long time, and quite frankly, I'm tired of living like this.

"I'm sorry," she murmurs. Shaking my head, I take a step away from the railing and turn toward my room.

I slip back into bed unnoticed and pull my sheets up to my chest, closing my eyes in hopes that sleep will quickly pull me under. Footsteps creak outside my room before the light in the hallway flips on. I make out the sound of my father's footsteps pass by my room before slamming his office door shut behind him.

It's another night of him sleeping on the pull-out sofa.

A few minutes pass and my heart rate returns to normal when my door cracks open, and my mom's short silhouette appears in the doorway.

"Everything okay?" I whisper.

She sighs. "I was hopin' you were sleepin', Son," she mumbles. "Everything is all right. You can get some rest. I'm about to crawl into bed myself."

We both know everything is far from being all right. She's trying to be strong for me, but the unmistakable trembling in her voice gives her away.

"If you need anything, I'll be here."

She brushes away another tear and exhales softly before she nods.

"I'll be okay, sweetie. I love you. Get some rest," she says, closing the door behind her.

I roll over onto my back and stare at the blades of the ceiling fan as they spin around above me.

I can't wait for the day when I can get out of here. The place where I grew up and fell in love with music no longer feels like home to me.

When sleep eventually pulls me under, I dream of the day when I pack up my guitar and leave without looking in the rear view. I don't care where I end up, as long as it's far away, and I don't have to deal with this shit anymore.

My mom stands over the stove the following morning when I race down the stairs. It's after seven, and I needed to be out the door five minutes ago if I didn't want to haul ass to the bus stop.

My dad's office door is open, and the house is eerily quiet. He must've taken off before the sun came up. I can't say I'm surprised.

"I made you some pancakes if you want some."

"I needed to be out the door already," I grumble. "Thanks anyway, Mom."

I slip past her and grab a package of Pop-Tarts from the cabinet.

"I'm gonna be late if I don't hurry."

She turns to look at me, and for the first time, I catch a glimpse of the bruise forming under her eye where her cheek is starting to swell. My hand tightens, crushing the pastry into my fist.

"Is that from last night?" I grit out.

"It's nothing, sweetheart. I accidentally smacked myself in the face with the cabinet. You know how I can be." She tries to laugh and winces. "I wasn't watching where I was goin' like normal."

I nod slowly, not believing a word she says.

"It doesn't hurt. Honest to goodness, it looks worse than it is. I promise." She tries to reassure me, but it's hard to believe her. She'll say or do anything to get me to believe there's nothing to worry about, not realizing I see through every word.

"I'll see you after school, Mom." I lean in and press a kiss to her puffy cheek.

She reaches her hand out and squeezes my forearm. Tears prick her eyes again, but she does her best to blink them away.

I take off out the door and down the three blocks to the bus stop. My father is lucky he took off already, or the anger pumping through me would've had me landing a few blows of my own to his face.

One for every time he's hurt her.

My feet pound against the pavement, and my chest burns from the cold winter air hitting my lungs, making it harder for me to breathe.

The bus stops near the corner, and I frantically wave my hand, trying to get the driver's attention. Thankfully, he sees me and waits.

He tends to keep a look out for me. Guess you could say this is another one of those things that have happened often lately.

I quickly climb the stairs and collapse into the first empty seat. I shrug my backpack off my shoulder and slide it onto the floor between my legs.

"You okay?" a soft voice whispers. Her eyes are fixed on the crushed Pop-Tarts still in my hand before she flicks her gaze to meet mine.

She clutches a book in her hand, pushing it to hide behind her bag. She tucks a strand of hair behind her ear, chewing on her lip, and looks away.

I've seen her on the bus before and around school, but I've never caught her name. Any time we've passed in the hallway, she ducks her head and scurries off to class or in the opposite direction.

Her eye makeup is heavy behind her black-frame glasses, and her bangs swoop over her forehead in an attempt to cover her face. Her soft voice is calming, and it dawns on me she's asked me a question before I slowly nod my head.

"I'm okay," I say.

I quickly bend down to shove my destroyed pastries into my bag before grabbing my phone and earbuds. I keep my face forward, counting down the seconds until we get to school.

I'm going through the motions. The sooner I get to class, the quicker I get this day over with.

I don't realize my leg is bouncing on the floor until her warm hand reaches out and rests on my knee to stop me. I glance down, staring at her pale skin, and peer over at her.

She nervously tugs on her sleeve past her knuckles, and I realize she's not wearing a coat. It's surprising, considering the temperatures in Nashville are below freezing, although thankfully, there's no snow on the ground yet.

I pull my earbud out and look at her.

"Promise me somethin', will ya?" she asks.

"Shoot." I nod, entertaining wherever this is going.

She hesitates for a moment and looks out the frost-covered windows before she continues, "Promise me if you ever feel like you're not okay, you'll tell someone."

Her eyes find mine again, and she must read the confusion on my face.

"It's okay not to be okay all the time."

I nod, understanding the significance behind her comment. My mom has been saying she's okay for a long time when we both know it's a lie.

I swallow hard before putting in the other earbud and turning up the music until the sound drowns out every torturous thought swirling through my mind.

She couldn't possibly understand the shit I'm dealing with, and I'm not about to put it on her either.

CHAPTER ONE

TREY

I think I've died and gone to heaven.

If I have a choice in how it happens, tits in your face isn't a rough way to go.

"Tell me what you want, baby," she purrs, brushing her hand up my thigh. "You know I can take care of you and give it to you the way you like."

We both know why I'm here. It's the same reason any other man hits up a club like Seven Sins. This sure as hell ain't our first rodeo, either.

She rakes her red-lipsticked lip over her teeth, and her sultry eyes darken on mine.

"You know what I fuckin' want, Daveny. Don't play with me."

Her lips purse together, fighting off a devilish smile.

"I know, baby." She sighs, brushing her hand over my dick and earning her a low hiss.

Her boobs spill over her too-tight top. Her curly, dark hair hangs around us like a curtain as she climbs on to straddle my lap. My dick strains hard against the zipper of my pants, and she's careful not to touch me there again.

"You're headin' out on the road for three months. Don't you want a little somethin' to remember me?"

The truth? No, I don't.

As I said, this isn't our first rodeo. I'm only here for one reason, and that one reason alone. If it wasn't her, it would be someone else. Someone to scratch the itch, and Seven Sins comes with its own perks.

I've toured with bands like A Rebels Havoc. Traveling from city to city. Sure, I've made *friends* along the way, ones who would be all too willing to fill in for her when I'm in town.

The ones who get more than one night with me understand what happens between these four walls stays here.

I could've stayed in Carolina Beach with the guys, found a strip club or two to hit up, and brought someone back to a hotel with me.

You won't ever catch me bringing a woman to my place, though. I don't like my flings in my space. My peace.

The last thing I need or want is for word to get out about where and who I spend my time with. Seven Sins comes with privacy and exclusivity, and that's what I need living the life I do.

"Quit teasing me," I growl, wrapping my palm around her throat. "You fuckin' know what I want. Now give it to me."

She pushes her throat into my hand and rolls her eyes closed. She bites the edge of her lips again and hums in appreciation.

"Mmm, I knew you would."

She grinds against my dick before she moves to stand. I flare my nostrils and grit my teeth. She's toying with me, and I give her a pass, waiting for her to give me what I'm here for.

She lifts her red high-heeled foot to the sofa cushion next to me, lifting her skirt in the process. The move gives me a glimpse of her bare pussy before she slides her hand down to block my view, rubbing her fingers over her clit.

I clench my jaw, waiting for her to cut it with the fuckin' teasing.

She smirks, lowering her foot and turning to climb the stairs onto the stage.

I'm seated on one of the leather couches facing the pole with two chairs on either side. Red neon lights are draped around the room with two lights illuminating the stage. A low, heavy beat pumps through the speakers.

Her eyes stay pinned on me with each step she takes, spinning in her heels around the pole. She drags her finger over her lip down between her breasts, stopping when she reaches the tie holding her top in place.

I grip my dick through my jeans, watching intently as she twirls the string around her finger and yanks it loose. Her tits bounce free, and she flings the material to the floor.

She cups her breasts, rolling her nipples between her fingers, and her eyes fall shut. Her hips rock in time to the beat.

She leans against the pole, sliding her body down until she's on her knees. She spreads her legs, giving me another glimpse of her pussy. I'm letting her drag it out, waiting impatiently for her to give me what I want.

"I want to watch you too," she says over the music.

Her eyes flick to mine, a coy smile lifting the edge of her lips when I pull my zipper down to reveal my hard dick. I pump it slowly in my tight fist before releasing my grip, letting it bob against my stomach.

She turns over on her knees, kneeling in front of me, hitching her skirt up in the process. Her body trembles when she presses her chest against the floor, slipping her hand between her legs into her pussy. She moans, pulling them out to let me see the juices coating her fingers, spreading her wetness over her clit.

My hand finds its way back to my dick, brushing the bead of precum over the tip. My eyes stay fixated on her—the way her body shudders while she gets off, and the low moan rumbling from deep in her chest.

She slowly blinks her eyes open, watching me as I jerk off.

Something about the sight of a woman pleasuring herself, drawing it out before I fuck them, is like a slow, torturous dance feeding all my sinful desires.

She turns over and leans against the pole. As much as I can't get enough of her ass in the air for me, she loves watching me as much as I get off on watching her.

"Come for me," she moans.

I blink slowly when she hits the delicious spot inside her, her release racing through her body, and I'm not far behind.

It takes the edge off, but it doesn't satisfy the need growing inside me.

I'm like a starving lion, and when it comes to sex, I can't ever get enough.

My phone blares from across the room, and I slowly blink my eyes open, cursing under my breath.

It dawns on me it's not the first time it's rung this morning. I should've known when I turned in after three that I'd have hell to pay when it came time to drag my ass up.

Madden's name flashes on the screen, and I hit answer.

"I'm on my way," I lie, rubbing the sleep from my eyes.

"Where the fuck are you?" he grits out.

His tone is curt, making it painfully clear he's in a mood already.

I squint, pushing my hair back and stare at the clock.

Fuck.

I should've been at his place ten minutes ago. No wonder he's pissed.

"I took the wrong exit," I lie. "Be there soon."

I end the call, tossing my phone on the bed, and force my ass into the bathroom to turn on the shower.

We've been waiting for this day for weeks now. It's been a fuckin' rocky road to get here. When I signed on with A Rebels Havoc as a guitarist for their sold-out tour, you could say the news was not well received.

Brix, Madden, and Tysin have played together since middle school. They put in years of work to get where they are, and I don't blame them for a second for being pissed off at having me thrown into the mix.

Brix and Madden warmed up to me quickly, especially after we met, and they realized I wasn't trying to come in and start any bullshit. At the end of the day, we all had the same goal.

Tysin, on the other hand, is a different story. He has it in his thick fuckin' skull I'm encroaching on his territory. It's been a pissing match between us since the beginning.

He'll have to suck it up and get over it if we have any hopes of making it through the next twelve weeks. I don't want to stir up drama or ruffle any feathers, but I won't sit quietly and let him talk shit either.

After I shower and throw on my clothes, I'm out the door like my ass is on fire. At least I had half a mind to pack before going out and lookin' for trouble last night, taking one thing off my plate this morning.

They're all standing outside Brix's house when I pull up.

"It's about fuckin' time you showed up," Tysin mutters.

No surprise—he's already in a mood. He's had a piss-poor attitude since Madden announced Kyla was joining us on the road as our tour manager. I'm beginning to think he has an axe to grind with every fuckin' person in his life. I'm not exactly excited about being crammed on a bus with them, but I'm not going to start complaining either.

I've lived in far worse situations.

After ten hours on the road listening to Tysin and Kyla bicker, we pull into Philly, and I'm ready to get my ass off the damn bus.

"Let's hit up the club tonight," I shout over my shoulder, swiping a few bottles of whiskey from the minibar and dropping them on the table.

Tysin collapses on the couch, lifting his leg to rest on the coffee table, and drapes his arm along the back. Madden stands across the room, staring down at his phone while his fingers furiously move across the screen.

"I'm down," he mumbles, not bothering to look up.

I twist off the cap to the bottle and toss back the shooter before taking a swig of cola.

"Count me in," Tysin grunts. "I need to get laid."

I smirk at him and bite my tongue, fighting off the urge to say what's on my mind.

He made the entire drive here miserable for everyone. He can play it off like it's not driving him insane listening to Kyla gush over her engagement. The fact Madden is clueless to the growing tension between them makes it even more entertaining.

I'll go along with it if that's the game he wants to play. Especially if he's down to hit up clubs with me at each city we stop on our tour.

It makes it easier to have a wingman with me. There are nights when I like to sneak away by myself, though, and I hate lying or coming up with new excuses. I don't owe anyone an explanation for the shit I do, but I don't want them to go digging into things, either.

It's a blessing and a curse going on the road with a touring band. There's always an endless line of beautiful women ready for one night of sin with a rock star.

Over the years, I've realized I have an unhealthy obsession with women and sex. If I wasn't hitting a club or a bar in search of someone to get lost in for the night, I was drowning myself in whiskey to numb the pain and distract me from my insatiable thoughts.

I'm convinced settling down is not in the cards for me. No serious relationship, no marriage.

It's not who I am, and it's not someone I'll ever be.

As many times as I tell myself to get a grip on my life, it's never been enough to convince me to stop.

A lion can only go hungry for so long.

CHAPTER TWO

LAYKEN

"I'm dressing like a filthy slut tonight." Mona grins at me through her reflection in the mirror. "If I'm lucky, I'll be goin' home with Madden fuckin' Cole."

She checks herself out, pushing her breasts together, and wags her brows.

I swallow past the lump forming in my throat. I'm so out of my element. Mona is my cousin and best friend. While our style is similar, our contrast is like night and day.

Only three weeks separate us, and we've been tied at the hip for most of our lives. Well, until she went off and moved across the country to pursue her career in radio.

I haven't seen her in months until she texted me when A Rebels Havoc dropped their tour dates. We planned for me to fly out to Philly this year and celebrate turning twenty-two together.

I've loved A Rebels Havoc for over two years now, back before they topped any charts or ever hit the airwaves.

"I want to drink my weight in cocktails and dance until I can't feel my feet anymore." She giggles, pouring herself another shot.

She reaches for another glass, adding it to the lineup before looking over to make sure I'm in.

"C'mon girl, maybe it'll help you loosen up a bit. Take one, maybe two with me."

I hesitate for a minute. If I told her no, she wouldn't pressure me on it. I'm not one to drink. I never have been. I guess after growing up the way I did, watching my father fight his demons, I never wanted to fall into the same path he was on.

She's right, though. Maybe it'll help me relax a little and ease my nerves.

It's not every night you get introduced to one of the biggest rock bands in the world.

I nod. "Pour me one."

"That's my girl," she sings, filling up the second glass to the brim.

We both lift our hands to cheers before tossing them back. I grit my teeth, the whiskey burning my throat and warming my skin as it goes down.

"How have things been in Nashville?" Mona asks, running her hand over her hair before untwisting the tube of lip gloss.

I know her like the back of my hand, which means she's easy to read. Judging by the quirk in her brow, she has a hidden meaning behind her question.

I shrug. "Not much to tell."

Leaning over the sink, I look in the mirror and trace my lips before adding my nude lipstick. I blot them together and tuck a strand of hair behind my ear, checking my appearance.

We both look damn good tonight.

I decided to go for a bolder outfit. I'm dressed in a cobalt-blue lace top with a pair of black denim jeans and high-heeled booties. My auburn hair is curled in waves framing my face.

Mona stands next to me in her black dress, dipping low to show off her cleavage, paired with black stilettos. She looks like she's ready to dominate someone and enjoy every second of it.

"What's going on between you and Rhys these days?"

I eye her in the mirror and roll my lips together. I knew this question would come sooner or later. Everyone likes to question our relationship.

I get it—our friendship is hard to explain to anyone on the outside looking in. How did the hotshot quarterback for Blackthorne University wind up interested in me?

I stopped trying to understand it myself. For years, he dropped hints about wanting us to be together. At first, I soaked in his smile and the way his green eyes stared into me, framed by his long lashes. He was beautiful for a man—tan, muscular, and looked like he stepped off the pages of a surfer magazine. His body was chiseled by gods.

I never could understand what he saw in a girl like me. I was all knocked knees and braces, with my frizzy red hair. I hated the freckles covering my arms and how my face would turn red for a multitude of reasons, making it impossible to hide behind a fake persona of being the shy and awkward book nerd.

We briefly dated before things went south. He was getting ready to leave for college after graduation. I felt pressured to move our physical relationship along, knowing it's what Rhys wanted. He tried to reassure me, saying he understood why I wasn't ready to give him or anyone my virginity. We went back to being friends, but I don't think he's ever given up on the idea of us being together.

"I haven't talked to him for a few days. He's supposed to be coming home for a few weeks this summer before training camp starts."

Mona leans against the wall in her small bathroom, eyeing me while I finish my last-minute hair and makeup touch-ups.

"Well, good. We're gonna hit up the club and have a blast. You can let loose and enjoy yourself, and maybe, if you're up to it, you'll find a hot man of your own to bring home."

As much as I'd love to strip myself from the label of being a virgin, I'm not the type to meet a guy and jump into bed with him after one night.

We show up outside the nightclub an hour later. You can hear the music pulsating from outside. A line of people wrapped around the front of the building and down the street.

If it weren't for Mona and her connections, we'd never get in. The bouncer near the door has stopped everyone from entering. When he spots Mona, he runs his hungry gaze down her body before nodding his head to let her in.

She fishes her hand behind her back, tangling our fingers together and pulls me with her.

"You lucky bitch!" a woman standing near the front of the line shouts as we pass by.

Mona glances over at her and laughs, tossing her other hand over her shoulder in a wave.

We make a beeline for the closest bar for a drink. The club is packed to the brim. The music is so loud it's almost hard to hear your own thoughts. Each corner is fitted with a bar, and there's a dance floor centered in the middle. It's overflowing with people. Their hands in the air, hips gyrating against each other while they dance and sing along to Lizzo.

There's a platform along the back wall, roped off from the rest of the club, with high-top tables and barstools. Two burly men in all black walk across the stage, followed by a group of people.

My heart is in my throat when I recognize one of them as Tysin, followed by Madden.

"They're here," I shout to Mona, tugging on her arm and nodding toward them.

"I told you they would be." She grins.

She's had a crush on Madden for as long as we've listened to him. The last time she saw them play, she was able to use her connections to meet Madden, and they became *friendly*.

Although, if Mona had her way, they'd get a whole lot friendlier tonight.

I don't know the dynamics between them, but it's no secret she's hoping to end up in his bed before the night is over.

When it comes to men, that's where she and I differ. She's never been afraid to go after what she wants. She goes out and lives life carefree. To be honest, I wish I could let myself relax enough to do the same sometimes.

I, on the other hand, have been holding out for this idea of love I've read about in my books. The type of man who makes your heart beat wildly and your pussy wetter than a slip 'n' slide.

I didn't have an example of what love should be growing up, and I guess you could say I'm starting to give up on ever finding it.

I stare in awe at the guys, watching them filter in. There are women flanked around them, draped onto their arms. My eyes are glued on the tall, buxom blonde who's hanging on every word Tysin says. He wraps his arm around her waist and pulls her into him. You can see her beaming smile from here.

I manage to drag my eyes away from them when another guy stalks up next to them. His hair is long, pulled up out of his face.

When he turns toward the crowd, his dark eyes and his beard make my mouth go dry.

Who the hell is that Adonis of a man?

It's hard to make out his features, but the sight of his muscular arms covered in tattoos and the curve of his mouth when he grins makes it hard for me to swallow.

"Do you know who the guy is with them?" I holler to Mona. "The one with the long hair."

She squints, trying to see through the flashing lights.

"Trey. He's their new guitarist."

My brows deepen. "New guitarist?"

I hadn't heard they added anyone to the band. It's always been the three of them—Brix, Tysin, and Madden.

"It's been all over the headlines. When they announced their tour, they mentioned adding a second guitarist."

The crowd starts pushing and pressing against us while we wait to order our drink. I wasn't planning on drinking much, but by the time we finally make it to the counter, I'm half tempted to order a double so I don't have to deal with the line again.

The bartender waves us in, and Mona shouts her order along with my whiskey sour.

My eyes find their way over to the stage, and my mind drifts back to Mona's comments. The mention of the name Trey reminds me of the boy I rode the bus with all those years ago. He never paid attention to me. In fact, until the one day we spoke to each other, I don't think he ever knew I existed.

I hardly spoke to any guys in high school other than Rhys. Any time a guy would come around, I'm pretty sure he was scaring them off with some sort of threat. I never knew for certain, but I started to put two and two together when I spotted him having a heated conversation in the hallway with a guy named Thomas one day.

Ironically, anytime I saw Thomas in the halls, he'd avoid looking my way and would barely mumble a word when I'd try to talk to him.

Rhys was used to getting what he wanted, when he wanted, with everything except for me. I think he was after the chase. I was the one person who didn't fall over themselves for his attention, and I didn't care in the least about his stat sheet or what name-brand clothes he was wearing.

The little I did know about Trey, though, I knew we had a lot more in common. I've heard rumbles throughout the hallway about his home life. We had more similarities than we did differences. The one day we sat next to each other on the bus, he blared his music so loud, I listened along with him on our way to school.

He lived in the nicer part of town with the big houses and manicured lawns. My mama couldn't afford much after my dad was gone. We settled for a broken-down apartment a few blocks away in a run-down neighborhood. We went two summers without air-conditioning. Our landlord would come by and say it was fixed, but a few days later, it was back to the way it was before.

She couldn't afford for us to move, so we stayed there until I graduated.

"Here." Mona bumps my arm, snapping me out of my thoughts to hand me my drink.

I glance up at Trey again as we weave our way through the crowd toward a row of tables.

He's dressed in a fitted black T-shirt, showing off his arms, and dark denim jeans. He leans against the railing overlooking the club, his gaze flitting around the crowd as if searching for his next prey.

We dance near our table, sipping our drinks and lifting our hands in the air while we sing. Mona urges me to finish the rest of mine before pulling me toward the dance floor, and I let the music flow through me as we sing and dance.

After a few songs, a strong arm slips around my waist, pulling me against a firm chest. The move catches me off guard, and my stomach twists with anxiety as my gaze darts over my shoulder to find a tall guy with short dark hair pressing his face into my neck.

He's cute, and the dimple in his cheek deepens when he grins at me. Normally, I would shy away from dancing with a random stranger, but I try not to overthink it and remember it's all about having fun.

At some point in all the dancing, Mona disappears, and my eyes search for her amongst the crowd before spotting her near where we came in. She runs her hand over Madden's forearm as he leans in, nodding along with whatever she's saying.

Trey stands next to him, and when our gaze locks, I suck in a sharp breath at the sight of him. His arms are crossed, and when the crowd parts, he catches sight of the stranger behind me and his hands gripping my hips.

It's him. It's Trey.

Not Trey from A Rebels Havoc, but the Trey from all those years ago.

Being this close to him and seeing him again sends my heart rate kicking into high gear.

He looks the same but different too. Gone is the tall, lean boy with the long hair and the rock band T-shirts. He's all man now, nothing like the clean-cut country boys you find back home in Nashville. Tattoos cover his forearm and chest, peeking through the button-down front of his shirt.

I wonder what other parts of his body have tattoos. Or a piercing. I've read about bad boys like him in my romance novels, and he seems like the type of guy who would have a piercing you'd only see if you were intimate with him.

I drag my teeth over my lip at the thought, and he clenches his jaw, his eyes blazing into mine.

He pushes his way through the crowd until he reaches me. The closer he gets, the more my heart begins to hammer in my chest.

"Time's up," he grits out, his eyes flashing to mine.

"Sorry, bro, but we're dancing here," the deep voice grumbles from behind me.

He drags his eyes away, locking on the stranger behind me. I step away from him, closer to Trey, and the stranger drops his hands from my side.

Trey is a lot taller than I expected, which says a lot, considering I've always been called a string bean growing up. A nickname that grated on my nerves.

He moves to cross his arms, leveling the guy with a stare that says, "try me." Meanwhile, all I can think about is those strong arms wrapped around me, and my fingers gripping his hair.

"No." He shakes his head. "No, you're not."

Trey flicks a glance over at me, and his face softens. Maybe he can tell I'm practically in heat at the vivid thought of his strong hands holding me in ways I've only read about in my books. There's a hint of a smile playing on the corner of his mouth.

"Is he with you?" he asks me. "You two together?"

I shake my head, almost too enthusiastically. He's probably waiting for my head to spin off my shoulders.

"There's our answer. Now take a hike."

The stranger looks back at me.

"Thanks for the dance," I mutter feebly over the music, not wanting to be rude while hoping he'll find someone else to dry hump for the night. He rolls his eyes before disappearing into the crowd.

Trey drops his arms and takes a step toward me.

"Don't you think that was a little dramatic?" I quip.

"No," he says matter-of-factly. "When I want something or someone, I don't mind being bold to get it."

I press my lips together, but it's no use. My smile breaks across my face.

He reaches for my hand, slipping his fingers between mine, and guides me through the crowd. He heads over to the table we claimed when we arrived and leans against the wall. We're out of the way, so there's more room, and we can hear each other talk.

"You here with that girl?" He leans his head next to mine, gesturing to Mona. "The one my buddy, Madden, is talking to."

"Mona. She's my cousin and one of my best friends. I'm in town for the A Rebels Havoc concert."

He leans back, studying me, and a slow smile spreads across his face.

"Is that right? You listen to A Rebels Havoc?" he shouts over the music.

I nod and grin. "One of my favorite bands."

The look on his face says he's pleasantly surprised. He tucks a strand of hair behind my ear, and my breath hitches at the move. It's something so simple, so innocent yet possessive at the same time.

My eyes flutter shut. He grips my hips and pulls me against him. This feels different than any guy I've been interested in before. The attraction, the tension between us. We're like two magnets pulling each other together.

There's a thought in the back of my mind, urging me to tell him who I am, to see if he remembers me from all those years ago. Maybe it'll be good to rip off the Band-Aid so I don't have to face his rejection when he changes his mind.

As much as I hate feeling like I'm hiding, I'm not ready to give up the way he's looking at me now.

Like he wants to throw me over his shoulder and carry me out of here.

He digs his fingers into my hips and turns me until my back is pressed against his front. Our hips start moving in time to the beat of the music, his hands slipping over my hips and down my thighs.

He pushes my hair away, his lips trailing over the column of my neck toward my ear. My knees go weak, and my body trembles when his warm breath feathers over my skin.

I start to envision all the other places I'd love to feel him touch me. I squeeze my eyes shut, tilting my head back against his chest.

"I'm only in town for the night, but I want you in my bed."

My breath hitches at the forwardness of his statement. He doesn't strike me as the type of guy to mince words, and like he said, he isn't afraid to go after what he wants.

"For tonight," he murmurs into my ear. "You're mine."

CHAPTER THREE

LAYKEN

Every nerve ending in my body is alive from his touch.

When he brushes his lips over the shell of my ear, his warm breath against my neck, tremors wrack through my body, and I go weak against him.

He moans when my ass rubs against the front of his pants. "Is that a yes?"

The heady feel of desire hangs over me like a cloud, leaving me floating in a daze.

I can't remember ever feeling this way in a man's arms. Even when Rhys kissed me, I never felt anything remotely close to how I feel with Trey.

After all this time, am I really going to do this? I've hardly been around him, and we've barely spoken to each other. Am I ready to take this step with him?

How do I tell him I've never been intimate with a man?

What if he changes his mind?

I've spent so long waiting for this day, to the point I've built up this moment in my mind, and now I want to escape the confines of the label and be free.

"Yes," I mutter breathlessly.

He slips his fingers into my hair from behind, massaging my scalp before pulling on the strands to tilt my head back. The move exposes my neck, and he nips and sucks at my skin.

"I'm gonna enjoy claiming every inch of you."

Good God. If this is how he talks to me now, I don't think I'm prepared for his dirty talk in the bedroom.

We head over to the bar and order another round of drinks. Trey leads the way, escorting me to the VIP section with Tysin and Madden.

Mona spots me with Trey, her eyes bulging when she catches our hands linked together before she grins, glancing back at Madden.

The wheels are turning in her mind already, and without a doubt, she's secretly hoping we'll both end up in their hotel room tonight.

Trey sits on one of the lounges and pulls me by my waist onto his lap.

He traces his finger up my calf and over my thigh before he leans into my ear and murmurs, "You're so fuckin' sexy."

I swallow a heavy drink of my whiskey sour, letting the effects of the alcohol take its course. In the back of my mind, I wonder if he's thinking about how the rest of the guys and the club can see us together?

I don't care, though.

He clenches his jaw, his eyes blazing into me when he runs his hand up my inner thigh. The move causes the muscle in my leg to tense, and I suck in a deep breath.

His gaze flicks down to my lips, and without thinking or second-guessing, I crash my mouth against his. He releases a slow growl, his hand slipping between where my legs are crossed, like he's fighting to hold on.

Perspiration dots his brow, and I feel it when I press my forehead to his.

His lips are warm and soft, and I can taste the hint of liquor. That, mixed with the smell of his woodsy cologne, is a heady combination.

Trey pushes my hair away from my neck and leans closer to whisper into my ear.

"As much as I wouldn't mind staying here and drawing this out, I'd rather dip out and get you alone, away from all these damn people."

I nod. We finish our drinks, leaving them on the table. Trey tangles our fingers together again before he leans down to say something to Madden and waves goodbye to Tysin.

"You two leavin'?" Mona grins, looking awfully cozy next to Madden.

"You don't mind, do you?" I rub my lips together, hoping and praying like hell she doesn't.

I try to hold back my smile. "Hopefully I'll see you later?" I mutter, hinting at maybe she'll be joining us wherever the guys are staying.

Her eyes glitter as she lifts her drink in cheers.

"Text me later tonight or in the morning," she adds.

Trey looks down at me and winks, nodding his head toward the door.

A black SUV with tinted windows waits for us outside. Security flanks us when we step out the back door, ushering us inside the vehicle

He reaches across the seat, urging me closer to him, and rests his hand on my thigh. I stare down at where it sits and fold mine on top of his.

"We should have the suite to ourselves. Well, until Madden and Tysin get back." He smirks.

Security escorts us to his room, making sure we get there safely.

"Thanks, Abel." He nods. "See ya in the morning."

He leads me across the suite and into his room. As soon as the door shuts behind him, he turns toward me. A giddy smile spreads across his face, and he reaches for my hand to pull me into him.

"If it were any other night, I'd be slow and take my time with you, but you've been drivin' me fuckin' crazy since I first saw you. I need you," he groans.

He sits on the edge of the bed, and I step between his legs.

"Under one condition..." I say bravely.

He grins, his brow quirking. "Shoot."

"Take your hair down."

He chuckles and obliges me, untying his hair. The hair underneath is shaved close to his scalp, with the rest of it long on top. He shakes his head, letting the strands fall into place before raking his fingers through it.

God, how is everything he does so sexy?

"Is that better?"

I bite my lip and nod, dragging my fingers through his hair to pull it away from his face. I tug on the strands until he tilts his head back to stare at me.

"Mmm," he moans. "Careful."

"Or what?" I whisper.

"The innocent look about you leads me to believe you're not quite ready for what happens when you wake that side of me."

He's right. I exhale a deep breath, trying to control my breathing to avoid giving away how much he affects me.

"Turn around," he orders.

I drop my hand and turn to show him my back. He slowly drags the zipper of my shirt down and mutters under his breath when he realizes I'm not wearing a bra underneath.

He leans forward, pressing a kiss to my spine, and my breath hitches. When I turn to face him again, he stands, slowly dragging the strap of my top down one arm, followed by the other.

All the air is sucked out of my lungs when the material falls to the floor.

"Fuckin' perfect," he rasps.

He leans down and flicks his tongue over my nipple before sucking it into his mouth. My fingers find their way back to his hair, holding him to me.

He blindly finds the button of my jeans and pushes them over my hips before kneeling on the floor. He unzips my high-heeled booties, helping me to step out of them before pulling my pants the rest of the way off.

Trey leans back to get a better look at me. I'm standing in front of him with nothing but my panties on.

Any other time, I'd be cowering away, covering my body in embarrassment, but the look in his eyes feeds something inside me that's been left unnourished.

He looks at me like he wants to sample every inch of my body, devouring me, leaving nothing untouched.

His fingers slowly drag up my leg. My eyes grow heavy, and my body tremors when he reaches my inner thigh, brushing along the edge of my panties.

"You wet for me?"

My tongue darts out, dragging across my dry lips. I fumble over my words, not sure what to say or do.

He grins. "I guess I'll have to find out for myself," he says, nodding behind me to the bed, urging me to sit.

He drags his shirt over his head and empties his pockets on the dresser, revealing what looks like two wings tattooed across his muscular back. He turns back toward me and smirks when he notices me staring at him.

"Lean back." His voice is deep and raspy.

I'm thankful he's calling the shots, guiding me through this, because my nerves would have me second-guessing myself without it.

He kneels on the floor, and I drop back onto my elbows, staring down my body at him.

Trey pins me with a heated gaze before slowly dragging his hand up my thigh until he brushes over the edge of my panties, then does the same down the other leg. Each time he gets closer to my pussy, I find myself desperate for him to touch me there.

He drags his finger over my mound before making the slow path down my leg again. This time, I'm left writhing beneath him.

When he goes to do it again, I can't take it anymore, and I lift my hips, silently begging him to touch me. He reaches for my panties, dragging them down my legs. His jaw clenches when I let my legs fall open.

"Spread your pussy open for me."

It takes a second for my mind to compute his request. His eyes finally break away from where he's staring, flicking up to meet mine.

"I want to see how wet you are for me. Spread your pussy open for me, baby."

I slowly slip my hand down my stomach and between my legs, brushing my finger over my clit and dipping it into my pussy.

I throw my head back, giving in to the pleasure. I can't take it anymore. I need and want more. I've never been so turned on in my life.

"Don't tease me," he warns, and his nostrils flare.

Doesn't he realize he's the one teasing me?

I push my finger in deeper, letting my wetness coat it, before slowly pulling out. He wraps his hand around my wrist, lifting my finger and sucking it into his mouth.

Mine drops open, my eyes growing heavy at the sight of him tasting me unabashedly.

"Fuckkk," he groans. "You taste as sweet as I knew you'd be."

This time, he lets his fingers do the work. He uses them to spread my pussy open before adding the other, brushing slowly over my clit before circling my entrance and sliding into me.

"Jesus, you're fuckin' tight," he chokes out.

My cheeks heat at his words. I'm afraid if I tell him the truth now, he'd pull away. I don't want him to stop, and I certainly don't want him to treat me like some delicate flower.

I want him like this, commanding and unrestrained, giving in to his pleasure.

He drops his face between my legs, sucking my clit into his mouth. The move is unexpected, unlike anything I've ever felt before. I clamp my legs around his head and grind against his face.

He moans and grips my thighs, holding me against him. He alternates between licking and sucking. My body trembles, unable to take the rush of desire racing through me.

Pushing my legs open, he adds a finger while muttering a stream of curse words in their wake.

"I need to feel your tight pussy around me."

The brashness of his words, the need on his face confirms he's right there with me.

He pushes himself to stand, reaching for the button of his jeans. When he frees his dick from the confines of his pants, it bobs against his stomach. The head is purple, and he squeezes it, brushing his thumb over the tip.

"You keep lookin' at me like that, and I'm gonna fuck your mouth first."

I flick my eyes up to his, snapping my mouth shut, my mind unable to keep up with him.

He nods his head, and he crawls up the bed with me. He pushes one of my legs back, keeping my foot pressed against his chest.

I don't even have time to think about what's about to happen when he brushes the tip of his dick over my pussy and positions himself at my entrance.

I throw my head back and squeeze my eyes shut, trying to slowly breathe through the sharp pain.

"Holy fuckkk," he groans, circling his hips. "You're gripping me like a fist."

He goes slow at first, easing himself out before thrusting all the way in deep. I bite my lip to keep from crying out, despite the pain shooting through me.

"Oh God, are you okay?" he asks, his concerned eyes searching mine.

I wrap my legs around his waist, holding him to me. I'm not sure if I'm afraid he'll pull away out of fear he's hurting me or if I'm desperate for him to give me more.

Or both.

"I'm okay," I breathe out harshly.

He pushes my hair away from my face, and his mouth captures mine. The kiss is slow and passionate. His hair falls around us before he pulls back.

He moves my leg to his chest, staring down between us to where our bodies meet. He rubs his thumb over my clit, and my eyes roll closed.

Everything hits me all at once, and my body relaxes.

When he pulls out and thrusts into me, what was once a sting of pain morphs into pleasure, and I'm begging for him to give me more.

His expert fingers brushing over my bundle of nerves and his steady thrusts have my need growing inside me.

"Trey," I moan. "Please."

His nostrils flare, and his breathing grows labored as he squeezes his eyes shut.

"I'm gonna come. It feels too fuckin' good. I can't take it anymore."

I don't know if it's his raspy words or the sight of pleasure on his face.

"Give it to me. I want you to come inside me."

The words are no further out of my mouth when he rolls his eyes closed and throws his head back. The sound of his low growl and his body tensing have me falling over the edge with him.

Everything about this night with him feels like a dream, and I don't want to ever wake up.

CHAPTER FOUR

TREY

I can't tell if the sound of knocking is the thumping in my skull or pounding on the door. I wince, flinging my arm over my face, and stretch my legs.

A slight groan follows, one that didn't come from me, and I peek my eyes open. My gaze trails over soft skin with light freckles covering her shoulders to the long, red hair lying unruly across the pillow.

I roll my eyes shut, mentally running through the events of the night before when my thoughts drift back to the nightclub.

Back to *her.*

I guess there's a first time for everything. I've never been one to let a girl stay over. Even if I'm staying in a hotel room, I'll take care of their cab and send them on their way before I crash for the night.

Except last night after we finished, she curled her body against mine and wrapped her arm around my waist, and I couldn't do it.

There was a softness in her face, an innocence and trust I've never felt with anyone. I could tell she was nervous with me. Maybe it was her lack of experience, or she was in her head at the thought of who I was, but she didn't let it stop her. She let me call the shots and did so without hesitation, as if she knew I'd take care of her.

It didn't feel right to push her out the door. Not only that, but I also didn't want to say goodbye to her. Not yet.

"Trey, I'm not kidding," Kyla hollers. "Get your ass up."

Her voice is muffled through the door. She's short and mighty, that one, and if I don't get moving now, she'll come barreling in here to drag my ass out of bed.

"I'm comin'," I shout, turning over to slip my arm around her waist.

I'm trying to recall her name, knowing she gave it to me last night, but after searching through the foggy memories, I come up empty. I hate myself for it too, but my thoughts quickly evaporate when she grinds her ass against my dick. I lean forward to nip at her shoulder.

"Careful," I growl.

She turns over and stares up at me from beneath her long lashes, pressing her palm to my cheek. Her eyes linger on my lips for a beat, as if she's thinking about kissing me before she pulls away.

"Kiss me, woman."

She wrinkles her nose. "I can't." The Southern twang is back in her sweet voice, and she shakes her head. "I need to brush my teeth."

"I don't give a shit. Kiss me."

She giggles and obeys, leaning in to press her lips to mine. I push her onto her back, moving to position myself between her legs again and grind my dick against her.

"I'm not fuckin' around, Trey. We need to get movin', or we'll be late," Kyla shouts, her fist hammering against the door.

I let my head fall against her shoulder. We had a good time last night, going another round before finally collapsing and letting sleep pull us under. I don't remember what time, but I know I heard Tysin and Madden come in at one point.

Tysin pounded on the door, announcing they were back, but I never heard a peep from Madden. I suspect he brought back the brunette he was chatting with before we left.

"Give me a second to use the bathroom, and I'll be outta your hair."

I sit up and swing my legs over the side of the bed, the sheet gathering around my waist. My eyes burn into her, watching her search for her clothes.

I note the familiar love bites marking her neck and chest and grin. I'm ready to forget the radio interview this morning and drag her back to bed, telling Kyla and the guys to fuck off, when she bends over and gives me a glimpse of her sweet pussy.

I grit my teeth and force myself to breathe slowly through my nose. Her eyes go wide, and her pale skin turns a sinful shade of pink when she catches me staring.

I'm dying to do the same when I bend her over and land a hard swat on her round ass.

"We have an interview this morning with your cousin. Will I see you there?"

She nods. "That's the plan. I need to head to my hotel and clean up before I meet up with her, though."

She motions over her shoulder to the bathroom before turning to scurry in there. When the door clicks shut, I search around on the floor for my underwear. I can't seem to find them anywhere, lifting the pillow and duvet from the bed, when I notice a small red stain on the sheets. My heart sinks, and my head snaps over to the door.

Fuck. I wince, storming over to the bathroom, and lean my head against the wood, listening for any sound on the other side. Was I too rough with her? Did I hurt her?

"Everything okay?" I grimace.

I try to think back to the night before, but some of the details are foggy.

"Yeah, I'm almost finished. I'll be quick."

"You're okay? I wanted to make sure you were doing all right, that you're not hurt or anything."

She's silent for a moment.

"No," she says, dragging the word out. "I'm more than okay. I'm just using the bathroom and splashing some water over my face, then I'll take off."

She must believe I'm trying to rush her out the door, and guilt rises in my throat. I press my palms against the doorframe and push off, spotting my briefs on the floor peeking out from under the dresser.

I need to jump in the shower before we take off. I'll walk her out and make sure she gets a lift back to her place first.

Someone knocks on the door again before Tysin pokes his head inside.

"We gotta leave here in twenty."

"Can you shut the fuckin' door for a second?" I grumble. "I'm not even dressed."

I quickly pull my underwear on before Kyla steps behind Tysin. She glances from him and around the room as if she's surprised he didn't bring someone back too.

I'm still trying to piece together their dynamic. Judging by his reaction to her joining us on tour and Madden's persistent harassing him to chill, there's undoubtedly history there.

Only I can't believe Madden would ever tolerate his sister messing around with the likes of Tysin for even a second.

"Is your guest still here?" she asks, flicking her eyes from me and down to her phone.

"Yeah, she's in the bathroom. Can you order an Uber to take her home for me?" I ask.

She nods. "Who am I calling it for? Please tell me you at least thought to ask for her name."

She turns toward Tysin, her eyes shooting daggers at him.

Her fingers skate across her phone, furiously typing before she glances up at us with a huff of annoyance.

I have no clue what I did to piss her off, nor do I think she gives a fuck who I hook up with. I humor her, though, knowing this is more about Tysin than me anyway.

I rack my brain for any mention of her name until it finally clicks.

"As a matter of fact, I did. Her name is Mona."

The bathroom door slowly drags open, and she tucks a fallen strand of hair behind her ear, her eyes avoiding mine. She falters when she notices the crowd and flashes me a hesitant smile. Her hair is tousled, and her eyes are sleepy, but even still, she looks fuckin' beautiful.

She's dressed in her clothes from the night before. My face falls when she moves past me as if she's trying to leave without saying goodbye. I grip her wrist to stop her and pull her into my arms.

"Hey," I whisper against the side of her head, wrapping my arm around her waist.

She seems different, shy. I chalk it up to all the curious eyes around us, or maybe it's the lack of sleep from the night before.

"Thank you for last night." I lift her chin, her gaze locking on mine.

She smiles softly. Something about the look in her eyes has me leaning in to kiss her again.

I don't think she expects it this time. She grips my forearms and hums against my lips.

"Kyla called an Uber for you. It'll take you wherever you need to go," I say.

She nods, smiling again, and whispers, "Thank you."

"Good luck at your show tonight." She pats her hand against my chest, moving past me. "I know you have to hurry, so don't worry. I'll see myself out."

She thanks Kyla for the lift before she disappears into the hall. She's not even a foot outside the door, and I already wish I could keep her here with me.

What the hell has gotten into me? I met this chick less than twenty-four hours ago.

Madden storms out of the room, his shirt off with a pair of jeans on, left unbuttoned at his waist.

"If you need me to call an Uber, tell me because we need to go soon," Kyla says.

"No one's here," he retorts, reaching into the fridge for a water, then unscrewing the cap and downing half of it.

"What happened to the brunette from last night?" Tysin asks.

"Mona? We're just friends," Madden clarifies.

Mona?

"Wait, what did you say her name was?" Kyla interjects, her gaze snapping over to Madden.

"Mona. She's the chick interviewing us at the radio station today. I met her last year on the Twisted Tour."

There's no way they'd have the same name, right?

Kyla turns, pointing her phone at me, her brows furrowing. "I thought you said the girl I called an Uber for is named Mona?"

"It is."

Madden finishes his water, tossing the bottle toward the garbage and misses. He curls his lip up in annoyance and shakes his head.

"Nah, man, that's not fuckin' Mona. The chick you left with last night is her cousin, River. No, wait, shit. Her name is Layken."

I roll my eyes shut and exhale a low growl. Are you fuckin' kidding me?

Kyla's face softens when she looks over at me. She releases a slow whistle and ducks her head, leaving us with orders to hurry up and meet her in the lobby before slipping out the door. I forcefully drag my hand through my hair, tugging on the strands. I eventually force my feet to move and slam the door shut behind me.

I don't have the time or mental energy to deal with this right now. I need to get ready if I have any chance of making it downstairs on time.

Steam fills the bathroom when I flip the shower on, and I quickly shed my underwear and step under the spray, attempting to wash my guilt and regrets down the drain.

If only it were that easy.

• • • • • • • • • • •

I don't say much on our way to and during the interview. By the looks of it, Layken is nowhere in sight. Thankfully, most of the questions are focused on the guys. Mona throws a few my way, asking how I felt about joining the band and what it's been like on tour. I keep it brief, making light of our early challenges. We'll work it out eventually, though. My relationship with the guys will grow with time.

Throughout the interview, every time I look over at Mona, I'm reminded of my foot-in-mouth mistake. I guess I fucked over any chance to see her and apologize because, as my luck would have it, she's nowhere to be found.

"Are you staying in town after the concert tonight?" Mona asks, her eyes lingering on Madden's.

I'm surprised she wasn't strolling out of his room this morning. Although, if I'm honest, it's probably for the better because it could've made the whole situation more awkward.

She was all too eager to have Madden's attention last night. Evidently, it didn't work out according to her plan, which would explain why she was batting her eyes and brushing her hand over Tysin's arm throughout the interview.

"We're loading up the buses and heading out right after our show," Madden says, shoving his hands into his pockets.

Disappointment shrouds her features, and she avoids his stare, not wanting to let on that it bothers her. She's clearly into him, but he doesn't seem to reciprocate those feelings.

I want to bring up Layken in hopes she'll be here soon, or maybe I'll be able to sneak her into my dressing room after the show. I won't deny I want to see her again. It isn't so much that I'm trying to ease my own guilt but more so that I didn't want it to end the way it did.

I guess I ruined it, though.

Before we take off to the venue, I ask Abel to keep an eye out for her or let me know if anyone who resembles her asks security for me.

Later that night, before our meet and greet, I'm pacing back and forth in my room with my headphones on, blaring some music. It helps get me amped up before we take the stage. That's where I'm at when Kyla pokes her head inside.

I don't notice her at first. She waits until I look up and turn my music down.

"You good?" she asks.

She chews on her lip, waiting for me to answer before she snickers and shakes her head, deciding to do the talking herself.

"All you're looking for is a hookup, right? Why are you being so hard on yourself? It's not like you did it intentionally. For all you know, she may not have even heard you. What are the chances you'll see her again anyway? We're about to head out on tour for the summer. You'll have hundreds of beautiful women ready to throw themselves at you. Some I'd be willing to bet wouldn't give a fuck what you call them." She smirks.

It's a joke meant to ease my frustration. Her face falls, picking up on the change in my demeanor.

"You didn't think to ask her for her name before you screwed her brains out?"

I stalk past her, annoyed by her question. Mostly because I hate the fact she's right.

"It was loud at the club. We were vibin', ya know? It was hard to hear anything. I was a few drinks deep before we even got there."

"What about when you got back to the hotel? You didn't ask for her name before you tore her clothes off?"

I drag my shirt over my head, spinning to stare at her in the mirror. Ivy pops her head in, looking from Kyla before turning to me. Brix steps in behind her, glancing at them staring at me shirtless.

"What the hell is going on in here?" he barks.

Ivy swats at his arm and tells him to chill before Kyla waves her hand to get them to be quiet. Brix rolls his eyes and crosses his arms, leaning against the wall.

"I've never been the type of guy who lets a girl sleep over, Kyla."

"Never?" Ivy asks.

I shake my head, meeting Kyla's gaze in my reflection. I press my fists down on the counter. "Never. I wanted to be alone with her, so I took her back to the hotel. I was drunk and caught up in the moment. I'm sure y'all know how it is, right?"

Kyla gets a distant look in her eyes before they meet mine again.

Whatever she's thinking about, whatever memory flashes through her mind has her face softening.

"I guess you're right." Kyla shrugs, seeming to understand my perspective.

"I'm sorry, Trey," Ivy adds. "There'll be plenty more like her, begging for the chance to take her place."

I nod, tossing my shirt over my shoulder, and stalk toward the bathroom, shutting the door behind me.

I want to tell them they're both wrong, but how do I explain why she's different when I don't even understand it myself?

CHAPTER FIVE

TREY

After the show, I'm drenched in sweat. Normally, I would hit the shower in hopes I could hook up with someone I know in the area or convince the guys to come with me to hit up a club.

"You good, man?" Abel asks, slapping me on the chest.

I nod. "I'm gonna step outside for a minute. Get some fresh air before I'm stuck on the bus again for God knows how long."

"Want me to join ya?"

"Nah, man. I'm good. I'll meet ya at the bus in twenty."

He hesitates as if contemplating whether to leave me alone but steps back, deciding to give me space.

I slip out the door of the arena in hopes of spotting Layken when she leaves. I pull my hair back and shove a baseball cap on, trying to fly under the radar.

I kept an eye out at our meet and greet earlier, thinking maybe I'd see her there, but she never showed.

A wall of heat hits me when I push the door open. I force a deep breath of the stifling air, and it's damn near suffocating. The sun has disappeared into the horizon. It's pitch black above me, with the lights in the parking lot and the buildings around me illuminating the midnight sky.

I step out of the way, watching people coming and going out of the side entrance, and lean against the wall. Pulling out my smokes, I lift one to my mouth. As I flick my lighter, I search through the stream of people for any sight of her.

After twenty minutes or so pass, the crowd begins to thin out, and I resign myself to the fact I missed my shot.

I regret not saying something to Mona at the station this morning. Maybe if I had given her my number or a message to pass on to Layken, I would've had a chance to see her tonight.

I lose track of time, standing there, letting my own guilt eat away at me, when the sound of the door opening pulls me from my thoughts.

"I thought I might find you out here." Kyla's sweet voice fills the silence. "I almost didn't notice you for a second with your hat on."

Her heels click on the ground as she joins me, leaning against the wall.

"You still in your head over this morning?"

I shrug, not sure what else there is to say. I'm not one to spill my thoughts and feelings. I tend to keep everything in until I work through it or, in some cases, until I explode.

It never ends well. I don't have much choice in this situation, though.

"What's the history between you and Tysin?" I ask, changing the subject.

She breathes out a slow sigh and chuckles. "You've only known me now, what, a week. What makes you think there's a history there at all?"

I return her laugh and shake my head. "Your brother may have his head up his ass, but you can't pull one over on me. I know two people who've fucked when I see 'em. Even with the ring on your finger, there's still something between you."

She pushes off the wall and turns to face me. She clutches her clipboard to her chest, and part of me wonders if she's trying to protect herself in some way.

"There's no history. Whatever you think you see between us is tension over him being an asshole for no other reason but to be an asshole." She shrugs before she glances down at the ground. "When Ivy and Brix got together, he stirred up drama, giving him shit for his relationship with her."

I don't believe her for a second when she says there's no past between them.

"I've heard about how he picked on her in high school and how their parents eloped. I couldn't believe she was his fuckin' stepsister." I smirk.

"Tysin and Brix had a bet going when she came home for the summer. The bet later tore him and Ivy apart." She shakes her head. "Brix did a lot of groveling to even convince Ivy to give him another chance."

Madden told me about the bet Brix and Tysin had going and how it damn near tore the band apart. I guess Brix became distant when it all went down, and they were worried for a while that he'd want to quit because of how tense things became between him and Tysin.

He reassured me if they could get through that time, we could get through Tysin's resistance to me joining them.

"Not to mention"—she sighs—"I've found my person. I've moved on, and I'm happy. Tysin doesn't know how to keep it in his pants. He couldn't stay faithful to someone if he tried."

If she wants me to help her pretend she hates Tysin, I'll let her continue to tell herself lies. She's engaged to Canon, and I don't doubt he makes her happy. Shit, I listened to her on the bus all day yesterday gush over wedding planning. Her face lights up whenever she talks about him.

I'm also not blind to the way she watches Tysin from across the room or his lingering stares when she's not paying attention. They move around like they're fighting and failing at proving their hatred for the other.

"Do you think there's only one person for everyone?" I ask, changing the subject.

She shrugs. "Do you?"

"Honestly, no. I don't. I think it's all bullshit. Although I'm not one for the lovey-dovey shit either."

"I don't believe in soul mates or that there's one perfect person for you. I think you can be compatible with many people, but it's all about finding the one you're not willing to live without. At the end of the day, it takes two people who love each other, who are all in and will give everything they've got because they'd never want to be without them," Kyla says.

I lift my cigarette to my mouth, taking a long drag before releasing a slow breath. I bend down and smash out the end, flicking it into the garbage.

"Is that what happened? One of you was all in, and the other one wasn't?"

She clenches her jaw. Like I said, she can't fool me. Even though she's fighting it, she can't disguise the hurt on her face.

"I'm serious, Trey. There's nothing between us."

I bump into her shoulder. "I'm giving you a hard time. Don't get all riled up on me."

"What about Layken? Is there something there between you two?"

I pull my hat off and rake my hand through my hair. I unclasp the band of my snapback, hooking it onto the belt loop of my jeans, and pull my hair out of my face in a bun.

"Nah, I guess I just wanted to try to talk to her and apologize for what happened," I say, trying to force a smile. "She didn't deserve the bullshit this morning, and she certainly doesn't deserve to deal with my shit out on the road. I'm not the relationship type, and I damn sure ain't ready to settle down."

"Ahhh." She nods her head. "One of those too, huh?"

"I grew up watching my parents always fightin'. My dad knows how to throw 'em back. I guess you could say I take after him there. Difference between us, though, is he has a nasty fuckin' habit of pushin' my mom around when he's had too many." I shake my head, flashbacks of the nights I'd wake up to him towering over her in the kitchen. "If they weren't arguin' over that, it was about him sneakin' around with the woman she caught him with. I don't know shit about being a good husband."

"What makes you think you'd be anything like him?"

I smirk. "You ask too many damn questions."

She shrugs. "Okay, well then what? You're just going to live your life from one meaningless hookup to the next?"

I push off the wall and head across the parking lot to lean over the railing overlooking Philly. She gives in, the clicking of her heels resume when she follows me over.

We both pause, taking a minute to look out into the city.

"I've never had anyone complain before. It's a mutually beneficial agreement. I'm not trying to hide what I'm looking for when I'm with a woman," I say, breaking the silence.

"Beneficial how?"

"They get to say they hooked up with Trey Whitt, and I get to feed the monster. It's a win-win in my book."

Her lip curls in disgust. "You know, you and Tysin may butt heads, but you have a lot more in common than you realize."

"Listen, I may only want the hookup lifestyle, but it doesn't mean I don't respect the women I'm with. Last night with Layken was just... it was different."

I don't want to tell her how I haven't stopped thinking about her all day or how the fact she wasn't at the interview or meet and greet today bothered me.

I won't get into how I came out here in hopes I'd catch her when she left the arena, either.

"Different how?" she asks, leaning against the railing.

A lot of women I hook up with frequent the strip clubs or gentleman's clubs I hang around. We're both looking for the same things, and when the night's over, we go our separate ways.

No strings attached.

"Well, for starters, I don't normally let women stay the night, and I've never cuddled with a woman, either."

The fact I let Layken stay over still hasn't sunk in with me. Let alone, even in my drunken haze, didn't stop to think about grabbing a condom. That's never happened.

"You make it sound so clinical. Wham, bam, thank you, ma'am."

I laugh. "Like I said, and trust me, I've never heard any of them complain."

"Maybe you don't stick around long enough to give them the chance."

I shrug. I guess she's right, but I've always made it a point to keep it that way.

I'm trying to tell myself that's what it is about Layken. She was the first woman I let into my space. I let a wall down with her and I hated the thought of her leaving feeling disrespected.

It's only sex, and sex is all I can give to a woman. I don't have room in my life for anything more.

If only I can convince the guilt coiling in my gut to accept this too.

CHAPTER SIX

LAYKEN
FOUR WEEKS LATER

I slam the lid to the toilet and fall back to take a seat, staring at the shampoo all over my floor.

"Dang you, Tater, look what you did," I holler, curling my lip as I lift my foot off the floor. "It looks like someone jizzed on my new rug."

Meow.

"Is that all you have to say for yourself, Potato?" I say in a stern voice, trying not to roll my eyes.

She rubs her head against my leg while I try to hop over to the bathtub to rinse my foot off. When I turn around, she's seated on the floor, staring up at me.

I should've expected this to happen. I flew home yesterday from a job I had out of town doing hair and makeup for a bridal party.

My cat, Potato Salad, is always like this whenever I leave town. If she's not walking under my feet or intentionally tipping shit over, she's finding other ways to drive me crazy, like tearing up an entire roll of toilet paper for me to find. I swear, she does it just because she's pissed at me. The moment I get my suitcase out, she knows I'm heading out of town, and she's at it again.

"You gonna clean this up?" I tap my finger on her nose, pointing to the spilled shampoo mess.

I should've known this would happen when the bottle broke. I'm too cheap, and I'll be damned if I'm wasting an entire bottle because the cap broke.

Leave it to Tater to find the one thing in the house that could make a mess and use it to get back at me.

I tighten the towel wrapped around my body and tiptoe around the mess into the kitchen to grab some paper towels. She cuts me off, taking her sweet time, leading the way.

"I swear, you're tryin' to make me late. Aren't you?"

Meow.

"That's what I thought," I grumble, ripping off several paper towels before deciding to take the whole roll with me. I'll have to wash the rug anyway, but at least I can try to get some of it out first.

I release a heavy sigh, adjusting my towel again after successfully cleaning the jizz off the floor, and grab my blow dryer. My hair is damp, and if I don't do something to tame it now, it'll be sticking up in six different directions.

Rhys will be here any second, and I'm still moseying around in a towel. I certainly don't want him getting the wrong idea when he shows up here, either. He's still holding out hope that something will come of our relationship, even though I've tried to tell him we'd be better off as friends.

As if sensing my thoughts, Tater circles my feet, doing a figure eight from one side to the other.

I've been thinking a lot about getting back into the dating game. I'm just finding it harder to even be interested in anyone else since the concert in Philly last month. Instead, I've kept my head down and stayed focused on work.

Anytime my mind drifts back to that night with Trey, I'm torn between letting my thoughts replay his hands all over my body, pleasuring me in ways I never could've imagined, to hearing him call me Mona before my walk of shame.

He's a rock star, for fuck's sake. He could have any woman he wanted. It reminds me of Rhys and the endless line of girls I've seen hang all over him. Even when I was with Rhys, he couldn't avoid the temptation, and eventually, he gave in to it.

I'm a fool for hoping the night with Trey meant anything to him or that he'd want to see me again. I guess I avoided the interview even after I told him I was going because I didn't want to face another round of rejection.

I quickly finish drying my hair, using my curling iron to give it some life before putting the finishing touches on my makeup. I'm not planning on this being a late night. Rhys is only in town for the rest of the week, so I'm sure he'll have other plans after anyway.

I unwrap the towel around me and toss it into the hamper. The clothes I picked out for the night were left lying on the bed.

"Excuse you," I say through my teeth, staring down at my heathen of a cat.

She peeks her head up from where she lays nestled into my red dress, as if she doesn't care about the layer of fur she left behind.

I wave my hand to shoo her away and grab my lint roller. After ridding the hair from my dress, I pull on a denim jacket and wedge heels, and I'm ready to hit the town.

Rhys wanted to bring me by Hazard Saloon, a local pub his mom has worked at for a few years. They serve some of the best food in town, so at least I know I won't be too disappointed.

The doorbell rings a second later. My heels click on the hardwood floor. I check the peephole and grin when I see Rhys standing on the other side.

"There she is." Rhys's mouth curves to the side in a lazy smile.

His bright eyes trail down my body, pausing on my legs. He sucks in a sharp breath before forcing his gaze to meet mine.

Rhys has always been handsome in a boyish sort of way. His hair is longer, styled in sort of a messy look. He's tan from hours of playing football out in the South Carolina sun. Those bright blue eyes and perfect smile are known for being dangerous around women.

Me? He's still the same wild child I knew back in middle school. The one who damn near broke his arm trying to show off on a skateboard and chipped his tooth opening a bottle of root beer for me.

He steps inside and looks around my small living room before turning to me.

"I've missed you." I sigh, pulling him in for a hug.

No matter what happens between us, he's always been one of my best friends. I hate to admit it, and I know he never will, but we've grown apart over the past year.

He's dressed in a gray T-shirt, a pair of denim jeans, and his scuffed-up boots. There's a hint of stubble covering his jaw, reminding me he's not the same boy he was growing up.

I can't deny the stark contrast between the man in front of me and the one I've been daydreaming about for the past few weeks.

Why the hell are you still thinking about him?

"I always miss you, Layk." He smiles. "Your place, I haven't seen it in person yet. It's nice, and it suits you. I like it."

He looks around at the cognac leather couches with ivory throw pillows. The walls are painted black, and two large windows add a lot of natural light. It's what made me fall in love with this place, along with how close it was to my mom and friend Kate.

Several potted plants are scattered throughout, including one on the coffee table in the center of the room.

It's a small cottage-style home, but it's enough space for me. I turned my other bedroom into a makeup studio, which has saved me several times when last-minute appointments have come up.

"Should we get going? I was hoping to see Mom before it picked up there."

I nod, ducking my head to pass him and follow him onto the patio.

Rhys presses his hand against my lower back and leads me down the stairs to his old pickup waiting at the curb. He's had it since high school, although he'll leave it here when he heads back to school.

He holds out his hand and helps me in. I hate how I'm comparing every little thing to how I felt with Trey, having his hands and eyes on me.

He was a fling. A one-night stand. Nothing more.

I try to distract myself on the drive to Hazard by replaying the jizz story from earlier. It's short-lived, though, when he asks about the concert.

"You never did tell me how the concert went. Did you have fun?" he asks.

I nervously chew at my lip, trying to figure out how much of the story to tell. I'm half tempted to ask him if he remembers Trey, even though I doubt he does. They ran with two different crowds. Now that I think about it, I don't even remember seeing Trey with any friends back in school.

Rhys hung out with the same crowd throughout high school. Most of them being guys he played football with and their cheerleader girlfriends.

Except for me. Everyone, including me, seemed confused by our friendship.

I doubt we would've ever become friends if it weren't for his mom watching me when I was younger. She was more of a parent than my own for most of my young life, at least until my mom got clean.

Our parents grew up together. Even though they had a falling out over my parents' drug use, she never turned her back on helping care for me. It's something I've always appreciated about her, and I've always thought of her like a second mom.

"It was a blast. Hands down one of my top three concerts ever. It's right up there with Blink 182 and Linkin Park."

His grip on the steering wheel tightens, and he turns to flash me a wide smile. We have never shared the same taste in music. Don't get me wrong, he wouldn't bat an eye if I asked to blare some rock music right now. He'll always be a country boy.

When we get to Hazard, he tells me to wait in the truck and jogs around to the other side to open the door for me. He leads me inside, holding the door, and even offers to pull out my chair.

I get the sinking feeling he may be misinterpreting this to mean more than it does. I'm relieved when his mom spots us from behind the bar and waves, holding up her finger to signal she'll be over in a minute.

"Are you gonna make it down for some of my games? My mom said you could ride with her if you want."

I avoid his gaze, moving to cross my leg over the other, trying to figure out how to break it to him.

I nod. "I want to try to make it there. You'll have to send me your game schedule or at least the ones your mom plans on coming for. I'll double-check my calendar to make sure I don't have any client appointments."

"You know, sometimes when I'm back at school and missing you, I'll check your social media and watch your videos." His face softens, and he avoids my stare, instead shifting his gaze to look around the bar.

"You do?" I ask, surprised.

He nods. "We don't talk as much as we used to, and sometimes it's good to hear your voice and see your smile. I can tell you love what you do, Layk. You seem happy, and I guess I just miss it, ya know?"

We sit in silence for a few minutes. I struggle when he's like this, opening up and trying to show his feelings. He's my friend, and I don't want to hurt him, but I also don't want to hurt him by not being honest, either.

"I can't wait to have you come down and introduce you to some of my friends and teammates. They'll love you. I forgot to tell you, but they hired a new conditioning coach, and he's been working with me on some drills. He told me last week after practice he thinks I have a real shot at being drafted in the first round."

"Are you serious? That's incredible." I lean over and pat the top of his hand.

He stares down at my hand, moving his to rest on top of it. He sighs and nods.

"It's all working out how I hoped it would. Now there's just one other simple matter." He smirks.

Guilt twists in my stomach. "What would that be?"

"You."

I smile and shake my head. "We've had this talk, Rhys. You know how I feel."

Pulling my hand away, I fold mine together on my lap.

"I know we have, and you know how I feel too. I promised to give you time. All I've asked is for you to wait for me, wait until after college, and I'll be back for you. It's all coming together how I hoped it would."

Wait for me. We both know what he means by that comment.

This isn't about him wanting me to wait for him in hopes of a relationship. He's asking me to save myself for him.

He's had his future planned out for as long as I can remember. I've always admired his perseverance. He's the type to set his sights on something, and he doesn't give up until it's his.

It's just frustrating that I've told him multiple times I want us to stay friends, and he still refuses to accept it as being my answer.

"You've spent the last how many years working toward this. I know you've busted your ass for it, Rhys. I'm proud of you, I truly am. I just think the life you want and the life I'm dreaming of are two different worlds. I'll always be here for you, cheering you on as your friend. You know that, right?"

"Only as my friend, huh?"

I swallow hard and nod.

He nods, flicking his eyes around the room. He's trying to hide the pain on his face, but I know him too well. I don't try to soothe him because even though I know it hurts him, I don't want him to get the wrong idea, either.

The thought of us living two different lives brings me back to Trey, and I wonder what he's doing right now. If I thought Rhys and I were different people, I can't imagine what life on the road with a touring band is like.

On the nights they don't play, I imagine him going out, drinking and partying. I bet countless women are eager and waiting for him to look their way, for their chance to fill my place.

Jealousy coils in my stomach when I picture his hands on someone else. I clench my jaw and try to swallow through the ball forming in my throat.

I hate I even feel this way. I've spent my whole life not feeling chosen—by my parents, by kids at school, even by Rhys. The one time I gave him a chance, it wasn't long until someone else came along, and he gave in to the temptation all too easily.

Hell, even my own father chose alcohol and drugs over me. In the end, they won out and took him from me forever.

"Something's changed with you. I can feel it. I could sense it the moment you opened the door back at your place. Is there someone else?"

He reaches his hand over for mine. I quickly snap myself out of my thoughts, fumbling to try to come up with a response.

"Hey, sweet girl," Joann sings as she squeezes past a group of people and flings her arms around me, pulling me in for a hug.

I bury my head in her neck, inhaling her familiar scent. There's something both calming and nostalgic about it, taking me back to when I was younger. She'd comfort me when my parents disappeared, and I hadn't heard from them in days.

"I've missed you," she mumbles against the side of my head, and I whisper the same back to her.

She takes her break with us, and I'm thankful for the distraction from our conversation. After dinner, I feebly make up a lie about not feeling well. Rhys suggests we cut our night short, and he'll take me home. He offers to swing by the drugstore to pick up some medicine and soup on the way.

I'm already feeling like crap about the lies, and it only gets worse when he walks me to the door. He agrees to drop by before he leaves town.

I didn't have the heart to tell him he didn't have to, at least not tonight. I nod and kiss him on the cheek, thanking him for dinner before waving goodbye.

He stands out on the front step, waiting for me to safely get inside before he saunters back toward his pickup truck.

Tater is right there waiting for me, perched like a princess, ready to pounce for having the audacity to leave her.

My phone vibrates in my clutch, and I pull it out to answer, seeing Kate's name flash on the screen.

Kate's my best friend and the keeper of all my secrets.

She's always been Team Rhys—at least until she heard all about my rendezvous with Trey. She's tried convincing me to give him a chance, if anything, to bury the memory of Trey under a heap of orgasms.

"You didn't hit me with a 911 text, so I take it the night went well?" she asks cheerfully, bypassing the greeting.

"Well, hello to you too."

"Yeah, hi. Don't give me that shit. I want all the juicy details. How'd it go with Cowboy Quarterback?"

I sigh, collapsing onto my couch. I don't even have the energy to take my heels off.

"Ugh ..." she grumbles. "Not good then, eh?"

"It's not that. It's just... you know."

"Are you kidding?" she scolds. "That boy is premium meat, okay? He's the prime rib of men. You mean to tell me you aren't interested in him because your pussy didn't hiss?"

"You are such an eloquent lady, you know that?"

I've tried suggesting she date Rhys since she seems to be more into him than I am, but she balked at that idea. She's as loyal as they come, and no amount of convincing would get her to date a man who was my high school boyfriend, no matter how short-lived it was.

"Oh, you shut it," she quips. "You're the one searching for the right man like your vagina is a compass or a fuckin' pinpoint doppler radar. You've hooked up with one man, a sexy as hell one, I'll give it to you. Now you're convinced if lightning isn't striking in your pants and the thunder isn't rollin' in, you're not interested."

"There's nothing wrong with knowing what you want."

She may be right, though. I can't keep comparing everyone to Trey. It doesn't change the fact I want to stay friends with Rhys, either. Maybe what I need right now is to get back in the dating game and see what's out there. Even if it's nothing serious, there's nothing wrong with having a little fun.

"What's that exactly? I don't think you know what you want anymore."

I huff. "As a matter of fact, I do."

I hear the telltale sign of a cork popping in the background. Evidently, she's over my shit and is pulling out a bottle of wine just to deal with me.

"Hit me with it, then. I'm waiting."

"I've decided to sow my wild oats. Take a few rides out for a test drive. Sample the platter."

"Yeah, yeah, yeah. I get it."

"I'm serious. I think, to a point, you're right. I don't know what I'm looking for right now, but maybe that's the point. I've given up the big V, and now I need to see what's out there. Enjoy myself and go wherever life takes me."

"It's too bad you couldn't do that with a hot, dominant rock star who gets off on claiming all your orgasms."

I sigh, remembering the look on his face when he ordered me to show him how wet I was.

Jesus.

"You're not helping," I grumble. "I'm trying to bury him under a heap of orgasms with other men, remember? That ship has sailed, so I need to stop thinking about him and comparing him to every man I meet. I mean, great for me. I lost my virginity to the sexiest man alive who has magic fuckin' fingers."

She giggles.

"It was a great experience. It'll go down as one of the best, I'm certain of it. Now it's time to move on and have more with other hot and available men. Ones who will ask me for my name and remember it in the morning."

"I'll drink to that," Kate adds. "We have the rest of the summer to live it up, too."

"Exactly." I nod like she can see me. "Life's too short to dwell on assholes and waste it on bad sex."

This is all great in theory, but even I know I won't soon be able to forget what it's like having Trey all mine for one night.

CHAPTER SEVEN

TREY

Every stop on the tour feels like more of the same.

We're closing in on our second month out on the road, and every day, I'm going through the motions.

Joining A Rebels Havoc and going on tour has been a dream. We fit together in ways I haven't with other bands before. The rush of adrenaline when I step on stage and the roar of the crowd can't be topped.

I've prayed my whole life for this moment.

So why does it feel like I'm living someone else's life? Why am I constantly searching for the next high?

We finish up our show in Irvine. It's the last of our three shows in California and on the West Coast before we start making our way back across the US. We have about three weeks left, and I've hit the point where I'm ready for it to come to an end.

As much as I love being out on the road and playing in front of fans, I live for the creative process. When I sit down with my guitar and the music and lyrics flow out of me.

We've been working on new music between stops and have ten songs ready for our record label. I'm pumped to get in the studio with the guys and start recording. We'll release our upcoming album in early spring if all goes well.

We decide to pull off and stay in a hotel for the night. I'm sick of being cooped up in this cramped bus and want to get away for a while. We'll be packing up and hitting the road to Phoenix for the Twisted Tour festival in the morning.

After we check in, I slip outside under the guise of needing to grab a smoke. I don't need or want anyone in my business. I sure as hell don't want them knowing where I'm going, either.

I lean against the wall outside the hotel and wait for the cab I ordered. When the car pulls up a few minutes later, I quickly snub out the end of my cigarette and stick it into my pack before climbing into the back seat.

"Where am I taking you, sir?" the older gentleman asks.

His hair is white and his voice gruff, likely from years of smoking too. I've been thinking about kicking the habit lately, although if I'm honest, it's the alcohol I should give up instead.

One thing at a time.

"Where's the closest strip club around here?" I grunt, rolling down the window and leaning against the door.

"There are a couple within a few miles from here."

The clock on the dashboard illuminates the time. It's after one in the morning. I don't have a lot of time to waste if I hope to get back without raising any suspicions.

"Whichever is closest is fine."

He nods, pulling out of the parking lot, and heads in that direction.

It doesn't take long to get there. There's not much traffic at this time of night, and the parking lot is thin. The black-painted building is outlined in pink and red neon lights, along with the sign reading 4Play.

I toss him two hundred-dollar bills, asking him to make a loop back around in an hour, and I'll double it. He agrees, saying he'll park in the back of the lot to wait for me, and I make my way inside.

I tuck my hair in my hat, pulling the brim down to cover my face, trying to fly under the radar. The club is dark, with blue lights around the bars and spotlights above each stage. It makes it easy to keep a low profile when it's hard to see the rest of the patrons.

A woman near the corner immediately captures my attention, stirring my dick to life. She's dressed in a red top and a matching black-and-red-plaid skirt, with stockings pulled up to her knees and heels. Her long red hair is curled in waves down her back.

She looks like Layken.

When she notices me eyeing her, she saunters my way.

This is exactly what I was hoping for when I came here. I'm not looking to mess around. I just need to feed the monster inside me.

"Hey, handsome." She flicks her tongue against her teeth, her mouth stretching into a slow smile. "How are you doing this evening?"

She drags her hand down my forearm and reaches for the waistband of my pants, taking a step into me. I lift my eyes to meet hers, raising my brow.

"Better now," I whisper low against the side of her face.

"Mmm," she hums. "What brings you in tonight?"

"I'm only in town for the night. Want to join me for a dance?" I nod toward the hallway leading to the private rooms. "I'll make it worth your while."

She winks and nods. Slipping her hand in mine, she leads me across the club and down the long corridor. The rooms are set up a lot like Seven Sins. You see one, you've seen them all.

There's a leather couch in front of a small stage with a pole in the center. She pushes her palm against my chest, urging me to sit, and I fall back on the sofa.

Her breasts spill over her top when she leans over and presses her mouth near my ear.

"You want a dance, or were you hoping for something more?"

I release a slow breath, inhaling her fruity scent.

She has an innocent look on her face, and if I had to guess, she couldn't be older than twenty-one. Freckles highlight the apples of her cheek, her long eyelashes fanning over them when she blinks.

"I like to watch."

Her teeth rake over her lip, and she grins before moving a chair to sit in front of me. She walks across the room and presses a few buttons on the wall, and the song changes to something slower.

She saunters over, biting the edge of her mouth, and takes a seat.

My eyes drink her in when she drags her finger up her leg. When she reaches her hip, she spreads her legs open and does the same again, only this time she moves slower, tracing her finger up her inner thigh.

Her eyes roll closed when she leans back, trailing her hand along her stomach and over her chest. She releases a heavy sigh, and the sight of her stomach trembling and her nipples beading beneath her top has my dick hardening in my pants.

I grip my cock through my jeans. She rolls her eyes open, a small smile playing on her mouth when she notices my obvious appreciation straining against my zipper.

She stands, reaching for the waist of her skirt and pushing it down her legs before taking a seat again. This time when she spreads her legs, she runs her hand down her stomach between her legs to brush over her clit.

Her eyes flutter shut, and a moan slips out of her mouth. Her hips move, seeking more of her touch. She presses her feet against the side of the couch next to me, giving me a better view.

"I know you want to touch yourself." She breathes out harshly. "Will you let me watch you too?"

I reach for the button of my jeans and slowly drag the zipper down, freeing my dick. Something about her sweet voice and her resemblance to Layken has my mind drifting back to that night.

When she slips her hand between her legs to touch herself, I tighten my fist around my cock, and in my mind, I'm back in the hotel room with Layken.

Her stomach quivers with her touch, slipping her fingers between her folds to rub over her clit again. I push my shirt up, sweat dampening my forehead.

She tugs her top down, freeing her tits, and I notice for the first time the hoop through her nipple. My fingers itch to touch her, but something holds me back.

She's not who I wish I was touching.

Something about that thought snaps me out of the moment, and I screw my eyes shut, forcing my mind back to Layken.

The sight of her spread out beneath me, her fingers dipping into her tight pussy, has my stomach clench. The thought of claiming every inch of her sweet body and showing her all the ways I could make her orgasm is so primal and arousing.

The way her innocent eyes stared at me under her long lashes, the soft look on her face whenever I instructed her what to do, and the look of desire on her face when I praised her gave me something I've never felt with a woman.

I slowly blink my eyes open, remembering where I am.

"There he is." She smiles, dragging her lip between her teeth. "Tell me what you want."

"I want to watch you come."

"Do you want to help me?" she questions.

We both know better than to think she offers this service to all her customers. I don't miss the way she looks at me, her tongue darting across her lips at the sight of my dick, or her eyes growing heavy when she speaks.

There's a hopeful sound in her voice, and I'm certain she knows who I am too.

I don't care, though. Not right now.

"I like to watch," I repeat.

It's the truth, I do, but I don't have any interest in her touching me.

The woman I want is gone. I'm left to fight off the memories and my demons tormenting me.

I keep telling myself if I can get off, get rid of this urge, it will rid me of this need for her I have growing inside me.

Sex has never been personal to me. It's a way of releasing my body's pent-up tension and escaping the world around me.

Until Layken.

She's the only woman I've ever let get close to me, and now I can't seem to get my mind off her.

My body craves her in ways I shouldn't. I'm an idiot for even letting myself think about her again, but there's no other way to chase away my demons. Not when I have no chance of seeing her again.

I fucked it all up the morning she left.

I snap out of it and force myself to live in the moment.

She reaches between her legs, using one hand to spread her pussy open for me, giving me a perfect view of her pink clit. The other slides through her folds, down to her pussy, fingering herself before spreading her juices over her.

The sight of her wetness coating her digits spurs something inside me, and I moan at the sight.

“Lick your fingers,” I command.

She drags her tongue over her lips before tracing her fingers over them, sucking the tip into her mouth. She slowly drags it out, flicking her tongue over the end. I imagine her doing the same to the head of my cock.

My balls grow heavy. I'm out of my mind turned on and need to come like I need my next breath.

All I want is to feel Layken's lips wrapped around me. The visual of her mimicking the same motion has me squeezing my eyes shut and fisting my dick hard.

“Aw fuck, Layken,” I moan.

Guilt creeps inside me when I realize I said her name out loud until I hear her hum in approval.

The sound of the chair moving draws my eyes open, and she kneels on the floor between my legs.

“Is that what you need? You need me to be her to help you get off?”

My chest heaves with the force of my breaths coming out in heavy pants.

She rakes her nails down my thighs, and I thrust my hips up into my tight grip.

“Ah fuck,” I groan.

She brushes her finger over the tip of my dick, wiping the cum leaking from the tip, and lifts her hand to her mouth. This time when she sucks on her finger, she rolls her eyes closed and moans.

"I can be her if you want me to be."

I tilt my head down to stare at her. Beneath the dim lights, it's almost as if my eyes are playing tricks on me, and it's Layken on her knees for me.

What is it about the thought of her giving herself over to me, letting me own her pleasure that's consuming me?

I need her. I need to see her, feel her, and hear her moans in my ear when we're both coming together.

She slowly cups my balls, and I growl, relaxing some when she wraps her hand over mine. She's barely touching me. Maybe she senses it's hard for me to give her my pleasure, but when she tightens her hand around mine and guides us over my cock, I choke out a throaty moan.

"Fuck, Layken," I growl. "Fuck, baby."

"I want you to come for me," she hums. "Come on my chest and mark me as yours."

She's playing the part, and we both know it. I let my mind picture it's her with those sweet innocent eyes staring up at me. I need it to be Layken, to be back in the room with her one more time.

When she moans under her breath about how she wants to taste me, I imagine it's her, and my orgasm hits me like a freight train.

She moves to sit up on her knees, and I aim my release at her chest.

I hoped coming here tonight would feed this insatiable desire growing for her. But when I open my eyes and see the evidence on her chest, it's the exact opposite.

The guilt is back, and it twists in my stomach like a venomous snake.

I've never felt more disgusted with myself than I am right now.

CHAPTER EIGHT

LAYKEN

TWO WEEKS LATER

"Ya know, I wouldn't be mad at all if we skipped VIP entirely."

"Like hell we will." Kate shoots a warning glance over her shoulder, pinning me with a look that says, "You've gotta be crazy."

I release a heavy sigh and grit my teeth. I entered the contest to win a pair of A Rebels Havoc tickets when they first announced their tour.

Back before I ever planned my trip to Philly with Mona or spent the night with Trey.

It's one of their last stops on the tour. I never expected to win. As excited as I am to watch them play again, I'd give anything to get out of this meet and greet.

The last thing I want is another walk of shame at the hands of Trey Whitt.

"You look hot as hell too. I think you should march right up there and tell him to fuck off," she quips. "I'll be right there with you, sister... right after I get my picture with the guys, though."

I roll my eyes, and she shrugs.

Kate loves the band as much as I do.

"Please, do it for me." She folds her hand and puckers her lower lip out like a blubbering child.

A line forming through the lobby is sectioned off with a sign signaling Havoc Harlots to join the line for the VIP meet and greet. Music is playing, and people are dancing and smiling like it's the best damn night of their life.

Security is stationed along the room's outer edge, and I'm trying to force myself not to be a total Debbie Downer. I refuse to let Trey ruin my night or the show, even if I wish I didn't have to face him again.

"My mama always warned me if you keep doing stuff like that, a bird will come right on by and shit right on that lip. So you best put it away."

She throws her head back and laughs.

"Well, I think your mama would've also said she didn't raise no bitch, so let's go."

Kate grabs me by the hand, pulling me toward the line.

The only thing I can do now is hope he doesn't remember me, and we can both move on with our lives.

I recognize one of the girls as Madden's sister, Kyla. She's the one who set me up with an Uber. The girl next to her is Ivy, Brix's fiancée.

Kyla's face lights up when she sees me, and my face heats as I recall the embarrassment of that morning.

So much for flying under the radar and hoping no one recognizes me.

"Hey, you're here!" She smiles, walking toward me. She unclips her walkie on her hip, clutching a clipboard to her chest. "Layken, correct?"

Kate's face turns to me, quirking her brow.

I nod. "That's me. You're Kyla and Ivy, right?"

She laughs. "You got it. I didn't expect to see you here."

"Yeah, I was in Philly visiting my cousin, Mona. She's the one who did the interview before the concert. We're both huge fans of the guys."

She gives me a sympathetic smile, and I wonder if it's because she knows now he called me by the wrong name.

I wish the ground would open and swallow me whole right about now.

"Here." She unhooks the belt sectioning off the line from the rest of the lobby and nods for us to follow.

There's a collective sigh from the rest of the women around us, likely wishing they were lucky enough to be pulled aside too.

"Come with me."

"No, it's okay." I hold my hand up to stop her. "We don't mind waiting."

"Nonsense. I have someone I'm sure you want to see." She chuckles.

It's a knowing smile, and I flash my eyes over to Kate. She bites down on the corner of her lip to keep from laughing, knowing exactly the thoughts swirling through my mind.

If she had listened to me and skipped the meet and greet, it could've saved me the humiliation.

"C'mon, Layk. Let's see who it is." Kate smirks, linking her arm in mine to pull me along with her.

It's a scolding look that your parents would give you for disobeying them in public, warning you you're treading on thin ice.

I release a slow breath, my heart rate picking up. I thought I had a little time to collect myself before we reached the front of the line. I'm not ready to see Trey again, even though I've been preparing myself for this night all week.

"Girl, those boots are fuckin' killer." Kyla stares down at my legs. Ivy pipes up behind her, echoing the same thoughts.

I'm dressed in light denim jeans and a pair of black over-the-knee boots. My tank top is black with the A Rebels Havoc logo on the front.

I took some scissors to it, much like most of my other tees, adding some slits to the neckline to spice it up.

I kept it subtle on the makeup by adding a longer lash and bright red lipstick. My auburn hair is down and is a bit messy after running my hands through it nervously a couple dozen times.

"Trey's gonna shit himself when he sees you." Kyla snickers, and Kate laughs.

She leads us through the doorway into the large room. The guys are standing on a red carpet with a black backdrop with their logo printed on the front.

Most of the women standing in line are barely dressed, their tits hanging out of their tops and their ass showing through the bottom of their shorts and skirts.

It's no wonder Trey couldn't remember my name. Look how many beautiful women throw themselves at him night after night. What could he possibly see in me that he couldn't get from any of them?

He had his night of fun before tossing me to the side and moving on to the next one waiting their turn.

The photographer finishes snapping pictures, and Kyla whistles to catch their attention. Madden seems to be the only one who hears her, turning toward us before elbowing Trey in the ribs. Tysin follows him.

"Is that who I think it is?" Tysin bellows.

Trey finally gives in and glances our way. His eyes are fixated on me, blinking slowly. All emotion drains from his face.

My stomach twists, and I'm more ready now than ever to get the hell out of here.

I break eye contact with him, turning toward Kyla.

"Thank you for doing this, but it's okay. I think we should get going," I say under my breath.

Maybe she didn't know what she was getting into by pulling us ahead, but I'm not about to do this again. My throat goes dry with a lump forming, making it impossible to swallow.

My eyes flash over to Trey one last time, unable to resist the urge to look at him, when he shocks the hell right out of me.

"Layken," he says.

He smacks Tysin on the chest, shoving him away. Tysin tosses his head back laughing, but Trey waves him off as if trying to tell me to ignore him.

"I didn't expect to see you here." He steps up to me and reaches for my hand, slipping his fingers between mine as if it's a natural gesture.

"Oh shit," Kate mutters under her breath.

His hair is pulled up, with a few strands falling around his face. He shakes his head, pushing them back, then leads me away from the rest of the group.

"Come with me," he urges. He looks around the room, searching for a way to disappear from all the watchful eyes around us, before turning his attention back on me.

"I was hoping I'd see you again after the concert in Philly."

I tug my hand away, needing to break my connection with him. If I hope to tell him exactly what's on my mind, I need to do it without feeling the electric current coursing from his body to mine.

I grit my teeth and steel my resolve. Why is it no other man I've ever met makes me feel the way he does? It drives me crazy.

"Why is that exactly?" I quip, crossing my arms over my chest.

His eyes search my face, sensing the change in my demeanor. He turns to Madden and says something to him under his breath before turning to face me.

"Will you come with me for a minute?"

I exhale a heavy sigh and nod. I don't bother turning toward Kate. She's heard everything and knows exactly how I feel.

Trey reaches for my hand again, and I give in, letting him lead the way.

A man jogs in front of us, reaching for the door handle.

I don't recognize him at first with the baseball cap pulled low. It's not until he speaks that I remember he's one of the security guards who escorted us from the club that night.

He joins us, taking off toward the end of the hall to block it off and give us some privacy.

I turn to face Trey, mustering up every ounce of courage to get through this conversation and put this all behind me.

Trey drops his head, running his thumb over his lower lip, the other over the back of my hand. He takes a step toward me until I'm pinned against the wall with nowhere to go.

"I owe you an apology."

"You can start there." I nod.

"I… shit, Layken. I fucked up, okay? I know you heard me call you by the wrong name that morning."

"At least you understand why I'm upset."

"I do know why. I knew why the moment you stepped out of the room, and Madden corrected me. I don't remember you ever telling me your name that night, which is stupid of me. You probably think I'm a total jackass for not asking, but also for taking you back to my room and calling you by your friend's name."

"Cousin. Friend and cousin."

The sound of a whistle comes from down the hall.

"A minute, Abel, please," Trey grits out.

He shakes his head, clenching his jaw.

"I'm sorry, I know this isn't the best time to have this conversation. I need to get back. Will you do me a favor, though? Please."

"What?" I ask, pulling my hand away and crossing my arms again.

I have a feeling I need to prepare myself to reject whatever he's about to ask me.

He reaches for my hip as if he's searching for some way to touch me before dropping his hand to his side.

"Will you stay after the show and come back to my dressing room? I'll have Abel bring you to me."

I exhale. "I don't think it's a good idea, Trey."

He gives in this time and brushes his palm against the side of my face, tracing his thumb over my cheek. I suck in a sharp breath at the softness in his gaze.

I can almost make out the thoughts creating a thunderstorm in his mind, like the ones swirling around in mine.

On the one hand, I want to push him away and forget he ever existed.

Yet when he touches me, I'm finding it hard to forget everything outside of the two of us.

I want to ignore every reason and fear as to why he's all wrong for me. Why I should tell him to leave me alone.

When his thumb brushes over my lower lip, every single one of them disappears.

"Please."

I open my mouth to speak before snapping it shut again.

"Give me this one chance. If you don't want to see or speak to me again after we talk, you can tell me to fuck off, and I won't stand in your way or stop you from leaving."

Abel whistles again from down the hall.

"For fuck's sake," Trey grunts under his breath, his nostrils flaring.

"Okay." I nod.

"Okay, you will?" His voice sounds hopeful.

"I will."

He sighs. "I'll have Kyla upgrade your tickets so you're in the front. Look for Abel after the show is over. He'll bring you back to me. Okay?"

I drop my arms to my sides, and he slips his fingers through mine. I don't fight him this time. As much as I want to be upset, my resolve is slipping away.

How can he so quickly make me forget how hurt I was after that morning?

"I have to get back, but I'll see you soon."

I don't know what more to say, pushing off the wall.

When he leans into my face, all the oxygen is sucked out of my lungs. He lifts my chin to meet his eyes, his warm breath feathering across my cheek.

"For what it's worth, Layken, I couldn't be happier to see you again."

He pulls away and flashes me a wink before reaching for the door handle, holding his hand out for me to join the rest of the group again.

It takes a second for my heart to catch up with my thoughts, still hammering out of control at the sight of his smile.

I'm in trouble.

CHAPTER NINE

TREY

I've tried to avoid coming back to Nashville. Something about being here reminds me of the painful memories of growing up.

Like everything else in life, I've learned to detach and avoid what's bothering me rather than let the pain sink in.

My mom moved home a few years ago. I haven't spoken to my father in years. After all the shit he put us through, the affair and moving us halfway across the country, only to leave my mom for her—I'll never be able to look him in the eye again without wanting to swing on him.

He'd never step up to me, either. He understands how deep my hatred for him runs. It's best we stay away from each other. Even if we did speak, he'd never admit or own up to his faults.

It's his way or no way, and I'm sick of his lies and excuses.

All that aside, though, something about being back in Tennessee and playing in front of a packed crowd was nostalgic. This is where I first fell in love with music. On nights like tonight, with the energy from the fans so electric, my guitar in my hands, it's easy to release all my cares and worries and let the music take control.

Maybe it's because Layken will be waiting for me after the show, and she's not far out of my reach.

I've tried to chase her out of my mind since the night we met. No matter what I do, I can't seem to escape her.

The lights on the stage go out, bathing us in darkness.

"Good fuckin' show, man!" Brix shouts, smacking me on my chest.

Sweat drips down from his face. He ripped his shirt off in the middle of the show, using it as a towel. He dabs it over his brow before slinging it over his shoulder.

"I never want this tour to end." Tysin grins, nodding his head.

He's bouncing on his feet, like a live wire of energy surging through him.

Madden stands from his drum set, tossing his sticks to one of the roadies before pulling his shirt off too.

We're all ready to hit the showers.

I jog off the stage and down the stairs, running into Abel standing in the doorway near the entrance.

"Will you do me a favor and find Layken, the girl I was talking to earlier, and bring her back to my dressing room? Kyla upgraded her tickets. She should be stage side in front, waiting for you."

He nods. "No problem, man."

I clap him on the shoulder, thanking him, and take off toward my room. I jump in the shower, making quick work of getting cleaned up. I'm just pulling my jeans on when two knocks hit the door.

"Yo, man. She's right outside. I wanted to make sure you're good before I let her in."

I nod. "All good. Thanks again."

Layken pokes her head around the door, stepping to the side when Abel disappears into the hallway, leaving us alone.

"Did you enjoy the show?"

Her eyes flash over to me, slowly trailing over the tattoos covering my chest and arms down to where they disappear beneath the waistband of my jeans.

Her throat bobs when she swallows before realizing she's waited a beat too long to respond. Her eyes flick back up to mine.

"I always enjoy watching A Rebels Havoc play."

Her voice has lost its anger from earlier, even though she still feels distant. I'm still taking it as a hopeful sign that maybe she'll warm back up to me.

"I didn't expect to see you again, especially in Nashville. I remember you saying you were visiting Philly but didn't realize you were from the area."

"I grew up here," she says flatly.

I nod. "Did you know I grew up here too?"

I swear there's a look of hurt on her face, but it vanishes in an instant. She clenches her jaw, rolling her lips together. I'm not sure if she's upset or ready to rip my head off.

After I rummage through my suitcase, I pick up my T-shirt, holding the cotton material in my hand. She stares at me for a second.

I can practically hear the seconds tick by as I wait for her to say what's on her mind.

"I did know that, Trey. I know a lot more about you than you think I do. On the other hand, you don't seem to remember anything about me."

Shaking my head, I take a few steps toward her. She follows suit, stepping back while holding her hand up between us to stop me.

"You should probably stay over there. I can't seem to think clearly when you're ..." She stops herself, waving her hand at me.

A slow smile stretches across my face. She flares her nostrils, dropping her hand to her side and clenching it into a fist.

I take the last remaining step toward her, reaching for her hand to pull her to me.

"Trey," she breathes out.

"Have you thought about me at all since that night?" I ask.

"No." She snaps her hand away and crosses her arms. "As a matter of fact, I haven't thought about you once."

I curl my lip into a sinister smile.

"Try again, sweetheart. I'm not buying it."

She rolls her eyes and shakes her head.

"Do you want to try again or keep lying to both of us?"

"I don't have to try anything, Trey. I don't belong to you."

Now I know she's trying to push my buttons.

I smirk. "You're damn right you don't." I grip her hip and lean into her. "Because if you did, I'd have you bent over that couch right now, reminding you who you do, in fact, belong to."

Her mouth falls open, and she quickly snaps it shut.

I chuckle. "Yeah, that's what I thought, sweetheart. Now let's try again, and you can tell me the truth this time. Have you thought about me since the night we spent together?"

My dick is strained against the front of my pants. I'm dying to pull her over to the couch and strip off her clothes.

"Yes," she mutters.

She takes another step back, propping herself against the concrete wall. I lean in, pressing my palm next to her head, and tilt my mouth close to her ear.

"What do you think about?"

She fumbles over her words, almost as if she's too nervous to tell me.

"You wanna know what I've thought about?" I ask, brushing my nose along the side of her face. I flick my tongue over the shell of her ear, and her breathing sputters.

She tries to act unaffected, or maybe it's more trying to convince herself she doesn't care, but her body gives her away.

Every. Single. Time.

"There's something about the sound of your voice when you moaned my name I can't seem to forget. I've closed my eyes countless times and pictured us back in that room. Or when you let out a breathy *fuck*."

"Trey..." She trails off.

"Yeah, baby, just like that."

Her breathing grows labored, her chest rising and falling rapidly as her eyes flick up to meet mine.

"Or the sight of you rubbing your fingers over that sweet pussy. Seeing how fuckin' wet you were for me."

I graze my lips along her cheek, reaching my other hand up to tuck her hair away from her face. She tilts her chin toward me, exposing the column of her neck.

Dragging my lip through my teeth, I slip my fingers into her long hair, pulling the strands at the base of her neck. The move forces her head back farther, giving me better access.

I flick my eyes down to her neck before meeting her gaze once more.

"If I were to reach into the front of your pants, would you be wet for me right now?"

She sucks in a deep breath, and I whisper, "I think you would be."

I brush my tongue over her earlobe and trail my lips down her neck, nipping and biting as I do.

Her hand juts out, holding my forearm, the other grabbing the waist of my pants.

She slips her fingers into the waistband of the denim, dangerously close to where my dick strains against my zipper. I release a slow hiss, pulling back to find desire glossing her eyes.

"Give me one more night with you, Layken. Let me make it up to you."

She seems to consider it for a second, a series of thoughts playing out on her face before she puts her hand up and pushes me away.

"I can't seem to think clearly when you're coming onto me, trying to distract me from the conversation."

My smile falls from my face.

"Listen, I'm sorry for what happened back in Philly. Fuck, I'd be lying if I didn't say I haven't thought about you countless times since. You say I'm distracting you, but dammit, look at you. You come in here, looking like you're ready to rip my heart out and stomp on it with those boots. It was the same way that night.

"I was captivated by you, by wanting to be close to you. I should've slowed down and not rushed it and, goddamn, asked for your fuckin' name. I've never been one to take things slow, though, and I sure as hell don't hold back from taking what I want."

She shakes her head, looking around the room as if searching for somewhere to escape. I don't feel like what I'm saying is making a difference.

"You're still missing the point, Trey."

"Is this supposed to be a guessing game? Jesus, baby, tell me what I did already because I have no idea."

"Philly isn't the first time we've met."

My brows knit together in confusion.

What? Is she saying we've hooked up before?

Immediately, my mind starts sifting through memories of being out on the road with Blunt Force Trauma. Shit, that was a dark time in my life. I did a lot of drinking.

A *lot*.

I got myself mixed up in some recreational activities I had no business messing around in before refusing to let that shit ruin my life too. And women.

There were *a lot* of women.

I'm not proud of my decisions, but I never hurt anyone, and I don't remember ever meeting her.

"When?"

"We grew up together in Nashville. You're a couple years older than me, but you didn't live far from me. I saw you every day for two years until one day, you were gone."

"Wait, what?"

She nods, a soft smile curving her lips. "To be fair, though, I don't look anything like I did back then."

I let my eyes trail over her body and smile appreciatively.

"I don't doubt you were beautiful back then, but trust me when I say, if I saw you walking around town, I'd remember it."

She smirks and smacks me against my chest.

"I have to be honest with you," I say, reaching for her hand and pulling her with me over to the couch. "Please don't take it personally, but I truly don't remember. I've blocked a lot from that time in my life out of my mind."

She moves to set her purse on the end of the couch, and she doesn't fight me when I pull her onto my lap.

"I've been told it's a trauma response or some shit." I shrug. "I've tried to stay away from here, not wanting to face those memories, even though I do miss it."

Her eyes soften, and she squeezes my hand. "I'm sorry," she whispers. It's not in a sympathetic way but more of an understanding.

I hate opening myself up to people, especially about deep shit from that time in my life. There's something so pure and genuine about Layken. It's comforting.

I brush my thumb over the back of her hand, soaking in the feel of her soft skin.

"We're staying in a hotel downtown off Broadway. Will you come back with me and stay for the night?"

"Trey, I don't know if it's a good idea."

"It's not about sex. I mean, not if you don't want it to be."

I'm almost surprised to hear myself say it, but it's true. I don't want her to leave just yet, and if she doesn't want it to be physical, I'm willing to accept it too.

"I find that hard to believe." She giggles, but her face falls when she sees mine.

"Don't get me wrong, I'd love nothing more than to make up for all the time I've been thinking about you, but I can live without it for one night."

"You could have any woman in this city you want. Why would you possibly choose to spend the night with me?"

"I don't want any other woman but you."

She seems surprised by every word out of my mouth. If I'm honest, I am too. It's true, though. There's no one else I want to be with tonight.

"Plus, I like spending time with you. I'm only here for the night, and I still have a lot of making up to do if I'm ever gonna convince you I'm not the asshole you must think I am. C'mon. One night?"

She fights the urge to smile, biting the edge of her lip before she nods.

"One night."

"You should know, though, Layken, I'm determined to convince you before the morning to give me more than one night."

CHAPTER TEN

LAYKEN

What am I doing?

Who am I kidding? I know exactly what I'm doing.

Although, I have to admit, I'm still trying to wrap my head around Trey wanting to spend the night with me for any reason other than sex.

I'm not naïve enough to think a rock star as sexy and confident as he is could have any interest in a girl like me. It's hard to ignore the butterflies in my stomach and the rapid heartbeat in my pussy because, damn, the bitches are back.

He's torturing me, though, when he rakes his hand over his facial hair, his smile when he catches my eyes lingering on him, or how he can't seem to hold himself back from wanting to hold my hand.

I rode with them to his hotel. The entire drive, I wondered if he was like this with other women he hooked up with when taking them to his room.

"Geez, you get her here, and you're already dragging her off to the bedroom." Kyla snickers.

Trey levels her with a glare, and I press my lips together to avoid smiling.

"Like you're not waiting for Tysin to do the same?"

Whoa. So the rumors are true, then. I didn't realize Tysin and Kyla were an item now.

Kate mentioned she noticed the ring on Kyla's finger was missing and how the two seemed overly affectionate toward each other. I'm not one to keep up with the tabloids, but Kate shared she read on Hollywood Tea how Kyla recently called off her engagement to FBX racer Canon West.

Trey raises his hand to wave everyone off and leads me to the room off their suite. He opens the door, then turns to face me, banding his arm around my waist and hauling me into the room before kicking the door shut behind us.

I giggle. He presses his forehead against my cheek and sighs.

"I can't believe you're here," he whispers.

I circle my arm around his neck, and his hold tightens.

"It doesn't seem real to me either."

He lowers me to the floor and leans away, cupping my chin. His large hand nearly wraps around the front of my throat. Something about it is commanding, possessive. I'd be lying if I didn't add incredibly hot.

His nostrils flare as he stares down at me. He looks like he wants to say something but thinks better of it before his lips crash down on mine.

I moan against his mouth, taken off guard, fisting the front of his shirt in my hand.

I'm lost in him, in this kiss. There's nowhere else I want to be. Once again, when we're together, he so easily makes me forget everything else but the two of us.

When he breaks the kiss, he brushes his finger over my cheek to my lips. The coarse skin ignites something inside me, making me imagine how they would feel on other sensitive areas of my body.

He furthers his path from my mouth, down my chin and over my chest. He pulls the front of my shirt down, getting a glimpse of my cleavage.

"Do you realize how intoxicating you are? The high I get from you is better than any drug, any drink I've ever had."

"Trey," I whisper.

"I'm sorry. I'm fuckin' tryin' so damn hard not to drag you over to that bed and beg you to let me recreate every vision I've had since the first night we were together."

When he said he's thought about me, I assumed he meant he was replaying memories from that night. I never expected to hear him say he's been envisioning us together in other ways.

He's not alone, though. No matter how much I try to force him out of my mind, he always manages to creep his way back in.

Like a drug.

"You make it hard for me to forget all the reasons I was ever mad at you."

He grins. "Looks like I'm well on my way to claiming more than one night with you."

"Maybe," I say, narrowing my eyes while attempting to stand my ground.

He shakes his head, leaning down to kiss me again, trailing a path down my neck.

"We'll see about that, won't we?"

He links our fingers together and pulls me into the room, stopping to open the blinds to the windows overlooking downtown Nashville. The lights are bright in the distance. I'm half tempted to ask him if he wants to do some exploring when he turns to face me.

"It's crazy as hell being back here," he says, shaking his head as he waves toward the window.

He's dressed in a black T-shirt and denim jeans and the same black combat boots he wore the first night. There's a leather bracelet around his wrist, and the sight mixed with his tattooed forearms disappearing beneath his sleeve is sexy on a whole other level.

"When was the last time you were here?"

He exhales a sigh. "Uhh, well, it's been a few years since my mom moved home, so I'd say then. She needed my help, and I had time off."

I suspect there's more to why he's avoided coming back, but I'm not sure I should venture down that road tonight.

"What about in the future?" I ask, trying not to sound too hopeful. I set my purse down on the dresser, my fingers itching to touch him again. "You think you'd ever come visit and maybe stick around for a few days?"

He flicks his eyes over to mine. "We only have a couple more stops on our tour before it wraps up. I can think of a few reasons I'd like to make the trip."

"Yeah?"

He smirks and nods, stepping away from the window. He saunters toward me at the foot of the bed. The look in his eyes practically lures me in.

There's that pull again between us. The voice in the back of my mind tells me to give in.

Give it one more night.

His eyes roam over my face and pause on my lips. His gaze burns into me, and I quickly drag my tongue over my dry lips.

He sucks in a sharp breath. "I'm finding it hard to resist touching you," he mutters.

"Don't."

"Don't?" His eyes flick over to mine, wanting to make sure he understood me correctly.

"Don't resist," I say on an exhale.

His fingers skate up my forearms, causing goose bumps to break out over my skin. He trails them over my shoulder and along the column of my neck, cupping my face.

The path is slow and torturous. With my face in his hands, his eyes move from mine down to my mouth.

"If we light this match, Layken, it's going to take a lot to put it out."

I want to ask what he means. The voice in my head shouts, "Be careful not to get burned." I don't care, though.

This isn't about wanting more or seeing a future with Trey. It's about giving in to the temptation, the desire unmatched by anyone else but him.

We already know how wrong for each other we are.

I've been the girl who doesn't get chosen, but tonight, he's choosing me. He wants to be with me, and dammit if I don't want to see the hungry look in his eyes and feel his firm hands on my body again.

I want whatever this night with him will bring, even if it's all I'll ever get.

Even if it's only for one night.

He brushes his thumb over my lip and leans in to kiss me. The spark causes me to gasp when his lips touch mine, and desire pools in my belly.

I'm ready to beg him. Beg him to touch me, all of me, wanting to feel all the ways my body comes alive under his touch.

His eyes are heavy when he pulls away.

"I want to feel those sweet lips wrapped around my dick, baby."

My mouth drops open before I quickly snap it shut. The last time we were together, I had a few drinks in me. It made me feel bold and confident.

Tonight is different.

The weight of his words and the need in his voice are heightened. I'm suddenly reminded how inexperienced I am compared to him, and I hate the thought of comparing myself to other women ready to take my place.

It's not like I'm completely clueless. I've watched porn a time or two, enough to know what I'm doing, but it's different when the roles change.

I swallow down my anxiety, wanting so badly to see the look of pleasure in his eyes again.

I run my palm over the front of his jeans, and he sucks in a sharp breath, flaring his nostrils before rattling off a string of curse words.

There's not a shy or nervous bone in him. He reaches for the zipper of his jeans, quickly unbuttoning them before shoving them over his hips enough to free his dick.

My tongue nervously darts out along my lips again.

"You keep licking your lips, I'm going to have you on your knees tasting me."

My eyes flutter, my chest seizing. A part of me wants to test him, desperately needing him to take the reins again and call the shots.

I instinctively drag my teeth over my lip before licking them again. His nostrils flare, and his eyes narrow.

"Is that what you want, Layken? Are you trying to tempt me?"

I hesitate for a minute, wrapping my hand around his hard length before I nod.

"Fuck," he murmurs. "You're fuckin' perfect."

He lifts my chin to kiss me. When I slowly drag my hand down him, he pulls back and hisses, staring down between us. I tighten my grip on him and brush my thumb over the head, rubbing the cum into his skin, and he grits his teeth.

"Jesus, Layken."

"I want you to tell me how you like it," I say meekly, taking a deep breath before saying it again, this time more confident than before.

"Is that what you want?" He tilts my head back to meet my eyes, and I nod.

He clenches his jaw.

"Get on your knees, Layken."

He takes my other hand while I slowly lower myself to the floor. I adjust my grip, and he wraps his hand over the top of mine.

"Twist your wrist like this," he grits out, showing me before releasing his hold, dropping his fist to his side.

His eyes bore into me, watching me repeat the same movement. He rolls his eyes closed and tilts his head back.

"Fuckkk," he says. It's low and throaty, and so fucking hot.

Something is so intoxicating, so heady, about seeing him turned on and knowing it's me who's pleasuring him.

He rolls his head back down, slowly blinking his eyes open.

"Open your mouth," he orders. "Stick out your tongue."

He holds the base of his dick, brushing the tip over my tongue. I lap at the head, licking and swirling around him, imagining he's like an ice cream cone and I want to savor every last drop.

I watch him from beneath my lashes, taking him in while he slowly slides into my mouth before flicking my tongue over the tip again.

"Tighten your lips around me, baby," he groans. "Fuck, just like that."

I suction my lips, and his nostrils flare as he thrusts slowly at first. My hands grip his hips, letting him set the pace.

He pulls out and squeezes the tip into his fingers and curses. "I'm so close to coming. You have no idea how fuckin' good it feels."

"This is my first time," I blurt out.

I regret the words as soon as they pass my lips. He steps away, his eyes staring down at me in wonder as his mouth falls lax. Heat warms my skin in embarrassment.

"Wait…" He trails off. "Are you serious?"

I nod timidly, wanting to cover my face and take it all back. It's like I just shouted, "I don't know what the hell I'm doing."

"C'mere." He holds his hand out to me and helps me stand.

"Oh God," I mumble.

"What's wrong?" he asks.

I massage my fingers into my forehead, trying to hide the panic from showing on my face.

"I shouldn't have said anything. Now you don't want to, and I just feel…" I shake my head, not wanting to continue my thought.

Rhys is the only guy who knows about my lack of experience. He was never an asshole about it. If anything, he was supportive and said all the right things, but when I wasn't ready to take the next step, he used it as an excuse against me when I found out he was with someone else.

"You think I don't want to?" he asks, his voice loud and more commanding than before. "Layken, look at me."

He reaches his hand out, lifting my chin to meet his eyes.

"Is that what you think? You believe I don't want to now that you admitted this was your first time?"

"Yeah?"

He pulls his pants up over his waist, and my heart drops when he moves me onto his lap.

I've ruined everything.

"Layken, you're wrong. I suspected you were inexperienced just by how nervous you are, but fuck. If I'm honest, it turns me on even more thinking about you..." He shakes his head, like he can't possibly fathom it. "You have nothing to be embarrassed or ashamed of. If anything, I'm ashamed of myself."

"Trey, please don't." I hold my hand out to stop him.

He wraps his arm around my waist, pulling me closer.

"I'm sorry, I'm fucking this up, aren't I?"

I smile and shake my head. "No, I mean, maybe a little, but only because you stopped me."

He pulls back, his brows deepening.

"I didn't want to stop. I wanted you to keep going, keep telling me what you want, and how you like it."

His mouth snaps shut.

"You want me to teach you how to suck my dick, baby?"

My breath sputters. How can he be so confident in himself and what he wants while I'm over here a fumbling mess?

"Say it, sweetheart." He smirks. "I want to hear you tell me you want to wrap those sweet lips around my dick."

My eyes flutter, and I nod. "I want you to show me what you like, to taste you, and to know you're turned on because of me."

He clenches his jaw, inhaling a deep breath through his nose. He moves me to stand and does the same.

He pushes his pants back down to free his cock from the confines of his jeans.

"Wrap your hand around my dick and suck me into your mouth."

Oh God. I swear, I could get off just listening to him talk. I squeeze my legs together, feeling a rush of desire at his commanding tone. I want nothing more than to make him feel as weak as he makes me when he touches me.

Like my knees are about to give out at any second.

I follow his instructions and grip the base of his cock. Wrapping my lips around him, I take him slowly into my mouth.

He softly brushes his hand along the side of my face.

"God, baby, that feels so fuckin' good."

He widens his stance and moans when I tilt my head back enough to stare at him. He slowly pulls out and thrusts back in. Each time he does, I take him deeper than before.

He curses under his breath, his fingers tangling in my hair to hold my head in place while he fucks my mouth.

When he hits the back of my throat, I choke and gag, blinking my watery eyes but not wanting to stop.

"Fuck, do that again, baby. Please. Take all of me and let me hear you."

His voice is strained, his neck tightening as he releases another deep moan.

I drag my tongue underneath him, letting him go farther again. He hits the back of my throat, and I gag around him.

"Good girl," he growls. "Just like that, baby."

I add my hand, following the path with my mouth, twisting my wrist with each pull.

"Dear God, I'm gonna come, baby. Tell me where."

I don't bother to let up, not wanting to stop. I'm addicted to the rush, the sight of his body tensing with desire, and the sound of need in his voice.

"You have to tell me. I'm about to come," he chokes out. "Tell me where you... oh fuck. Layken, baby," he rattles off.

His hands fist at his side. When I take him again, letting him feel the back of my throat, he comes. It surprises me at first, but I'm too turned on by his reaction to think about anything else.

He throws his head back and groans. His body tenses until he eventually relaxes. When he pulls out, he pulls me into his arms and kisses me.

“That was... you’re fuckin’ unreal.” He shakes his head, a look of awe in his eyes.

I drag my tongue over my lips, not thinking about his warning earlier. His eyes widen as he stares at me before he kisses me again.

“You’re fuckin’ dangerous.”

I smile. “How so?”

“I don’t think I’ll ever get enough of you.”

CHAPTER ELEVEN

TREY

It was different waking up the following morning next to Layken. We spent most of the night awake, and I didn't care. We were hitting the road for our next show in Tampa.

I could sleep on the road, or I could sleep when I'm dead.

I'm not used to the feelings stirred up by being around her, but I meant it when I said I wanted to earn more than one night with her. If I was going to, I had to start making up for the last time we were together.

"Breakfast in bed?" She smiles, pushing herself up against the headboard.

She pulls her legs to her chest, eyeing the large tray in my hands when I set it down on the bed. Her eyes widen when she looks at the platter of food before blinking up at me.

I shrug. "I didn't know what you liked to eat, so I ordered a little of everything."

She snags a strip of bacon, takes a bite, and moans.

When did watching a woman eat become so sexy? I guess I can't be surprised. Everything she does is somehow sexy to me.

"You keep that shit up, and I'll shove this food off the bed and roll you around in it."

She presses her lips together and shakes her head before taking another bite.

I flare my nostrils and growl under my breath before crawling in next to her. I cup the side of her face in my hand. Her gaze softens, her body relaxing when I lean in to kiss her.

"They're gonna need to drag me out of here when it's time for us to hit the road. You, naked in my bed, making noises like this will make it impossible for me to leave on my own."

"Man, if you want to stay here for the next couple of nights, it's no problem." Madden taps his elbow against my arm, lifting his beer to his lips, effectively snapping me out of my thoughts.

I exhale a heavy breath, gritting my teeth, and try to bring myself back to where I'm at.

Every day for the past few weeks, my mind has been back in Nashville with Layken.

I was hoping our schedule would slow down when our tour wrapped up, and I could follow through on my word to visit her.

After a short break, we immediately headed out to LA to start recording our album that was dropping soon. We were busting our asses in the studio from sunup to sundown. Now that we have a few days off in Carolina Beach, I'm beat and desperate to slow things down for a while.

"I might need a place for the night. I can't believe I got stiffed by my Airbnb."

Madden shrugs. "It's all good. No sense in you finding a place when we're about to head out on the road again anyway. It's not like I don't have the space."

He has a point there.

We have a photo shoot for our album in NYC before we fly out to LA to promote the music video for our upcoming single.

"If you're up for it, maybe we can grab a few beers after practice at Whiskey Barrel."

Certain parts about being here, like hitting up the bar with the guys, make me miss Nashville. When I was little, my dad would bring me with him to work. That was how I was first exposed to the music scene. He'd park me at a high-top table, and I'd watch wide-eyed at the live music playing. I grew up listening to rock, blues, and country.

For my birthday that year, I asked for my first guitar and started teaching myself how to play. It took a while to get the hang of it, but from that day forward, I've been playing and never once have I doubted if this is what I was meant to do.

We're still waiting for Brix to arrive. I crack open a beer and park it at the high-top table. Kyla slips in and climbs onto the barstool next to me.

"You look like you have a lot on your mind," she says, nursing a whiskey on the rocks.

She's not wrong, but I shrug, playing it off.

"You tired? Homesick? Or missin' Layken?" She smiles, like she has all my problems figured out.

I shrug. "I'm good. It's been a long day, and we have another long day ahead of us tomorrow."

She shakes her head. "I'm not buyin' what you're tryin' to sell."

"I guess that makes me as good of a liar as you are." I nod toward her and Tysin.

I smirk, and Tysin lifts his beer to cover his smile. When I flick my gaze back to Kyla, she narrows her eyes on me.

A lot has changed since the end of the tour, one being their relationship. She's trying to act like she's calling me out for hiding the fact I'm missing Layken. I'm not hiding anything, but even if I was, I'd be about as terrible as she was saying she hates Tysin.

"Quit tryin' to read me and everything I do," I quip.

She curls her lip into a smile. "You make it too easy. So when're you goin' to Nashville to see her?"

"What makes you think she'd even want to see me if I did?"

"You're kidding me, right?" Kyla asks. "Please tell me you're joking."

"Why would I be joking?"

"The real question is why you're trying to convince me or anyone else she wouldn't want to see you. Anyone with eyes and half a brain could see how bad she has it for you. I could see it before you ever kissed and made up."

I shake my head. "She was pissed at me that night. It took some sweet-talkin' to even get her to hear me out. I'm lucky she gave me the time of day, much less came back to the hotel with me."

Tysin chuckles, looking down at Kyla and back over at me.

"What?" I bark.

The two of them look like they're in on something.

"Hate to break it to ya, man, but Kyla's right on this one."

"Since when do you have a clue about women? You left this beautiful woman waiting for two fuckin' years. You think I didn't see how *she* looked at *you* the very first day on the bus?"

Tysin fights off the urge to smile. "I guess we can both agree we don't always see what's right in front of us, huh?" he retorts.

Kyla reaches for my arm, her face softening. "I'm serious, Trey. I think she was hurt after the first night, but I do think she's into you. A lot more than you might believe."

I tilt my head back, downing the rest of my beer. We have a few minutes before we take the stage. We don't plan on doing a full set, but we'll play a few songs.

"Even if she does," I say, setting the bottle down on the table, "I don't deserve a woman like her. Not ever, not in this lifetime."

Kyla huffs. "Why don't you let her be the one to decide instead of making the decision for her."

I wanted to tell her because she's the first woman I've felt this way for, and I don't want to go down the road and face the fact when she realizes she deserves more.

I didn't, though, because arguing with Kyla is an endless battle. She'd die on this hill just to prove she's right. It's who she is, and I have a feeling her last statement may have more to do with her relationship with Tysin than my situation anyway.

"Maybe you're right. I guess we'll have to see where it goes."

It's the best I can come up with. She wants to push me on it. Tysin's waiting for her to continue. He steps in and whispers in her ear, and I use it as an opportunity to make a break for it.

I slip off my barstool and disappear into the crowd, heading for the back room we have reserved for us when we play at Whiskey Barrel. I love how the guys still always play here even though they have achieved success.

Madden steps in from outside and nods his head in greeting.

"It's about showtime." He grins, reaching for another beer from the bucket on the table. He bounces on his feet, twisting the cap to take a heavy swallow.

"I'm ready."

I've kept in touch with Layken. She's been busy with work, and I've been bouncing from one place to the next, working on our new music. We've exchanged a few texts here and there. The last one was a few days ago.

After my conversation with Kyla, I'm itching to reach out to her. I tell myself it's innocent, just to see how she's doing.

This is unfamiliar territory for me, and I don't want to hurt her if it doesn't work out. I also don't want to keep my distance from her, either.

I open our message thread and read through our last conversation before I quickly type out my response.

Me: I'm about to head out on stage but want you to know I'm thinkin' about you.

I hit send, and a few seconds later, the message is read, and the bubble appears, signaling she's typing out a response.

What the hell is this feeling? My heart's practically in my fuckin' throat.

Layken: I was hoping you didn't give up on wanting more than one night...

Layken: I've been thinkin' about you too

She's been thinking about me.

Me: I guess I need to step up my game, then.

Me: Would it help if I told you I'm planning a trip to Nashville?

A loud whistle comes down the hallway, and I glance up to find Brix standing near the stage. He looks down at my phone, then back up at me and smirks.

"You comin', schoolgirl? Or you gonna keep sendin' hearts and kissy faces all night?"

"Listen, I've seen all the romantic shit you do for Ivy. Rose petals down the hall and all over the bed in the back of the fuckin' tour bus. Don't come throwin' that shit at me."

He grins. "You're right. I'd fuckin' do anything for that woman. Although I try to hold off until after the show."

"Yeah, all right, I fuckin' got it. Give me a sec."

Layken: You're coming back to Nash?

Me: Yeah, baby, I'm thinking I'll head your way next week.

Me: I gotta get on stage, though. Can I call you later?

I grit my teeth and pocket my phone, wishing I didn't have to get on stage right now. I grab my guitar before I climb the steps to join the guys.

At one point, I swear my phone vibrates against my leg, and for the rest of our set, all I can think about is reading her message. If I wasn't staying with Madden, I would've dipped out right after we wrapped up and turned in early for the night.

After I hit the shower to clean myself up, I pull on my boxer briefs and climb into bed in the guest room at Madden's place. It's almost two in the morning when I click on her name to connect the call.

"I was wondering if I'd still hear from you." She sighs when she answers.

"You said I could, and I wasn't about to miss the chance to hear your voice again."

She hums. "I did, but I was starting to think maybe you forgot or had other plans."

"I don't want anyone but you."

There's a rustling sound on the other end, and I picture her curled up in bed. Her soft voice filters through the line. I'd give anything to have her next to me.

"I wish you could see how damn big my smile is right now."

I think back to my conversation with Kyla. I guess I downplay what I'm feeling because I don't want to hurt her, and I don't want to get her hopes up.

I haven't thought about hitting up my usual spots now that I'm back in Carolina Beach. It hasn't even crossed my mind.

"I'm not very good at this, ya know. I've messed up a few times, and I'm sure I'll mess up a few more. I've never done this with anyone."

"Talked on the phone?"

"No." I chuckle. "I've never pursued a woman. I don't get close enough to even see where it would go. I want to see you again, though, and spend more time with you away from everyone else when we're not on the road and in town only for a night or two."

"Trey," she whispers.

"Yeah?"

"I want that too."

I suck in a deep breath. "You do?"

"Yeah." She giggles. "I guess you need to hurry up and get back to Nashville then, huh?"

"We fly out in the morning to shoot our album cover, but right after that, I should be able to head your way."

"Kate asked me to help with a styling gig she has, but things will slow down next week, so it works out perfectly."

During the night we were together in Nashville, she told me about her job doing hair and makeup, mostly for weddings and other events. She's started using social media to teach other women and young girls too. I was captivated by the way her face lit up while she talked animatedly about it.

"I'll need you to schedule a couple nights with me if that's all right with you?"

"Is that right?" she says, giggling. Her Southern twang coming through in her voice.

"I'm trying to win you over, and the best way to start is by taking you out on a proper date."

CHAPTER TWELVE

LAYKEN

"You're still not gonna tell me what's going on?" I whisper, gritting my teeth, and lean over into Kate's seat.

She's been wearing the same smug grin all morning.

I've lost count of how many times I've asked where we're going. All she'll tell me is it's a job of a lifetime, and I can't let her down.

I fell asleep on the phone with Trey sometime around three this morning. Trey ended up video calling me in the middle of our conversation. I still smile when I think about him lying back against the headboard. His messy hair reminded me of the times he wore it down and let me drag my fingers through it. I woke up to a photo text from him of my face before he hung up. The smile on his face when he watched me sleep is not something I'll soon forget.

It made for a rough morning dragging my ass out of bed to make our flight. It didn't help that the nausea I've been feeling lately was back, making it even harder to get up and around for our trip.

"Good morning, ladies and gentlemen. Welcome to International Airlines. My name is Cody, and this is Emmy. We are your cabin crew here to ensure you have an enjoyable flight to New York City today."

"All right, so you're hauling my ass clear to New York City," I start to say, but wince, feeling my stomach roil once again.

"Are you sure you're okay?" Her brows deepen in concern.

I nod and wave my hand at her. "Yeah, I think it's just pre-flight jitters."

"Pre-flight jitters? Since when are you ever nervous when flying?"

She has a point. We take trips together often, and I've never been one to get anxious.

She leans in close to me again. "Are you sure you're not pregnant? How long has it been since you and Trey first hooked up?"

My mouth drops open, the concern still showing on Kate's face.

"Let's not go throwing those words around or putting that out into the universe. There's no way I'm pregnant," I defend. "Besides, I'm on birth control. I'm telling you, I'm just anxious lately. Maybe you could help a girl out and tell me what the heck this mystery trip is about?"

She sighs and shakes her head. "If I do, it'll ruin the surprise."

"Surprise?" I pull back, studying her face. "Why would this be a surprise for me? I thought I was helping you with a job?"

She nods. "Oh, you are, but my clients may include someone you might know too."

My face falls before a slow smile curls the edge of my lips.

"It's Trey, isn't it?"

She shrugs. "Maybe."

"You got a job with A Rebels Havoc?" My eyes widen, and my mouth drops open, realizing how big this is for her.

She bounces in her seat and nods. "Oh my God, do you know how good it feels to finally tell you? I've been dying."

I smirk. "When we saw them play in Nashville, I started chatting with Kyla when Trey dragged you away. I mentioned I'd love to help style them for any upcoming appearances or events they have. I didn't expect her to take me up on it."

When I spoke to Trey on the phone last night, he said they were taking off to shoot their album cover this morning. I didn't know he was going to NYC or that our trip would bring us back together.

"When you told me this morning about how you were up late talking on the phone, I knew I couldn't break the news until the last minute even though it was killing me not to tell you."

I lean against the window, staring out at the ground as the plane taxis down the runway. Closing my eyes, I think back to the sound of his voice on the other end of the line.

I swear, something about the deep, throaty sound is something I'll never get tired of hearing.

It takes me a while, with the anxious excited feeling bubbling back up inside me, but I managed to force myself to sleep on our flight. If I didn't get some rest, I'd be useless when it came to helping Kate. Over the past few weeks, I've started to feel so run down with all the traveling. I can't seem to get enough sleep, and I'm often up all night with insomnia, which isn't helping things.

An SUV waits for us outside after we grab our luggage. I'm glad I packed appropriately for the weather. It's warmer than I would've expected it to be in late August. As soon as I step outside the sliding doors, I'm met with a wall of humidity.

Twenty minutes later, we're driving through an industrial part of the city when we pull up outside of what looks like an old, abandoned warehouse.

"Where the hell are we?" I ask, leaning over Kate to peer out the window.

She's nervously gnawing on her lip, glancing outside and back at me.

"This is the address Kyla gave me. She said to go through the side door with a sign on it saying ARH2." Her brows knit together, her gaze darting over to the driver.

The windows along the top of the building are broken and dusty, adding to the eerie vibe.

"Is this the right place, ma'am?" the driver asks. "It's the address you gave me on the GPS."

"I think so," she mumbles. "It's the right door."

Right as she says it, the door opens, and Brix saunters outside. He has a cigarette hanging from his lip and his hand in his pocket when he pulls out a lighter, lifting it to his mouth.

Behind him is one of the guys I recognize from their tour. It's the bodyguard who escorted me back to Trey's room after their show.

"Looks like it's the place," Kate says, and I reach for my door handle.

"Can you be back here around six, please?" she asks the driver, and he nods.

We leave our bags in the back of the SUV since we won't have a chance to check into our hotel until later this evening.

I'm thankful for my nap on our flight. Maybe it's the adrenaline and excitement over seeing Trey again, but as soon as I step foot outside, I feel like I've got a second wind.

"Layken," Brix says when he notices me.

He takes another drag, his lip curling into a knowing smile.

"Trey's gonna lose his shit when he sees you."

I press my lips together to smother the smile, but it's no use. I can't contain the grin or the butterflies taking off in my stomach.

"He's back in his dressing room." He nods toward the door. "If you wanna go in and see him."

"I'm actually here with Kate." I motion to her next to me. "We'll be helping get you guys ready for your shoot today."

His eyes bounce from me and over to Kate, nodding.

"Nice to see you again," he says, recognizing her from the meet and greet.

Kate bounces on her feet. "You too. Thank you for the opportunity to work with y'all."

Her accent comes out with her nervous jitters. She spent the whole drive to the airport this morning telling me how great of an opportunity this was for her, and I promised not to let her down.

We slip past their bodyguard, who directs us down the hall and to the last door on the right.

I help Kate lug her bag and her carrying case with her stuff inside. She arranged for all the pieces she needed to be sent ahead, and everything was set to arrive before we arrived.

We make it down the long corridor before I hear Trey's voice filtering into the hallway, halting my footsteps.

"You can go talk to him if you want," Kate whispers. "I don't mind, I promise."

"You're sure?" I spin around, clutching my hands against my chest. "I promise, I'll make it quick, and then I'll come find you and help you with whatever you need."

She nods, reaching her hand out for me. "I wouldn't be here without you anyway. Now go."

She pushes me toward the door, and there's a spring in my step. I glance at her, my smile damn near beaming like the sun. I force myself to relax and shake the nerves when I turn back toward the room his voice is coming from.

"Go," she whispers loudly, and I take a deep breath, then peer around the corner.

Kyla is leaning against the counter, and Ivy stands across from her, her arms crossed over her chest. Tysin pulls a shirt over his head, and Trey is busy staring in the mirror. His hair is down, and he has a backward baseball cap on.

My breath hitches, and I nearly fumble over myself as I stare at him. Ivy and Kyla notice me first. Their eyes go wide, and mischievous smiles spread across their face like their evil plan worked.

"Hey, girls." I grin.

Trey's eyes snap over to me at the sound of my voice, and his mouth drops open. He takes his hat off, tossing it onto the counter, then turns to face me.

Kyla reaches for Tysin's hand, pulling him toward her.

"We'll get out of your way. I bet Kate will be looking for the guys to get started soon," Ivy says, already heading for the door. Tysin and Kyla are right behind her.

When I hear the door click shut behind me, I don't need to check if they're gone, leaving us alone together again.

"What are you doing here?" he asks, his brows knitting together.

He takes a step toward me, his breathtaking grin making my heartrate stutter.

"Turns out the job Kate needed my help on was styling you guys for today."

"I'll be damned." He reaches out and pulls me toward him.

My heart is stuck in my throat when he brushes his lips along the back of my hand.

He blinks slowly. "I swear it feels like I'm dreaming right now. I want to kiss you so fuckin' bad," he adds, never one to hold back.

"Well, what are you waitin' for?"

He catches me by surprise when he lifts me into his arms. I circle my arms and legs around him while he carries me into the room, setting me on the counter so I'm at his eye level.

He shakes his head to move his hair out of his face. I press my lips together, slipping my fingers into the long strands and pulling them away from his face. Only this time, I mimic the move he's done before and tug on it until he tilts his head back for me to kiss him.

His eyes narrow, darkening on me, and he pulls me closer to the counter's edge. He steps between my legs and growls.

"Are we back to this?" he asks.

I quirk my brow.

"I have no problem moving you over to the arm of that couch if I need to remind you who's calling the shots."

"What if I want to call the shots?"

I bite down on my lip, dragging it between my teeth.

He shakes his head. "Not gonna happen."

I tighten my legs back around his waist and pull him closer to me again. He grips my chin, his large hand nearly covering my throat in the process. I tilt my head back and moan, letting him feel the vibration against his palm.

This time, he isn't sweet and doesn't ask for permission. He kisses me hard, moving his other hand to my hip, digging his fingers into me. He releases his hold on my chin and grinds his hardness against me.

"What is it about being around you that turns me into a ravenous animal?" he mutters, shaking his head.

The look on his face says part of his admission bothers him.

"I happen to like it when you're this way."

His eyes meet mine, and he raises his brow. "You do?"

I nod. "You think I wouldn't tell you if I didn't?"

"You deserve someone who isn't always thinking about how badly they want to rip your pants off and fuck you against the counter."

I suck in a sharp breath, and my tongue quickly darts out to wet my dry lips.

"Is that what you're thinking about right now?" I question.

"Are you kidding me? When am I not thinking about it? I'm not talking about just anyone, either. It's you. It's only you. You consume my every fuckin' thought, and it's driving me crazy." He pounds his finger against his temple, and he shakes his head.

I grin, sliding my hand over his chest and wrapping it around the front of his throat. He clenches his jaw, his eyes turning serious when he meets mine.

"You drive me crazy too," I whisper. "I haven't been able to stop thinking about you since the last time we were together."

He flares his nostrils and kisses me. I brush my tongue along his lip, and he opens for me. His hands find my hips again. Only this time, they keep moving, reaching into my jeans to grip my ass.

The move forces me to grind my pussy against him, and I'm desperate to reach between us and cup him through his jeans.

When we break apart, he leans his head against mine before moving his lips to press a kiss on my forehead.

"I can't wait until I can have you to myself without work or other people interrupting us. Just you and me."

I nod. "Soon, though, right?"

"Not soon enough." He presses another kiss against my lips.

"I should get back to Kate," I whisper. I know she needs me right now, and I don't want to keep her waiting.

He nods, stepping back, and I slip down off the counter.

"Good luck out there," I whisper.

He leans in and presses a soft kiss against my lips and along my cheek until he whispers in my ear, "Thank you."

When I reach for the door, he clears his throat before he says my name to stop me.

I turn back toward him. He's looking at me in the mirror. His face is serious, his eyes hungry when he says, "One of these days, I'll have you bent over, your ass in the air for me, and when I do…" His voice trails off.

"I'll belong to you."

CHAPTER THIRTEEN

TREY

Every time I look in her direction, her hungry eyes are on me. Watching me.

She'd quickly flick her eyes away a few times, but not without me noticing first.

"Let's redo this last cut one more time, then we'll call it a wrap for the day," our director, Shannon, hollers from behind the camera.

The audio recording dials back to the beginning, and we run through the song one last time. We've put together a few shots of us playing all the way through, with different angles, each one focusing on a different guy.

My eyes drift over to Layken. She's standing near the back with her friend, nodding in time to the music. She looks like she's having a good time, dancing and singing along.

What gets me is every time she notices me looking in her direction, she doesn't fight off her smile. Fuck me, man, if watching her isn't doing some crazy shit to my heart.

Maybe Kyla was right. Maybe I should see where it goes and let Layken be the one to decide if this is what she wants.

After we call it quits for the day, I head to my dressing room and quickly get cleaned up in hopes of catching Layken before she takes off. I don't know how long she'll be in town or what her plans are for the night, but I want to sneak in some time with her if I can.

Two knocks hit the doorframe, and Layken pokes her head inside. Her eyes trail down my body when she sees me. I'm dressed in a maroon T-shirt and a pair of dark denim jeans with my combat boots. I pulled my hair out of my face and put my chain back around my neck.

"We're getting ready to take off. I thought I'd come say goodbye," she says, looking a mixture of happy to see me but disappointed to go.

She drags her lip between her teeth, staring down at the ground waiting for me to reply.

"What are your plans for the rest of the time you're in town? When does your flight leave?"

"We don't head back to Nashville until tomorrow afternoon."

I nod. "Well, I know you're in town for the night with Kate. Maybe we can go out for dinner or grab a drink?"

She grins. "Kate made dinner reservations for us with a friend of hers who lives in Brooklyn. It's been a while since they've seen each other, and they are meeting up with some other friends they know. I was gonna tag along, but maybe, if you're up for it, I can sneak away and meet you instead."

I reach my hand out for her, and she crosses the room, moving to stand between my legs.

"You mean to tell me I could have the chance to get you all alone with no one around?"

She nods slowly, staring down at our linked hands.

"Tell me where and I'll be there," she whispers.

I brush my thumb over her lower lip and lift her chin. I lean in to press a kiss against her lips.

She sucks in a sharp breath and drops our hands, quickly reaching out to grip my forearms. I cup her face, her eyes hooded with desire. I wish I didn't have to wait until later to have her to myself.

Hell, it would be so easy for me to lock the door, lift her onto the edge of the table, and take her right here.

It's a weird feeling, though, because as much as I want her, I also don't want to rush it.

I need her to know this is more than sex to me. I want this time to get to know the Layken underneath more than just her clothes, although I would love the chance to explore her in ways I haven't yet too.

"There's a bar down the block from the hotel we're staying at tonight. I've been there before when I've been in the city. Blackbird. Meet me there, let's say around eight thirty. How's that sound?"

She blinks slowly and nods.

"I'll be there."

I lean in and press a kiss against her mouth.

"I'll be waiting."

Blackbird is a swanky bar with low lights, black bars and tabletops, and gold accents scattered throughout. Large chandeliers hang from the ceiling, and the band playing has a blues vibe to it, reminding me of the music I listened to when I was younger.

I claim a seat near the end of the bar, facing the door, so I can catch Layken when she walks in.

She's wearing a black dress with her hair pulled up in a high ponytail, a gold necklace, and a pair of black heels.

My eyes pause on her feet. I get the vivid picture in my mind of those heels wrapped around my back, her nails digging into my skin while I fuck her rough and hard.

She must pick up on where my thoughts are because when I glance up, she flicks her tongue against her teeth and winks.

I toss back my shot before signaling to the bartender for another. My gaze burns into her. I'm going to need more if I have any hope of making it through the night without hauling her off to my suite.

On second thought, another drink could make it more dangerous now that I think about it.

"I'll just have a water, thank you," Layken adds.

"You know what, I'll have you change mine to a beer. Whatever craft beer you have on special." The server nods.

I get my taste in beer from my father. Something I'm not quite sure if I'm proud of.

He always appreciated and respected the brewing process, especially after he opened his bar. We talked about it often, even when I was younger.

"Thank you for inviting me out tonight." She slips her hand onto my shoulder, and I turn my head, coming face-to-face with her.

She leans in and presses a soft kiss against my cheek, and her perfume hits me like a punch in the gut.

"How's the new music coming along?" she asks, resting her chin on her palm, eyeing me.

I told her about recording a demo for our label and how we've been working on some new music during our late-night phone calls.

"It's going well. Our new single comes out next month. We'll be back on the road promoting that before our album releases next year."

She grins. "I can't wait for more music."

"Writing music, the creative process, is one of my favorite parts about what I do. Don't get me wrong, I love going on stage and playing for a full house, but there's something raw about sitting alone in a quiet room with my pencil, paper, and my guitar."

"I'd love to hear one of the songs you've written sometime…" She pauses, seeming to second-guess herself. "If you'll let me."

I nod. "You know, I've written probably close to a hundred songs. Most will likely never be heard by another person."

She reaches for her glass of water when the server sets it down in front of her, taking a drink. I do the same with my beer.

She's not drinking tonight, and a part of me wishes I wasn't either now.

"You can play them for me." She smiles.

"I've never had anyone I wanted to share them with," I say. She leans against my shoulder, slipping her arm around mine. "With you, though, it's different."

She blinks slowly, staring at me, and I want so badly to kiss her. I wish we were away from here. Somewhere where it's quiet, and we're alone.

"I think you're staying in the same hotel as we are," she whispers as if reading my thoughts.

I quirk my brow, and she nods.

"I saw Kyla and Ivy when I was walking through the lobby to meet you. I ended up walking here since it's so close."

"What do you say we get out of here then?" I ask, my voice coming out husky.

A smile plays on her lips, and she nods. "I like that idea."

I wink at her and turn back to the server. I signal to him and hand over a hundred-dollar bill, telling him to keep the rest.

Sliding off the barstool, I turn toward Layken, slipping her hand into mine to help her down.

We're in the corner, away from most of the room, when I lift her chin and kiss her softly. It's quick, and when I pull back, her breath hitches.

"Let's get out of here," I whisper, pulling her with me.

She giggles from behind me, watching me sway as we bob and weave through the bar until we reach the front. It's not too far from our hotel, thankfully. I'm starting to feel the effects of the alcohol.

She grins every time she catches me looking at her, unable to keep my eyes off her and those legs. After the third time, I drag her into a small alcove near an office building we pass by. It's out of the way from the hustle and bustle of downtown. It's late in the evening, and the lights are dim inside.

"What are you doing to me?" I whisper, pushing her back against the wall.

"Me? Why are you putting this on me?" She smirks.

I brush my finger along her jaw until my hand presses against her cheek. She leans into it, briefly closing her eyes as if soaking it in, before slowly opening them again.

"It is you. It's you, and it's all your fault," I rattle off.

She turns her face into my hand and places a soft kiss against my palm.

"What did I do?"

I sigh, my eyes trailing down to her lips before moving back up to meet hers. "You... you're perfect. What could you possibly see in a mess like me?"

"I'm not perfect," she says, her voice changing, going from soft to stern.

I nod, moving my hand down her jaw to grip her chin. "You are. So fuckin' perfect."

I flare my nostrils, leaning in again to kiss her. It's different than the kiss back at Blackbird. This one is heated and fueled with passion.

Her fingers reach up to grab my wrist, holding on.

When I pull back, I look down at her face and add, "So perfect, and I'm going to fuckin' ruin it. I know I will." I shake my head. "I don't want to hurt you."

"I'm not perfect, Trey," she grits out. "I have my flaws and insecurities. What you see on the outside is only a small part of who I am. Just like you. I know there's more to you that you don't want to talk about or show me."

She holds her hand up between us, pressing her palm against my chest.

"I want more of this Trey, the one under here, that you don't share with other women, fans, or even the guys."

"What if I do and you don't like the man you find underneath?" I grit out.

"How could you possibly think I wouldn't?"

"What if I'm not the man you think I am? You deserve someone who will love you. What if I can't?" I blurt out. "Huh? What if I can't give you that? What if I don't know how?"

"I've never been in love before." She swallows, pulling back. "This, with you. You've had all my firsts. We can take our time and figure it all out together."

I nod, leaning my head against hers. She moves her hand up my chest to wrap around my neck, pulling me down to kiss her again. I grip her hips, soaking in her words and the feel of her body pressed against mine.

You've had all my firsts.

I lean back from her. "What do you mean I've had all your firsts?"

She told me the second night we were together she's never given a blow job before. What other firsts is she talking about?

Her throat bobs as she swallows hard, breaking eye contact.

She looks away from me before she drops her hand to her side. She looks hesitant, like she's struggling with how to break whatever it is she's about to tell me.

"Layken," I ask, lifting her chin to look me in the eye again.

Whatever she's about to tell me, I want her to look me in the eyes when she does.

"There's something about the first night we were together I never told you..." Her voice trails off.

My brows deepen. I have a feeling I know where this is going, but I wait, letting her continue.

The alcohol that was once coursing through my veins seems to have evaporated, her tone sobering me up.

"It was my first time."

CHAPTER FOURTEEN

LAYKEN

"Trey, where are we going?" I ask. My heels click on the concrete, trying to keep up with his long strides as we turn the corner in front of the Granite Hotel.

When I told Trey I was a virgin on our first night, his face turned a mixture of shock and humiliation. He kissed me, reached for my hand, and told me we had to go.

"What's the matter with you? Will you please slow down?" I blurt out as we step into the vestibule.

He slows his strides but doesn't utter a word until we're standing at the front desk.

"Hello, sir. How may I help you?" The brunette standing behind the counter looks at us and smiles.

"Uhh, yes, hi. My name is Trey Whitt, and I'm staying in another suite tonight, but I'd like to reserve another room if I could?"

"Certainly." She nods.

There's a slight curve to the edge of her mouth, glancing from him over to me. The look insinuates she has an idea what he plans to use the room for, and my face heats at the thought.

Trey glances over at me, picking up on my embarrassment, and pulls me closer to him.

"Hey," he whispers against my temple. "Will you do something for me?"

I nod. "Anything."

He curls his lip. "Call Kate and tell her you'll be staying in my room tonight."

I swallow and nod again. I flick my gaze over to the woman behind the counter, and she looks at us.

"I'll meet you by the elevators," I say, releasing his hand.

His eyes roam over my face, pausing on my lips before dragging them away.

"I'll be there in a couple of minutes."

The receptionist rattles off the total, and Trey pulls out his credit card from his wallet.

I slip my phone out of my purse and take off across the lobby to the bank of elevators. There are two benches across from them, and I take a seat, waiting for him.

My heart leaps when I glance at Trey to find his eyes on mine before returning his card to his wallet and signing the screen in front of him.

I quickly hit the call button next to Kate's name, and the phone rings before going straight to her voicemail. She's out to dinner, so I don't think anything of it, and when the phone beeps, I leave her a message.

"Hey, it's me." I sigh. "I'm back at the hotel now with Trey, and, um, he asked me to stay with him for the night. I hope you're having fun with your friends and don't mind. I'll be back in the morning. Okay?"

I glance up to find Trey walking toward me.

"Text me when you get in, though, so I know you made it back safely. Love you. Thank you for bringing me with you today."

I hit end and grin when Trey reaches me.

"She okay with me stealing you away?"

"She didn't answer, but she won't mind. Guess I'm all yours tonight."

He steps toward me, pulling me up to wrap his arm around my waist, and I press my palm against his hard chest.

"Yes, yes, you are," he whispers. "Now, let's get out of here and away from all these damn people."

His eyes are on me during the entire ride up to our floor. My face warms from the heat of his stare. With every step we take down the hall, it's as if my body is hyperaware of his.

When the door slams shut behind us, his face turns serious. He takes my purse from my shoulder and hangs it on the hook near the door.

"Trey." My voice comes out low.

He turns back to me. "Why didn't you tell me before tonight it had been your first time?"

I suck in a sharp breath, knowing it may only bother him more when I tell him the truth. I didn't want it to turn into a big deal like it is now.

"I didn't want it to change the way you looked at me."

He presses his lips into a firm line, and his throat bobs. He reaches for my hand, massaging it between his fingers before lifting it to press a kiss to the back. He turns it over, holding my hand against his face.

He closes his eyes like he's soaking in the feel of my skin before he slowly blinks his eyes open again.

"I understand what you're trying to say," he whispers, "but you should know, nothing could change what I see when I look at you, or how badly I want you when I do."

I brush my thumb over his cheek and pull him down to kiss me.

Rhys is the only other man I ever thought I'd give my virginity to until I found out about him hooking up with other girls. He played it off like he understood and was being a supportive boyfriend, the picture-perfect Rhys he put on for everyone to fit the image they had painted in their head.

"You deserved better for your first time," he says, breaking the kiss.

"I thought it was perfect," I say truthfully.

The fact he understands how big of a moment it was for me and how thoughtful he is about wanting it to be meaningful to me tells me everything I need to know about Trey.

I wouldn't change a thing about that night. Maybe what happened the morning after, but we've moved on from it, and I'm not going to hold it over his head anymore.

He shakes his head and pulls away.

"How can you think that way? I treated you like all I cared about was getting you back to my room and tearing your pants off. When I did, I was rough and…"

He winces, rubbing his hand over his face.

I drop my hands to my side and walk farther into the suite. There's a large king-size bed with a dresser and a minibar.

I step in front of the bar, turning around to face him again.

"Will you look at me, Trey?" I cross my arms over my chest.

He finally turns to look at me.

"This." I point at him. "This is exactly what I'm talking about. You're treating me like I'm some fragile piece of glass. You didn't hurt me. I didn't break."

He shakes his head again, stalking toward me, and he doesn't stop once he reaches me.

"Turn around," he whispers softly.

It's such a stark contrast to the man he normally is. I follow his orders and he pushes my hair to the side to unzip my dress.

He trails a line of kisses from my neck across my shoulder. Each one amps my heart rate, causing my chest to rise and fall with each struggled breath.

He peels the strap down my arm before doing the same to the other, letting the material fall to the floor around my feet.

His hand grips my hip, and he murmurs again for me to face him.

His nostrils flare at the sight of me with nothing but my dark-orange lace bra and panties with my black high heels.

My fingers itch to reach out and touch him when he brushes the back of his hand over my stomach, causing my body to tremble. I don't, letting him continue his slow and torturous perusal of my body.

His eyes flick back to meet mine, and he lifts my chin to kiss him. I sway to the side, feeling unsteady on my feet, and his hand darts out to hold me.

"I'm going to take my time and enjoy every inch of you like I should've the first night."

"I don't want to re-write that night with you. It was perfect," I whisper, hating how he's trying to cover it up or take it back. "I want you in every way I can have you."

He stares at my lips and nods, meeting my gaze once more. "And you will."

I wasn't talking about sex.

I meant what I said earlier tonight about wanting more of the man he holds back from everyone.

I reach my hand up to unhook the clasp between my breasts, letting them fall free, sliding my bra down my arms to the floor.

"Let me," he says, kneeling in front of me.

The sight of Trey on his knees peeling my underwear down my legs will be forever seared into my memory.

He helps me step out of them. I lean back against the bar to keep my balance when he reaches for my heel, unhooking the strap before doing the same to the other.

His eyes darken when he stares up at me, my waist coming right at eye level. His gaze drags over my body, and I want to recoil from him to cover myself up.

I'm not used to being on display like this, certainly not for a man.

He presses a kiss against my ankle, continuing his path up my legs until he reaches the apex of my thighs before draping my leg over his shoulder.

I shudder when he slowly laps his tongue over my clit. As much as I love Trey's soft and passionate side, I miss the wild and frantic lovemaking too.

I slide my hand into his hair, holding him against me, and he hums in appreciation.

He watches me, his eyes glazed over with desire as he licks and sucks my clit. When he leans away, he brushes his finger through my folds down to my entrance.

"Does it feel good?" he asks.

I nod almost too enthusiastically, and he grins.

His eyes move back between my legs, and he sucks in a sharp breath when he buries his finger deep inside me.

He curses under his breath. "Fuck, you're dripping, baby."

I tremble, rolling my eyes shut, relishing the feel of his hands on me.

When he flicks his tongue over my swollen bud again, I'm ready to beg him to give me more.

He's giving me what he thinks I want, what he thinks I deserve, but I want the real and raw Trey.

"Trey," I whisper, pulling him back.

He pushes himself to stand.

"I meant what I said," I murmur.

His brows deepen in confusion. I reach my hand out toward him, sliding them into the waistband of his jeans to drag him closer to me.

He clenches his jaw, and his nostrils flare at the sudden move.

Something about it spurs me on, not wanting to lose the confidence or the heat in his eyes.

I reach for his belt, unhooking it before slowly sliding the zipper down. When I kneel on the floor in front of him, pulling his pants along with his boxer briefs down with them, he lets out a deep groan.

He kicks off his shoes and his pants, nearly tripping as he does. I giggle, quickly standing to wrap my arm around his waist.

"I meant what I said when we were outside earlier. I want you, the real you. Not the man you think I want. Just you."

He nods, leaning in to kiss me again.

"The real Trey doesn't do soft and sweet. I love that you're trying for me, but it's not what I want."

"I do, but only for you."

I wrap my hand around his hard length, and he sucks in a breath, curling his lip in a snarl.

The look in his eyes changes, and it fuels something inside me. When I tighten my grip, pumping him slowly with a twist of my wrist, his breathing falters.

"Sit down," I order, motioning behind him to the bed.

He turns to look at the bed, then back at me with a quirk of his brow.

This is the quietest I've ever heard him, but he obliges, moving to sit on the bed.

I lean forward, releasing my grip on him, and kiss him hard before climbing on his lap to straddle him.

"Layken," he growls.

"This is what I want," I whisper.

He grits his teeth when I reach between us, guiding him to my entrance. I brush the tip of his dick over my clit before lining him up where I want him.

His hands make their way to my hips, and as soon as they do, I slam down on his lap in one hard thrust.

My eyes roll closed, and my arms snake around his neck as Trey releases a string of expletives.

"Fuck, baby," he groans.

When I move my hips to pull back out, I slide down him slowly. This time, his mouth drops open, and he stares at me in wonder. I do it again, changing between slow to hard, throwing him off each time as his fingers dig into my hips.

"Is this what you want, baby? You want to drive me fuckin' crazy?"

I moan, throwing my head back.

"You want me so turned on that I give in and fuck you the way I want?"

I don't answer or change what I'm doing. Each time my ass smacks against his thighs, his breathing picks up more.

"You keep this up…" he warns.

A smile curves at my lips, baiting him.

"And what?" I ask, staring down at him.

"What happened to my sweet Layk?" He groans as I take him hard again.

My fingers slip between us, brushing around his dick and up to rub over my clit. He falls back on his elbows to watch me.

"You woke up my demons," I moan. "And now they're dancing with yours."

Lifting his thumb to his mouth to wet it, he pushes my hand out of the way and replaces it with his.

When he brushes over my clit, it feels different this time. The roughness of his hands against my sensitive flesh has me squeezing my eyes shut, moaning his name.

I push him flat on the bed. I crawl up his body, kissing his mouth before I turn around. The move gives him a full view of my ass.

"My fuckin' God," he curses.

He spreads my ass open for him, brushing his finger over my puckered hole. The move sends tingles shooting through my body. My arms go weak, and it takes everything in me not to stop what I'm doing.

I crawl over him, lining him up at my entrance again.

"Layken," he warns. "I told you, if you keep this up..."

"And I said, *or what*?" I grin, slamming back down on him. The move, this angle, hits deeper than before.

He quickly sits up, wrapping his arm around my waist like a rubber band, holding me to him and turning us around to toss me on the bed.

I'm on all fours and turn to look over my shoulder at him. His chest heaves, and he pulls me back to him, thrusting into me from behind.

"Trey," I moan.

Just when I think he's going to take it slow, not giving me what I want, he plunges in hard and deep.

"Is this what you want, baby?" he asks, pushing my shoulders down until my face and chest are pressed against the mattress.

"Mmm, yes," I moan, moving back against him.

"Fuckin' greedy little thing, aren't you?"

"Only for you."

He leans over, folding his body over mine, and groans into my ear.

"You're fuckin' right," he mutters. "This pussy, you, it's only for me."

"Yesss."

He pulls out, only this time, when he thrusts out and back in, it's the Trey I remember. Wild and unrelenting.

The only way I want him to be.

He lands a loud smack against my ass, and I moan, desperate for more.

I don't want him any other way.

CHAPTER FIFTEEN

LAYKEN

Saying goodbye to him the following morning wasn't getting any easier, but it helped knowing it wouldn't be long before I saw him again.

One week. I could make it one week.

Even though the days seemed to drag by slowly, I've been living on a cloud.

We started talking through text messages and phone calls, but ever since he called me the night before my trip to NYC, he insists on video calling me as much as we can. Our conversations only seem to be getting hotter and hotter.

I'm trying not to overthink where things are going between us. Since we're both busy with our careers and life, we agreed to take our time and see where it goes. After our date at Blackbird, I've been trying to remember to keep it fun and not expect it to get serious.

The past few days have been nonstop go, go, go. I was booked to do hair and makeup for a bridal party yesterday. I've been telling myself it's from traveling and work keeping me busy, but I'm starting to feel like my tank is on empty. I decided to take time off while Trey was in town.

I've been a nervous ball of energy all day waiting for our date tonight. I do one last glance in the mirror to check my appearance when I hear two knocks on the door.

My heart leaps to my throat, and my hand flies to my chest, unable to stop the smile from spreading across my face.

Trey.

He's been all I can think about since the photo shoot. Every time we're together, I never know if or when I'll see him again. The more time we spend together, the harder it is for me to leave, knowing I won't know when the next time will come.

My heels click on the hardwood floors as I cross the living room. I turn the lock and take a deep breath before I open the door to find him standing on the other side.

He's holding a large bouquet of lilies in his hand. His eyes widen, slowly trailing down my body. His mouth falls open before he snaps it shut, his gaze lifting to meet mine.

"Dear God almighty," he growls.

I smirk, noting the twang back in his voice.

"I'd say Nashville is starting to rub off on you already."

He chuckles. "I guess you're right. You opened the door, and I damn near forgot how to speak."

He takes a step inside and reaches for my hand to pull me into his arms. He sets the flowers on the arm of the sofa, his eyes flicking around the small living room.

I'm willing to guess it's nothing like the big fancy hotel suites and luxury apartments he's used to staying in out on the road. I don't need much to make me happy, and it's perfect for Tater and me.

He circles my waist, lifting our joined hands to his mouth to kiss the back.

"On my way over here, I told myself I was going to take you on the date you deserved a long time ago. When you opened the door, I couldn't think straight and forgot where the hell I was. You look ..." He shakes his head. "Beautiful. You're beautiful."

I rub my hand over his chest. I've never been the best about accepting compliments, even if I love to hear what he thinks when he looks at me.

"Thank you," I whisper. Heat spreads over my face and neck.

I know without checking the mirror the blush highlights my freckled face, giving away exactly what his words do to me.

He's dressed in a pair of distressed black jeans and a white T-shirt, his silver chain hanging from his neck. His hair is down, and I can't help but think about pulling on it like he does mine when he kisses me.

He notices me staring at him, his eyes roaming over my face before stopping on my lips. I'm waiting for the moment when he gives in and gives me what I want.

"If I kiss you right now, I won't be able to stop."

His voice is low and gravelly, almost as if the statement is causing him physical pain.

"Okay." I nod.

"I'm trying to show you I want you for more than sex."

This isn't the first time he's mentioned it. I know it bothered him to think he somehow ruined my first time by not taking things slow. I don't want to bring it up again, even though I appreciate how he wants me to know he wants more than the physical aspects of our relationship.

My arms slip around his neck, and I pull him in for a hug, kissing his cheek.

"I can wait until the end of the night, then," I whisper into his ear.

His hands find my hips, his fingers digging into my waist at the mention of later. It's awfully bold of me to say, but even if nothing else happens before the night is over, I wasn't about to let him leave here without kissing him goodbye.

I step back, and he drops his arms, fisting his hands at his side. He takes the chance to look over my body, pausing on my tan legs and beige suede booties.

I paired them with my black romper. It's light and flowy, with a belt cinching the waist. The neckline plunges deep. It was going to make for a long night, though, with the way Trey's eyes burn into me. It's light and simple, considering the warm temperatures in Nashville today.

"We should get going," Trey says, his voice cracking before he clears his throat.

I smirk. I quickly lock the door behind us, hollering goodbye to Tater, who's probably passed out at the foot of my bed, before shutting the door.

Trey walks me out to the black Range Rover parked at the curb. Holding out his hand, he helps me inside before slamming the door shut behind me.

We talked about going downtown to check out live music on Broadway. He let me pick out the restaurant. He was sold as soon as I mentioned them having the best steaks in town.

The entire drive there and throughout dinner, his hands are on me, touching me in some way. He's either holding my hand and gripping my thigh in the car, touching my lower back when he walks me inside, or brushing his arm along my shoulder when he rests his arm along the back of the booth.

It makes it hard for me to focus on anything he says.

"It's crazy being down here again. Seeing everything while you're driving through town on a tour bus is different. Now that I'm here…" His voice trails off as he glances out the restaurant window at the people walking past.

I debate ordering a cocktail with my dinner, thinking maybe it'll take the edge off my nerves, but decide against it. While I felt better earlier today, the last thing I want is to wake up with a hangover on top of it.

"What does life look like for you now that you're not on the road?"

He shrugs. "Outside of gearing up for our next album, I guess I haven't thought that far ahead. I'm not one to plan out the next steps in life. I take it day by day."

There's a sinking feeling in my stomach. As much as I try not to get ahead of myself, it's hard not to wonder where he sees this going. If it's not looking at the future, does this mean he isn't thinking about where I fit into his life too?

He must pick up on the change in my mood. He moves his hand over and slips it over my thigh. His fingers dip between where my legs are crossed, clenching his hand as if he's holding on to me.

"What's that look for?" His brow furrows.

I attempt to shake myself from the mood. I don't want to ruin our night together.

Who knows what could happen after this trip when he goes back to North Carolina. Hell, for all I know, this could be our last night together.

"Nothin'." I smile. "Just thinkin' what life must be like as a famous rock star."

"It's not as glamourous as you probably think it is." He laughs dryly. "Especially life on the road. Don't get me wrong, it's fun, and I love getting up on stage and playing. But being in a new town every night while living crammed on a bus? After a while, it starts to get old, and you miss home."

"Where is home now? Carolina Beach with the guys? Back in Virginia where you grew up?"

"Ya know, I don't think I know anymore. Ever since my mom moved back to Nashville, Virginia doesn't feel like home anymore either. I guess I'm still trying to figure it out."

He moves his hand to reach for mine, lifting it to his mouth before he brushes it over his cheek. The feel of his facial hair on my skin does wicked things to my insides.

"I think I could get used to life in Nashville, though. With you. You think you could see yourself in Carolina Beach with me when I need to be closer to the guys?"

"I'm not trying to think too far ahead..."

His eyes narrow, and I press my lips together, trying to contain my smile. There's no use in trying.

"I wouldn't mind living near the ocean. Having you nearby wouldn't be so bad either."

He smirks and leans over to press his lips to mine. He releases my hand, brushing my hair back from my face to deepen the kiss. My fingers blindly reach for him, gripping the front of his shirt.

I'm thankful for the high booth seats, keeping us hidden from the rest of the restaurant, but I don't care. Let them look and stare. I'm so lost in him right now, and I never want to come up for air.

When he pulls back, he presses his forehead to mine. My breath hitches, trying to calm my rapidly beating heart.

"Let's get out of here," he mutters, and I nod.

He pays for our dinner, and we make our way outside. A cool breeze sweeps in, and Trey pulls me into his arms off to the side, away from people.

He brushes his nose along my cheek, his warm breath heating my skin.

"There's nowhere else I'd rather be," he whispers. "Thank you for tonight."

The sincerity in his words and the softness in his eyes have me reaching up to wrap my hands around his neck and pull him in for a kiss.

His fingers brush through my hair, and the other reaches for mine, linking our hands together.

"Let's go." He smiles against my mouth.

We decide to make the walk a few minutes downtown since it's not too far. A few people recognize Trey, pointing at him as we walk by, and a couple stop us and ask to take pictures with him.

Each time they do, I offer to take their picture and one woman even offered to take ours. Trey slips his hand around my waist, holding me tight against his body, as they snap a few photos. Before I can pull back to thank them, he lifts my chin to look at him and kisses me.

Everything about tonight is a dream. It's almost hard to believe Trey's here, and we're out in public on a date like it's everyday life.

Maybe I'm overthinking things, it certainly wouldn't be a surprise, but I swear Trey is growing more relaxed as the evening goes on. As if this has given him a chance to break away from life, and for one night, he's not Trey the rock star.

The closer we get downtown, the more people spill out onto the sidewalks. People huddle into groups, going from one spot to the next, with music blaring outside as we pass by. Trey stops when we get to Bottoms Up, glancing in through the window at one of the bands playing. They have a country blues vibe.

Trey smiles and nods toward the building. "Want to check them out?"

His eyes are bright with excitement. "Let's do it!"

There's a bar in the middle of the open space with high-top tables scattered throughout, with booth seats lining the edge. A large stage spans the front where the band plays. We get in line to order a few drinks, and I grin when I notice Trey tapping his foot in time to the beat.

"You mind grabbing a drink for me while I run to the restroom quick? We can grab a table if you want," Trey asks, pressing his mouth to the side of my face.

"Of course, I'll wait for you here."

I stand in line, watching the guy on stage. His eyes are closed, and he grips the mic, singing with every breath in his lungs. He's an incredible singer, and my eyes are fixated on him.

It's later in the evening, and the crowd is thick. A few minutes pass before an arm circles my waist. I lean into Trey, slipping my hand down to hold his and sway with him.

"His voice is incredible," I shout over the music, lifting my eyes to meet Trey's.

His hand travels lower, gripping my ass in his palm. I twist my body to wrap my arm around him, coming face-to-face with a man I've never seen before. I shove him away, spinning at the sound of Trey's voice to find him standing behind me.

Trey's footsteps falter, clenching his jaw tight when his gaze flicks from me over to the stranger. Everything from there moves in slow motion when Trey shoves his way through the crowd separating us.

The man is drunk and stumbles back. He doesn't seem to realize I'm not interested in him and reaches out to grope my ass again. I elbow him in the gut and step closer to Trey, who storms past me, coming nose to nose with him.

"I don't know who you think you are," he growls. "But you better keep your fuckin' hand off her before I rip your arm clean from your body."

My mouth drops open, staring wide-eyed back and forth between the two of them.

The guy throws his head back and cackles, causing beer to slosh over the mug in his hand and onto Trey. He fumbles, holding his hand up as if it will somehow stop Trey or his threats.

"All right, man, chill. I didn't realize you pissed on her already and marked your territory."

Trey grits his teeth and snatches his arm, dragging him outside. He stumbles over himself, his beer sloshing onto the floor, causing him to nearly trip.

"Trey," I shout after him, ducking my head to avoid all the people staring at us as he hauls him out to the sidewalk.

"Get the fuck out of here before I beat the breath right out of you," Trey shouts.

The man curls his lip, bellowing a sinister laugh. "It's cool, man. Sooner or later, you'll step away, and I'll slide back in again. She'll be mine whether you like it or not."

Trey narrows his eyes and clenches his jaw. "'Scuse me?"

"You heard me." The man grins, running his hand over his beer-soaked shirt. His face morphs into one of anger, finally realizing he's lost his beer all over him. "Scumbag," he spits.

Trey lunges for him, and I reach my hand out to stop him. He stumbles for a moment, his face softening when he realizes it's me, and he shakes his head.

"You and your pussy fuckin' threats don't mean shit to me," he cackles, leaning against a light pole. He's barely able to stand up straight. His eyes shift over to me, and he winks, moving his eyes back to Trey.

Trey shakes his head, grabbing him by the front of his shirt to hold him up and look him in the eyes.

"If I ever find out you come near her, I'll beat you within an inch of your life. You hear me?" he growls. "Trust me, it's no fuckin' threat. It's a promise."

I've never heard him so angry before.

He steps back, and I think he's going to let it go from there, but then he clenches his hand into a fist and hits him in the jaw. My eyes blur with tears forming. I shout Trey's name, begging him to stop when he pulls back and lands a second and third.

"All right, man, all right. You got a good one in on him," the bouncer grumbles. He's calm, pulling Trey back and steps between them.

"You better get the fuck outta here because if I hear you say one more stupid thing to him like you did, I won't step in next time," the bouncer says to the stranger. "You hear me? Don't bother coming 'round here either. We don't want you at Bottoms Up."

Trey turns, his eyes falling on me.

Lights flash around us. It takes me a second to notice the crowd forming, holding up phones to snap photos and videos. I'm no stranger to the power of social media and how quickly rumors can spread and words get twisted, doing anything to tear you down.

There's a thought in the back of my mind how this could come back to bite both of us, but more Trey than anyone.

All I care about right now, though, is making sure he's okay.

CHAPTER SIXTEEN

TREY

On the drive back to Layken's, my mind is a fucked-up mess.

I'm pissed some prick took it upon himself to grope her without permission, and I let my anger take hold of me and ruin our night.

The fact people stood there, snapping photos and videos, I know it won't be good. I'm not used to the risk of being associated with a band like A Rebels Havoc.

When I first joined and we went out on tour, I didn't feel like I was as much a part of the band as the rest of the guys. Whether they liked it or not, their label forced them to accept it, which meant they were stuck with me.

As time has gone by, we've all gotten closer. Like Tysin has said before, it's water under the bridge. Still doesn't change the fact that having my name plastered across headlines or having videos circulating on social media of me getting into a fight could bring a shitstorm to our door. I can imagine how pissed Madden will be already.

Layken shifts in her seat, and I glance over to find her staring out the passenger window at the lights and sounds of downtown passing by.

I didn't even get a chance to crack open my beer. I guess it's a good thing, considering where our night ended up. I wanted to get Layken out and enjoy an evening together—just the two of us—with no friends and no tour plans interfering.

It was over before it ever got started. Every time I'm with her, I'm fuckin' it up left and right, ruining my chances with her. Sooner or later, she's gonna be sick of the bullshit and end things with me for good.

She clutches her purse in her lap, her back sitting ramrod straight. I don't know how to fix things, or even more if she'll let me.

"I'm sorry for what happened back there," I whisper, turning down the music.

It falls silent around us, and I hold my breath, waiting for her to give any clue as to what's on her mind.

She shifts in her seat again and leans her head against my arm, resting her palm against her thigh.

"I remember you," I whisper. She leans her head back to look at me, but I keep my eyes fixed on the road.

I've never told her or, hell, anyone about my life back then. If I do, I want to say it without having to question or second-guess the look in her eyes.

"I remember riding the bus with you. The day we sat next to each other was the day my dad packed us up and moved our family to Virginia. We didn't know it at the time. He said it was for work. I think my mom secretly hoped the affair he was trying to hide from her was over. It wasn't until we settled in that she found out the truth."

I give in and glance down at her. She rubs my forearm soothingly, concern marking her features.

"My dad was an alcoholic and had a nasty habit of stumbling in late at night and pushing her around. There were nights when I'd wake up to find him towering over her in the kitchen, and I'd step between them to keep him from hitting her. What happened back there, I guess you could say when I saw him put his hands on you, I couldn't control myself. All I saw was red."

Layken sucks in a deep breath. "I'm sorry," she whispers. "You shouldn't have had to go through that as a kid, much less have to step in to protect your mom from your own father."

She slips her fingers between mine.

"You're a good man. You don't have to be sorry. I know you were just doing the same thing. Looking out for me, protecting me."

She leans her head against my shoulder, and for the first time since we left Bottoms Up, the tightness in my chest eases.

"You know," she murmurs. "You and I aren't as different as you may think."

I swallow hard at her words.

"My dad had an addiction problem of his own. Both my parents did. My mom was able to pull herself out of it before CPS took me away. My dad, though, he was too far in, or maybe her leaving him pushed him over the edge. It wasn't long after my dad passed away."

"Shit." I grit my teeth, squeezing the steering wheel in my hand.

I hear the hitch in her breath, and I'm thankful we're close to her place.

"So like I said, we're not so different from each other. It's why I didn't like it when you told me I'm perfect too. I'm not perfect. I'm the furthest thing from it. We've both gone through shit at the hands of our parents, and it shaped who we are now. Right?"

I pull up outside her house and shift the truck into park, turning off the ignition.

Now that we're here, I'm struggling to come up with a reason not to leave.

When I open the door and hold my hand out to help her down, there's a glisten in her eye. All I can do is hope it's not over between us yet.

I don't let go of her hand, and instead, I use it as a chance to pull her into my arms and against the side of my truck.

I tuck my nose into her neck and inhale her scent. She smells like warm vanilla, and the urge to run my tongue over her soft skin to see if she tastes as sweet as she smells nearly consumes me.

"I'm sorry I keep ruining all our firsts," I whisper into her ear.

I release her hand, moving to grip her hips. She relaxes some, her arms sliding up to wrap around my neck.

"You didn't ruin it," she mutters calmly. "Besides, the night isn't over yet."

I pull back to meet her eyes, and she runs her hand down to cover my heart.

"I won't stand here and promise you I'll always be the man you deserve. I'll make mistakes, but one thing I can promise you is I'll always protect you."

She smiles and nods. "I know."

My eyes bounce down to her lips. Dammit if I don't want to kiss her hard and forget everything else. I need to get lost in her like I need my next fuckin' breath.

"Trey," she says. "Are you gonna kiss me or what?"

I smirk, lifting her chin. My lips pause a hairbreadth away, and she tilts her mouth, attempting to reach mine. She grits her teeth and clenches her jaw, showing her sweet Southern attitude.

"Trey." She swats my chest.

She barely pulls away before I grab her hand to stop her, holding her hips against mine.

"I had to make sure you wanted it."

"You kiddin' me—" she mutters as I crash my lips down on hers.

She releases a heady moan that vibrates against my lips. I lift her into my arms. Her legs circle my waist, followed by her arms, and it takes everything in me to keep us both upright as I carry her toward her house and up the stairs to her porch.

Her mouth peppers kisses over my cheek and down my neck. I'm too focused on how the thin material of her outfit leaves little to the imagination. I swear I feel the warmth of her pussy rubbing over my dick.

The more she grinds against me, the more I find myself wanting to tear it off her just to taste her.

"I'll unlock the door." She exhales a heavy breath.

I give in, letting her down as she fumbles to open her purse in search of her key. Her chest heaves, and her hands shake before she finds it.

I reach over and kiss her, taking the keys from her. She giggles and mutters a quiet, "Thank you," under her breath.

We're no more than a foot inside before I'm pulling her back in my arms, slamming the door shut behind us.

"Layken," I growl. "I know earlier tonight I told you I was tryin' to be a gentleman and give you the date you deserve. Right now, I want you to help me forget. Everything."

She nods, stepping up to me, and I lean back against the wall.

"I don't want you to hold back with me. I want all of you," she moans when I reach down to grab her ass. She returns the sentiment, slipping her hand down to cup my dick through my jeans.

I thrust my hips against her, desperately seeking more. I'm tempted to ask her where her bedroom is, but I can't be bothered with asking her questions right now.

"I want to taste you," I growl against her mouth.

Her eyes flutter closed, and she nods.

She quickly turns around. "Unzip me."

She pulls her hair over her shoulder, out of the way, and I quickly peel the zipper down. I follow the same path with my lips until I'm kneeling on the floor behind her.

She lets the material fall to the floor, leaving her standing in front of me in nothing but her bra and thong. She braces her arms against the wall, arching her back so her ass is right in front of my face.

I spread her ass cheeks with my hands before releasing them, watching the way they jiggle when I do. I do it again before nipping and licking her soft skin, then following it up with a hard smack that earns me a low moan.

I reach my hand up and push on her back, urging her to bend over. She follows suit, giving me better access to her from behind.

I clench her supple ass and bury my face between her cheeks, running my tongue through her folds to flick her clit. She releases a heady groan, pushing back against me to ride my tongue.

"Oh my God," she exhales. "Trey, that feels so fuckin' good."

Her sweet voice has me nearly busting through my pants with how hard I am.

Knowing she's untouched by any other man releases something animalistic inside me. I want to mark her and claim her as mine. She arches her back, desperate for more.

When I pull away, I smack her ass cheek, loving the way her tan skin turns red.

I stand and pull her with me over to her couch. Getting an idea, I recline back to lie down. My tall frame nearly takes up the entire length of the couch. She stands in front of me, pausing to watch me in rapt confusion.

"Take your panties off, Layken," I order.

The edge of her mouth curls before her fingers push them over her hips, letting them fall around her feet. She kicks them off near the rest of her clothes.

"Your bra too."

She smirks, shaking her head. "What about you? Don't I get to see any of you?"

"Right now, it's all about you. Let me see those beautiful tits. Now."

She sighs. "Always so bossy."

"You're damn fuckin' right."

She reaches for the clasp behind her back, letting the straps fall down her arms before she flings the bra behind me. She resists the urge to cover herself up, but with the intensity of my gaze, she doesn't.

"Good girl," I moan. "You're so fucking beautiful. Fuckin' perfect. Perfect for me," I add, remembering her comment in the car.

Her bare feet pad across the floor toward me, and she bends down to kiss me. Her hair surrounds me like a curtain.

"Now come here." I motion over my head, and her brow furrows in confusion.

"Sit on my face, baby."

"Trey," she whispers.

I shake my head and nod behind me toward the side of the couch. "Nuh-uh. I said sit."

She moves to the side of the couch, and I adjust my head on the armrest. As soon as she's within reach, I wrap my arms around her thighs and bring her closer.

"I said sit, baby, not hover. I want you to ride my fuckin' face."

She hesitates for a minute until she feels the swipe of my tongue over her clit. I bury my face between her legs, licking and sucking. Eventually, any reservations of embarrassment she was hiding fall away as she begins riding my face.

I stare at her from between her legs, loving the way her tits bounce. She reaches her hands up, cupping them in her hand. Her fingers play at her nipples, tweaking and plucking them.

"Your tongue, your beard," she moans. "Feels so good."

Her words are choppy. There's no keeping up, her movements growing urgent, frantic. One of her hands slips into the strands of my hair, gripping it into her fist as she stares down at me.

She blinks slowly, her mouth dropping open as she struggles to catch her breath.

"Trey, I think I'm—" she chokes out.

She keeps the same pace, rocking back and forth over my tongue. My cock is so hard, I'm about to bust through my damn jeans.

I grip my dick through the denim, blindly unzipping them to free me from the confines. I squeeze the tip, knowing it's only a matter of time before I come too, and I want desperately to be inside her when it happens.

I use my other hand to grip her ass. Her breath grows labored, and her thrusts are jerky and wild. I brush my finger through her folds from behind, getting it nice and wet before trailing up toward her puckered hole.

"Trey, please," she snaps.

It's not scolding. She's curious, and even if she doesn't say it, her begging tone tells me she doesn't want me to stop.

I moan against her pussy, letting her know how much I love touching her ass. One of these days, I'm going to claim her there too.

I want every inch of her body in every way I can have her.

When I brush my finger over her tight hole again, she thrusts back, seeking more. She slows her movements, easing up off my face.

She stares down between her legs at me before her eyes roll closed.

"More. I need more."

"I know, baby," I mutter before leaning up to flick my tongue over her clit. I dip my finger into her pussy, coating it in her wet juices before trailing back to her ass and easing the tip back inside her.

She moans loudly, tugging on my hair again, urging me to keep going. I slowly ease my finger out before sliding back inside her. She rocks against me, taking more each time.

"I'm going to come," she mutters quickly. "Oh God, don't stop. I'm gonna come."

I slip my finger all the way inside her and take her clit in my mouth, sucking hard until a wave of tremors wracks through her body, sending her frantically bucking over my face.

I'm about to come myself from the sight and sound of her alone.

She releases a deep breath and attempts to stand, circling the couch before she collapses on me. Her eyes are hooded, her movements lax as if every ounce of energy has been sucked right out of her.

I lean in to kiss her, and she hesitates at first before she gives in, crashing her mouth on mine.

We lie there for a few minutes before she eventually comes out of her lust-fueled haze.

"Now it's my turn." She grins, pressing a quick kiss against my mouth.

"Is that right?" My voice drops low.

She nods, crawling down my body to where my dick rests hard against my stomach.

"I want to make you feel as good as you make me feel," she whispers.

My nostrils flare at the sound of her sweet voice.

I brush my thumb across her lips, and she grips my wrist, sucking the tip into her mouth. I clench my jaw, and my nostrils flare.

When I pull out, I quickly replace it with my finger. She opens her mouth, her eyes staying locked on mine, giving me a view while she takes it all.

"On your knees. On the floor," I command, and she pulls back.

She bites down on her lip to try to hide her smile and obeys.

I push myself to stand, shoving my jeans down to my knees. Her eyes blaze with desire watching me tighten my fist around my dick, jerking it hard and fast.

"Let me see your tongue."

When I take a step close to her, she flicks her tongue out, swiping at the tip, but I pull back.

"Nuh-uh." I shake my head. "I call the shots, remember?"

Her eyes narrow, and I can tell she's covering up the urge to smile. She doesn't say anything more, though. Instead, she follows my order and sticks her tongue out.

She moans when I smack my hardness against it watching her drag it down the underside of my dick. I tap the head on her cheek and she tilts her head to the side, letting me.

"I want you to take me so deep it makes you gag."

Her tongue darts across her lips, wetting the dry skin.

"I want to watch tears form in those beautiful eyes while you stare up at me."

Her nostrils flare and she nods, waiting for me to continue.

"When I'm close, you're gonna crawl onto my lap and ride my dick just like you did my face."

"Trey," she mutters, digging her nails into my thighs.

"You want this dick, Layk?"

She responds by opening her mouth, her hands falling to her side.

"Mmm, good girl."

"I love it when you call me good girl." She swipes her tongue over the tip. "'Cause we both know it's a lie."

CHAPTER SEVENTEEN

TREY

The next morning, I wake to the sound of my phone blaring. It takes me a second before I remember where I am. The subtle scent of vanilla envelops me before an arm tightens around my waist.

I wince, opening one eye, and am met with Layken's soft smile and sweet eyes staring back at me.

"It's the third time your phone has rung. I'm surprised you didn't hear it until now."

"I was dead to the world." I chuckle.

It's true. After last night, I was. I had every intention of being buried deep in her tight pussy the first time, but when she begged for me to come on her chest, I lost all coherent thought.

Who was I to even think about denying her another first?

Not gonna happen. I was a weak man, where she was concerned, and I wasn't afraid to admit it.

The first time we had sex was on her couch, and she rode me just the way I told her I wanted her to. Then we ventured into her room, and I fucked her on the side of her bed with my dick in her pussy and my finger in her ass.

She was slowly turning into a sexy little minx. I'm starting to wonder if I'll be able to keep up with her.

The phone stops ringing, only to start up a minute later.

"I guess I should answer it then."

She giggles. "Yeah, sounds like it would be a good idea."

I saunter across the bedroom, not a strip of clothing covering me, and pick up my phone from where I left it along with my wallet on her dresser. Madden's name flashes on the screen.

"Hello?"

"It's about time you fuckin' answered," he grumbles.

"Yeah, well, I've been busy."

"No fuckin' kidding," he barks. "You happen to check the text messages I sent you?"

I hold my phone up, swiping away from the phone call to notice five missed calls from him this morning and ten text messages.

"I just woke up."

"Hollywood Tea reported on your little brawl outside the bar last night. When were you gonna tell me about that going down, or were we supposed to find out when the rest of the world did?"

"Shit," I mutter.

It's not that I forgot about it. Okay, maybe I did. I think the better explanation would be I was distracted.

Blissfully fuckin' distracted.

I glance over at Layken curled up on her bed. Her arm is tucked under her pillow, and she's watching me. She wears a concerned look on her face, so I attempt to give her a reassuring smile.

The sight of her naked body spread out makes it hard to care about being mad, though, if I'm being honest.

"What's it say?"

"Pull up my messages. I sent you the link."

I release a deep breath and open the message, clicking through to the Hollywood Tea link. I swear they're always up in people's business, constantly gossiping about every little detail in celebrities' lives.

TREY WHITT INVOLVED IN FIGHT OUTSIDE OF BAR IN DOWNTOWN NASHVILLE

Trey Whitt was involved in a bar fight outside of Bottoms Up in the late evening hours on Saturday. The crazy scene was caught on video obtained by Hollywood Tea.

The altercation happened around 11 p.m., shortly after Whitt and his date arrived. Whitt was spotted at dinner earlier in the evening where the couple was seen kissing and cuddling together in their booth.

We're told the rock star was using the restroom when an unidentified date joining Whitt was approached by another man. Witnesses say the interaction set Whitt off, leading him to pull the man outside of the bar where the fight began.

You can see in the video that Whitt swung at the man, appearing to connect with his jaw multiple times before bouncers intervened and broke up the fight.

This comes weeks after the new guitarist for A Rebels Havoc was spotted at 4Play Strip Club while out on tour. Witnesses say Whitt is a regular client of the club, and it's reported this isn't the first time he's been spotted out with an unidentified woman in recent months.

We reached out to local law enforcement, but they state they were not called to the scene and are not currently investigating.

Whitt, meanwhile, has yet to publicly comment on the incident.

"Shit," I mutter. I drag my hand through my hair and wince. "They're making it sound worse than it was. Well, what the hell do we do now?"

"Kyla has been on the phone all morning."

"Dammit, I'm sorry."

Layken sits up, putting the pieces together from the night before. We were so lost in our own world, we hadn't thought about everything going on outside these four walls.

"You wanna tell me what the hell happened?" Madden grits out.

"I was out on a date with Layken. We went to grab dinner in downtown Nashville before we walked over to hit up some bars on Broadway. We were going to listen to some of the live music. I ran to the bathroom while Layken stood at the bar to order our drinks. When I walked up a few minutes later, I saw this prick fuckin' gropin' her, man."

"You fuckin' kidding me?" he growls.

"Hell no, and you can't tell me you or none of the other guys wouldn't have done the same fuckin' thing if it was Ivy or Kyla."

It's the damn truth. There's no way Brix would let anyone get away with pulling a move like that on Ivy. Kyla would have Tysin and Madden ready to throw the fuck down too.

"You're damn right we wouldn't let 'em get away with it. They'd be a dead man walking."

"Exactly," I grumble. "So what the hell happens now?" I ask, massaging my fingers into my forehead to ease the pulsing tension. My head is pounding thinking about all this.

"I'll fill Kyla in, and we'll figure out what we need to do to put out the fire."

"Okay," I grunt. "I'll be flying back later tonight. I guess keep me updated on what you hear."

We end the call there.

I take a seat on the edge of the bed, pushing my hands into my hair.

I'm not used to this life. All the bands I've played with before weren't even close to the level A Rebels Havoc is in their career. I didn't think through how much my life would change when I joined them.

My life's constantly under a microscope with every one of my decisions and mistakes open to be ridiculed by anyone and everyone.

Layken escaped when she heard our conversation. As soon as the call ends, she appears in the doorway, holding my clothes in one hand.

She's dressed in a red silk tank top and matching shorts. Her toenails are painted black, and her hair is pulled into a messy bun on top of her head.

She was wearing her contacts the night before but has since switched them out for a pair of black frame glasses. The sight of her dressed in her comfy clothes makes it hard not to pull her back into bed with me.

I can't deny how incredibly beautiful she looks without a trace of makeup on, her hair still wild from the night before, and her glasses.

"Everything okay?" she asks, nervously chewing on her lip.

I take a step toward her and toss my clothes onto the chair at the end of her bed. I quickly slip my boxer briefs on and nod, pulling her into my arms.

"It is now," I whisper, burying my face into her neck.

"Well, it sure didn't sound all right. You wanna talk about your phone call with Madden?"

I sigh. "The media is already stirring up shit about the fight last night."

She quickly steps back, her eyes snapping up to meet mine. I take a step toward her, removing the distance separating us, and reach for her hand. I need to touch her, feel her right now.

"It's not a big deal, though. We'll figure it out."

It's a lie. It is a big deal. Not only are they reporting on the fight but they're also stirring up rumors about my past and making insinuations about my relationship with Layken. I wasn't happy about them spreading lies about visiting 4Play either. I hadn't been there since before I saw her on tour in Nashville.

"You know how the media can be. They'll spin anything to draw attention," I add.

"What are they saying?"

I massage my temple with my fingers, wincing from the pounding in my skull.

My phone beeps again, this time with text messages. I don't want to deal with it now, so I push the button on the side and power it down.

It can all wait until after I leave.

I know before I do, I need to sit down and explain to her what was said about me at 4Play. The last thing I want is for her to read it and think it was while we were seeing each other, or that they are speculating I met her there.

After I called her the wrong name, I didn't think I'd ever see or speak to her again. A part of me is afraid she'll still be upset and won't want to hear me out. Or worse, she'll start to view me like my father.

Nothing but a womanizing prick with a temper.

I'm nothing like that fucker, though. Even if I let my anger get the best of me last night, I would never turn it on her.

I've had my fair share of one-night stands and flings, but I've always been respectful to the women I've been with. I'd like to think they'd agree.

Still, trying to explain myself to her is starting to make me second-guess every decision I've ever made.

I'm nothing like Layken. She's too good, too pure. She's everything I'm not and will never be.

"I need to talk to you about something." I slip my fingers between hers and lead her over to the bed.

She releases my hand and crawls onto the bed. Before I have a chance to hold her again, she crosses her arms over her chest as if protecting herself from me and whatever I'm about to say.

"Come here." I reach for her, but she doesn't move.

"Trey, whatever it is, please just tell me."

I move to stand, turning to face her, trying not to let her cold stare get to me.

"There's more to the article I need to tell you about. They brought up shit that has nothing to do with last night or our relationship."

Her brows knit together, and she swallows hard. "Like what exactly?"

I fumble over my words, not sure where to start. I wish I didn't have to tell her, but I need her to hear it from me and not anyone else.

"After the first night we were together, I didn't think we'd ever see each other again. If I did, I never expected for you to give me the time of day. I felt like shit about that night and—"

"We've already talked about that night, Trey. There's no sense in drudging it up again. What's this about?"

"Well, after we were together the first time, I hit up a few strip clubs while I was out on tour."

"Okay…" Her voice trails off. "Were you with someone else? Is that what this is about?"

My throat feels like it's on fire. Nothing good could possibly come from answering that question.

"Define *with*."

She breaks eye contact, staring down at the bed.

"With them in any way, Trey. Were you with them in the ways you were with me last night?"

Tears prick the corner of her eye, and I hate myself for knowing I'm the cause behind it.

"I didn't touch or fuck anyone, if that's what you're asking."

Her eyes narrow. "What's the problem then?"

"I may have got off watching one of the girls pleasure herself."

Her mouth falls open before she quickly snaps it shut. I hate thinking how our first night we spent together was similar. She presses her lips together and shakes her head as if she's trying to rid herself of the visual picture and emotions bubbling up inside her.

"Anything else?" She blinks through her tears, her eyes finally lifting to meet mine again.

"Like I said last night, I don't claim to be a man who deserves you. I'm not perfect. I've hooked up with other women. Don't ask me how many because I can't answer that question. What matters is since the first night we've been together, you're the only woman on my mind. You're the only woman I want."

Her face softens, and I pray I'm finally getting through to her.

"Even when I didn't think I'd see you again, I couldn't imagine being with anyone else. You can ask Kyla and Ivy—they both know how torn up I was. It's why Kyla knew I'd want to see you at the meet and greet. I didn't want anyone but you."

"You really mean it?"

I nod. "Of course, I do. I'd never lie to you."

She crawls across the bed toward me, sitting up on her knees. She wraps her arms around my neck, and I bury my face into hers.

"Promise me somethin', will you?"

"Hmm?" she asks, and I pull back.

"Promise me no matter what happens, no matter what shit gets printed in the media or what is said about us online, you'll give me a chance to talk to you first. Don't run, don't push me away."

I remember when my mom first learned about my dad's affair and how broken she was. We came home after she picked me up from my new school to find the letter from the other woman. He wouldn't even talk to her or give her a reason for why he moved us all the way to Virginia, only to turn around and leave us for someone else.

This is different, though. You hear all the time what lengths people will go to blackmail you if they think they can get a payout.

The last thing I want is for someone to print lies about me and for her to believe them without hearing me out.

"I promise," she says.

I lean down to kiss her. "I promise to always protect you, no matter who it is and what lengths I have to go to do so."

CHAPTER EIGHTEEN

LAYKEN

"It was a last-minute trip to visit a friend of mine," Trey says.

His mom called shortly after our talk this morning. News was starting to spread quickly, and it didn't take long before she found out about the fight or figured out her son was in town without telling her.

My phone vibrates on the couch next to me, and I see another text message come through from Rhys. It's the third one this morning, followed by one from Kate.

Kate: I heard about what happened last night. I hope you're okay. Call me when you can and tell me what happened.

"I have to be at the airport at two," he says.

I clutch the throw pillow from my couch in my lap, tucking my feet underneath me and watch Trey pace back and forth in my bedroom in his underwear. He runs his hand through his hair.

He doesn't have to say it. I can sense already he feels guilty for not telling his mom he's in town, but why didn't he? What would be his reason for keeping it from her?

"I'm heading back to Carolina Beach today, and we have a short break before we'll be back out on the road promoting our single, but I promise I'll make a trip home to see you soon."

Trey glances into the living room, his eyes connecting with mine.

"Yes, that's her." Trey shakes his head. I suspect she's asking if the woman in the article happens to be his *friend* he's in town visiting.

"I'm sure one day she'd love to meet you too, Mom." He smirks.

I let them finish their conversation and decide to take the risk of scrolling through social media, reading comments posted on Hollywood Tea's Instagram page.

Several of them speculate who I am, our relationship, and what happened leading to the fight.

fashionistaqueen: *She looks like Layken Grant. She's a makeup artist all over TikTok.*

havoc.harlot69: ***@fashionistaqueen*** *I think so too. WTF is he doing with her? She's not even pretty?*

rockergirl33: *He could do so much better*

After reading several more comments like it, I sag against the couch and close out of the app, tossing my phone absentmindedly onto the cushion next to me.

Do people even care about the impact their words have on others? Who in their right mind thinks it's okay to go online and say such hurtful things?

The hardwood floors creak, and I glance up to find Trey sauntering toward me. His brows knit together when he kneels on the floor in front of me.

"What's wrong?"

I shake my head. "It's nothing. I just made the mistake of going online to read what was being said about last night and..." I sigh. "It's nothing."

He studies me for a moment, and I force a smile, reaching up to push his hair away from his face and press my hand against his cheek. He leans into me before kissing my palm, and I pull him down to kiss me.

"Can I make you breakfast?" I ask, resting my cheek against his chest.

"I don't have to be at the airport for a few hours, and I'm hungry. Sounds good to me."

I'm not ready for this weekend with him to come to an end.

We both stand. He reaches his hand underneath my silk pajama top and up my side until his finger brushes under my breast, and I squirm from his touch. He laughs, continuing to let his hands roam over my body.

I lean away and cross my arms over my chest, his eyes dropping down to the hint of cleavage.

"Why do you get shy on me sometimes and cover yourself up?" he asks.

I hesitate for a second, twisting in his arm and linking our fingers together to pull him with me into the kitchen.

He releases my hand and circles around the bar, taking a seat on one of the barstools while I pull out the eggs and butter from the fridge.

"I've told you before, Trey, I'm not perfect," I admit, thinking back to the comments online. "I have my flaws and insecurities. Growing up, kids liked to pick on me. They'd make fun of me for my eyes or my crooked teeth. It wasn't until after I had my eye surgery that they let up on it, even though the occasional 'four eyes' comment was thrown in there."

Even after I had surgery to correct my vision, I still wear contacts from time to time. I've always preferred wearing my contacts, but sometimes when I'm tired or in a hurry, I'll toss on my glasses.

"You look different than what I remember, but I'll be honest, some of my memories from back then are hard to remember."

"I remember you." I smile. "You and your long hair with your Chuck Taylors or your black combat boots. You look different too, but some things never change."

He smirks.

"I'll be honest, my job doesn't help with it either. I started doing makeup because it made me feel good about myself, and I love thinking I'm helping other young girls out there who are first getting started in makeup. I hate how it gives people a chance to critique your looks. People on the internet don't think about the weight of their words. They aren't standing in front of you and forced to deal with the consequences of their actions. They can tear you down, and because you've put yourself in the public eye, you're expected to accept it. It's just not fair, you know?"

I unhook the skillet hanging from the rack of pans and fire up the stove, tossing some butter on it and using the distraction to deflect from the vulnerability of our conversation.

I hate for him to see me as this weak and insecure woman. I'm not perfect. I have my share of insecurities, and a lot of them started with the hurtful things people said to me growing up and the fear of letting people in for them to eventually walk away.

"Anyway, you know, I was nervous during our first night together. I didn't want you to know it was my first time because I think in the back of my mind, I thought if you did, you'd change your mind. Maybe it was the alcohol or the look in your eyes, but I didn't feel so nervous."

I drop my hand to my side and turn back toward him. My shirt dips down, and he slowly trails his eyes over my body, pausing on my chest. His shoulders tighten, and his nostrils flare before he flicks his eyes back up to mine.

I walk around the bar toward him, and he turns to face me. His eyes darken, and when I'm close enough, he reaches for me and pulls me between his legs.

He tilts his forehead against mine.

"It's the way you look at me. I'm addicted to it. If you tried hard enough, you could burn my clothes off."

He laughs, and I smirk, running my palm over his bare chest.

"It's true," I giggle, pressing my hands to the side of his face to look at me. I lean in and kiss him before pulling back to say, "Like right now, you look like you'd singe this top off me if it meant getting me naked."

He brushes his finger along the waistband of my shorts, and I turn back to the butter melting in the skillet. He follows me to the stove and I crack two eggs.

"You should tell me how you want these," I whisper, his arms wrapping around my waist, his fingers disappearing into the top of my bottoms.

I release a shuddered breath when he whispers in my ear, "I like them however you like it, baby."

"I'm gonna end up burning them if you don't knock it off," I say, earning me another laugh.

I spin in his arms, and he moves his hands with me, reaching down to grip my ass inside my shorts.

The look in his eye is back, and it's making it hard for me to focus.

"Am I wrong?"

"You're not wrong, Layk," he says, his finger brushing along the seam of my ass cheeks, and I flash a warning look at him before we wind up frying these damn eggs.

He looks like a kid who just got told to keep his hand out of the cookie jar.

"Whatever you see when you look in the mirror that makes you think you're anything less than beautiful, I don't see it. You asked me to show you more of me, and I'm trying. You should know, though, the woman I see under here." He leans down and presses a kiss to my chest, trailing his lips up to my ear. "She has no reason to cover herself up or hide from me. When I tell you that you're perfect, I mean you're perfect to me. Perfect *for* me."

He leans in, and I crash my lips on his. The kiss is hard and full of passion, and I relax when he circles his arms around my waist, holding me tight against him.

"I wish you didn't have to go," I murmur.

"I'm not ready to leave you," he whispers, tucking his face into the crux of my neck. "I don't think I'll ever be either."

CHAPTER NINETEEN

LAYKEN

It's been over a week since Trey returned to Carolina Beach, and I've been counting down the days until I see him again. The time is ticking by at an agonizingly slow pace.

Maybe it's because I've been feeling like shit the past few days or being away from him while the media still stirs up shit has been torture. Either way, I can't wait to see him and be in his arms again.

I'm still dealing with constant nausea and fatigue, and I'm fighting to ignore Kate's comment suggesting I could be pregnant. I've held out long enough, hoping my period would come, proving why all my worries and fears were for nothing.

It's mid-October, and the weather is starting to quickly change. We've had nonstop rain all week, making it feel more and more like fall every day.

I pull on a pair of leggings and an oversized hoodie. I don't have the energy to get ready, so I don't bother with my hair or makeup.

My hair is twisted up into a bun. I throw on my glasses before taking off to the drugstore a few blocks away.

I'm trying to make the trip quick, but it's impossible to fly under the radar these days, and they don't make it easy when buying a pregnancy test. After the pharmacist helps unlock the cabinet for me, I quickly have her ring me up and fly like a bat out of hell back to my car.

I've been putting this off for long enough. I want to get this over with and put my worries to rest. The more I think about it, the more I'm going out of my mind with anxiety.

I race home, up the stairs to the house, and into the bathroom. I fumble with the box, tearing open the package, and read the instructions.

Five minutes? You have to wait five minutes?

If I thought that the hours felt like minutes before, nothing compares to waiting for the results of the little test sitting on the vanity counter.

I force my feet to move, opting to keep myself busy by making a cup of coffee and firing up the stove to cook some eggs with toast. It's the only thing I've been able to eat lately without upsetting my stomach.

The eggs on the skillet sizzle, but my eyes stare at the timer, and I count down the seconds until the alarm goes off. I release a heavy sigh, mustering up the courage to check the test. I carry it with me into the kitchen, pacing back and forth. Tears well up in my eyes, and I squeeze them shut.

"No matter what happens, everything will be okay, Layk. Everything will be okay."

I exhale a heavy breath and open my eyes, finding two lines appearing on the screen. It takes me a second to realize what I'm looking at, and I curse myself for not going with the digital ones eliminating the doubt and panic in my mind.

"What the hell does it mean?" I blurt out, frantically pulling out the discarded box from the garbage.

Two lines is positive. One line is negative.

Two lines is pregnant.

Two lines.

There are two lines.

"Holy shit, I'm pregnant?" I mutter.

My stomach roils. I toss the test on the counter and slap my hand over my mouth. I nearly forget about my eggs before I come barreling to a stop, turning the knob and moving the hot pan to the other side of the stove before racing to the bathroom.

Like every other day this week, my morning starts with me kneeling on the floor bent over the toilet emptying whatever contents are left in my stomach. When I'm positive I have nothing left to give, I lean back against the cool wall, helping to soothe my heated skin.

I pull my legs up to my chest and wrap my arms around them, resting my head on my knees. Perspiration dots my brows and a wave of fatigue and nausea hits me again like a Mack truck.

I have a long list of things to get done today before I fly out to see Trey. It will all have to wait until later, though. After a few minutes pass, I pull myself to stand and head into the kitchen to clean up the food and turn off my coffee pot.

With a glass of water and crackers, I drag myself to my room and crawl into bed.

It's after three in the afternoon when I wake to the sound of my phone ringing and six unread messages. Several are from Rhys, and the rest are from Trey.

I haven't opened Rhys's messages all week, but I know without checking that he knows about my relationship with Trey. It's been all over social media, and he already admitted he's been keeping tabs on me while he's been away at school.

"Hey," I answer, attempting to sound more chipper than I feel, hoping to avoid him noticing something's off.

"Hey, baby. Everything okay?"

"Yeah, of course. Why wouldn't it be?" I ask, swallowing down the panic as if the secret is out, and he somehow caught me out buying a test earlier.

It's not that I want to keep it from him. I just want some time to wrap my head around it and figure out how to tell him. I certainly don't want to do it over the phone when he's hundreds of miles away.

"I messaged you earlier before practice and didn't hear from you. We just finished a little bit ago. I was gonna jump in the shower and realized I hadn't heard anything."

"Sorry, I spent most of the day getting ahead on some projects before I leave."

I feel guilty the moment the lie passes my lips. It's a white lie, though. Soon, I'll tell him the truth and make up for everything.

"Can I ask you something?" I blurt out without thinking.

I almost wish I could take it back and push all doubt aside.

"Anything."

"What is this between us, Trey? What are we?"

There's rustling on the other end of the line.

His voice drops. "Where's this coming from, Layk?"

"It's just a question," I say honestly. "It's been on my mind for the past few days."

"I've never been in a relationship before. Any sort of relationship I've had with a woman doesn't compare to what I have with you."

"What does that mean, though?"

"Are you asking for a label? Is that what you want, baby?"

"I don't care about labels, Trey. I'm asking what we're doing. Is this serious to you, or am I someone to pass your time? I want to know, seriously, if you see me in your future."

"I told you, Layken, I don't think that far ahead when it comes to life. I never have, but I know I want you in it. I want to figure it out with you."

"Okay." I squeeze my eyes shut and sigh.

"What do you want, baby?" He turns it around on me.

I should've expected it. I can't ask him without him questioning me too.

"I want it all. The husband, a family, a house we call our own. I don't need a lot in life to be happy, Trey. Oh, and Tater. It's a package deal, and Tater tot comes with it. It's me and the sack of potatoes."

He chuckles, and the sound soothes all my fears. "I wouldn't dream you ever would."

The line falls silent again until he whispers, "I want what you want. I want it all with you."

My heart seizes. "You do? You're not just saying it because I'm telling you it's what I want?"

"Yeah, baby, I do."

I hate the distance between us. Sooner or later, we'll need to figure out a way to be together. If I'm pregnant and we're doing this, I don't want to keep this long distance, and I sure as hell don't want to raise our baby alone.

I'm not going to let myself consider it any other way. One thing I know about Trey is how much resentment he carries for his dad after his affair. I don't believe he'd ever put me in the position to do this alone.

"Can we FaceTime later tonight when you're not busy?" he asks.

I hesitate for a second, wishing I could see him now. I never bothered to get ready, and he could get suspicious if he sees me like this.

Before I have a chance to respond, the phone rings with a video call from him. I shoot up in bed and grit my teeth, staring at my reflection. Surprisingly, I don't look as bad as I expected, aside from the mascara smeared under my eyes and the acne breaking out on my chin.

I giggle, hitting the button to accept the call. "I guess I should warn you I haven't gotten ready yet for the day."

His hair is pulled back, and his cheeks are red. He looks like he's been out in the sun. His eyes light up when he sees me. Sometimes I wish I knew what he saw when he looks at me, but the heat in his gaze puts any worry in my mind at ease.

"You're fuckin' beautiful," he murmurs, and I can't help the grin beaming on my face.

"You always look handsome." I wink, and he shakes his head.

"I wanted to see you quick, but I probably should've thought this through and called you after I got out of the shower."

"Oh, don't mind me, you can prop your phone up, and I'll sit here and watch. I mean, wait."

"Is that right?" He smirks but obliges, setting his phone on the counter facing the shower.

He reaches for the hem of his shirt, lifting it over his head. I wasn't prepared for the sight of him, my eyes trailing down his body, waiting for him to continue.

My fingers itch to touch his hard chest.

He keeps his eyes on me when he unbuttons his jeans and shoves them down his legs. I suck in a sharp breath, watching his tattooed fist wrap around his hard dick.

He pays extra mind to the tip, rubbing his thumb over it.

"I wish I was there so you could use my mouth."

He clenches his jaw, and his nostrils flare. "Dear God, what have I done to you?"

"What's that supposed to mean?"

"Don't act like you weren't shy and nervous our first time. Now listen to you, offering up your throat to me like a good girl."

"I'll always take care of my man."

He grunts, jerking himself off. The sight does crazy things to me, and I clench my thighs together to alleviate the ache between my legs.

"Don't go thinking I was planning this either. This is all you. Look what you do to me," he groans.

I shrug. "I like to watch you."

"Mmm, good." He leans back against the wall, gripping his dick in his hand. My eyes zero in on his movements and the way his veins pop out of his forearms.

Arm porn.

"Layk, I need you, baby."

"Get in the shower," I mutter. "I want to watch you put soap all over your body."

He releases his dick, and it bobs against his stomach. He turns on the water. The shower door is glass from floor to ceiling. He's close enough to give me a good view of him.

He leaves the door open and steps under the spray, letting the water beat down on him as the bathroom fills with steam. He reaches for the loofah hanging from a hook on the wall and squirts a copious amount of body wash on it.

First, he starts rubbing it over his chest, trailing down to his stomach where his dick stands at attention. He runs his hand over his abs, following the same path, wrapping his soapy hand around his hard length.

He hisses and rolls his head back.

"Layken," he groans.

"Keep going. You're turning me on."

He growls. "Fuck, baby. Need to feel that tight pussy so bad."

He lifts his leg onto the bench seat and tosses the loofah beside him. He turns to the side so I can see how hard he is. He leans his back against the wall, letting the water rinse all of the soap from his body.

His hips start to move, and I imagine I'm bent over in front of him while he fucks me from behind.

"Oh God," I moan, unable to take it anymore. I reach into my sweatpants and push my underwear to the side. "Trey, I'm touching myself now while watching you. I want you to picture me kneeling on the bench in front of you, and you're fucking me from behind. Make me come with you."

He releases a deep, throaty groan, picking up the pace. His eyes roll closed.

"I'm so close, baby. I want to fuck you until I come, and you're on your knees licking up every drop. You know how I like it, don't you?"

My chest heaves. "Yessss," I hum.

I can't get enough of him. Sometimes I wonder if it'll always be this way with him. Will I always be addicted to having him in every way I can?

Stars dance in front of my eyes, and I beg him to come, needing him with me when I do. His hips start to buck, his hand picking up pace, and I stay with him.

I squeeze my eyes shut when I go crashing over the edge. Even though I can't see him, I can hear him shouting my name.

Even with him hundreds of miles away from me, he still knows how to get under my skin, in all the best ways.

CHAPTER TWENTY

LAYKEN

Trey is leaning against the side of his SUV, waiting for me outside the airport when I arrive.

I'm dressed in a pair of jeans with my favorite cognac boots and a lacy oversized tunic top. I'm still early in my pregnancy, but I'm nervous Ivy and Kyla may notice I've put on a few pounds since they last saw me. My hair is down, curled, knowing as soon as we land, we're heading to Whiskey Barrel to meet up with everyone before the guys play.

When the door opens, the warm North Carolina breeze hits my face. The sun is starting to set in the distance, and the sky is turning various shades of purple and pink. Trey smiles when he sees me coming. I take off toward him, ditching my suitcase when I'm a few feet away, and fling my arms around his neck to hug him.

He reaches down to lift me into his arms, and I circle my legs around his waist.

"Damn, I fuckin' missed you," he growls against my neck.

I push the hair out of his face, staring down at him before my lips crash on his. He moans against my mouth. I wish we were far away from here without the prying eyes around us.

"I've missed you too," I say, inhaling a deep breath when I pull back, and he lowers me to the ground.

He lifts my suitcase and carries it around to the trunk. He opens the door for me before jogging around to the other side to join me.

"Wait." I stop him from pulling out of his parking spot and lean over to kiss him.

He hums in appreciation.

"I've been waiting to kiss you all week. We're good now. We can go."

He chuckles under his breath. "Feel free to keep doing that whenever you want." He winks.

I giggle, shaking my head. After his trip to Nashville, Trey ended up finding a place to rent while he's been in town. When his Airbnb fell through, he stayed with Madden for a while until Kyla hooked him up with something closer to the water.

I rest my arm on the center console and stare at his profile, his hand firmly clenching the steering wheel as he weaves in and out of traffic.

"You sure we don't have time to make a quick stop?" I ask, biting my lip.

"Baby, I'll blow off this entire show and take you back to my place. Just say the word."

I smirk, but his face stays stone serious. I don't think he's kidding at all, either.

"We might have time if you want me to find somewhere to park, and you can climb over here on my lap. Otherwise, we'll have to wait until we get home later tonight before I can bury myself deep inside you."

His phone rang, and Madden's name appeared on the dashboard screen. Neither of us says a word while he lets it go to voicemail, his hand tightening on the steering wheel again.

I want to watch them play again, even if I wish we had more time before their show started.

"How long will it take us to get there?" I ask.

"We're about ten minutes out."

He tenses when I lean over to whisper in his ear, cupping him over his jeans. "This center console raises, right?"

His breath hitches, his eyes flicking over to meet mine when I start to lower his zipper.

• • • • • • • • • • •

"I'm so happy you're here with us." Ivy smiles, snapping me out of my thoughts from our drive here. I cross my legs to ease the ache. She rounds the high-top table and pulls me in for a hug, Kyla following her to do the same.

"Trey has talked all week about how excited he was to see you," Kyla adds.

I'm unable to contain my smile. I search the heavily packed crowd, spotting him near the stage. His guitar is slung across him, plucking the strings as he nods his head to the beat.

"I'm happy to be here too." I smile, captivated as I watch him, lost in his own world until he lifts his head and his eyes connect with mine.

His eyes narrow, and he drags his lip between his teeth. I smile at him, wondering if he's thinking about earlier too. He flashes me a wink. I'm ready to take him up on his offer from earlier and drag me back to his apartment.

"The past month with him has been amazing. I'm excited we have more time together while I'm here."

It's a short trip before he takes off to LA for the release of their single.

"I won't be ready to go home on Monday." I sigh, turning to Ivy and Kyla.

Kyla sips her cocktail, finishing the rest.

"I'm gonna go grab another drink before the guys start their set," she shouts over the music.

Ivy nods, looking down at her glass. "I'll join you. This one is about to be finished here in… two seconds." She winks, swallowing down what's left.

"You want anything while we're there?" Kyla asks.

I glance at the water I've been nursing since I got here. I worried if I didn't order something, they'd be onto me.

"Yeah, sure. I'll take one of what you're having. It looks good." I smile, thanking her.

Ivy nods, and they wave, muttering they'll be right back.

Madden approaches a few minutes later, pulling one of the bottles of beer from the ice bucket at the end of the table. He pops the top open and takes a long swig.

"How've you been holdin' up with everything going on in the press?" he shouts over the music.

I shrug. "I've been trying to tune it out. It's easier said than done, especially when I was there, and you know they're painting Trey as the bad guy. I saw how it truly went down."

He chuckles and shakes his head. "I swear, it's the one thing I'm learning not to let get under my skin while working in this industry. We've had our own family try to use us for money. Fans will lie and say they hooked up with you when they never did.

Countless women have come out of the woodwork claiming to have hooked up with Brix when he and Ivy were together."

My heart sinks for Ivy. After what I went through with Rhys, I couldn't even imagine what it would feel like to go through the same, not to mention in the public eye.

"People will make up stories and try to sell them to the press. There are few people you can trust, and anyone will throw you under the bus if it means earning themselves a quick buck. I hate being told to stand by and shut my mouth when I see the people I care about getting their name dragged through the mud."

"I can imagine after you reach the level you and the guys have, you can't help but question everyone and their motives."

He nods, eyeing me. "Exactly. I'm not someone who wants to deal with it, though. As soon as someone shows their true colors, I'm out."

"Well, for what it's worth, you should know I'd never do anything to hurt Trey or any of you, for that matter. Even if what we have right now doesn't work, I'd never say a bad word about him, certainly not to the press."

He smiles, flashing me a wink before he lifts his beer to his mouth again. "You don't strike me as the type to do something like that anyway. Lord knows you've had plenty of times with how you two got started."

Trey comes up behind Madden and claps him on the shoulder. "What the hell are you two talkin' about?"

"You two." Madden grins, taking another swig.

"What about us?"

"I told her she didn't strike me as someone who would betray you or try to come between the band."

"Nah." Trey shakes his head, circling the table. He wraps his arm around my waist and pulls me against him. "She's a damn good woman with a good heart."

I swallow hard. Even though I'm not intentionally trying to keep this pregnancy a secret, I know I'm dragging my feet about telling him. A part of me is worried about how he'll take it. What if he doubts me and my intentions? Or thinks I did this on purpose to trap him or take advantage of him for his money?

It's the furthest thing from the truth, but still. That's what people in this industry have proven to them.

Trey growls near my ear. "Too damn sweet for me, but I still want a taste."

I pull back and lift my eyes to meet his. He's teasing me, knowing we can't do anything while we're here with all these people surrounding us.

His eyes lock on my lips, and I quickly dart my tongue across them, wetting my dry skin. His nostrils flare, and his hold on my hips tightens.

"You keep that shit up, I'll be tempted to pull you in the back room away from all these fuckers and finish what we started earlier."

"Guess you'll have to wait until we get back to your place."

With a grunt, he shakes his head, lifting my chin in his fingers, and kisses me hard.

For all the concern about what the media has to say about us, he doesn't shy away one bit from showing me affection, even with a packed crowd around us. Although I'm surprised many of the people here seem to show the guys respect and give them space to enjoy themselves while they're here.

After our shower fun the other night, Trey has been teasing me by telling me all the places he wants to claim me in his house while I'm visiting.

"I'm thinking tonight we'll go out on the balcony," he whispers in my ear.

The butterflies in my stomach have returned in full effect.

He lifts my mouth to kiss me again.

"We have to get on stage now."

"Good luck, baby."

He kisses me again right as Ivy and Kyla approach, claiming their seats on the other side of the table. Brix and Tysin come up behind them, giving them a hug and a kiss before taking off toward the stage to set up.

"Here you go, love." Ivy squeezes my shoulder, coming up behind me. She sets my drink down in front of me.

I reach for my clutch to give her money, and she waves me off, insisting she pay for it. The knot in my stomach twists. It's one thing for me to buy a drink and decide not to drink it, but I'll feel terrible if she notices.

They lift their glasses in the air and wait for me to join them in cheers. Panic sets in, trying to come up with a way around it. So much for trying to fly under the radar. I should've told them I didn't feel like drinking tonight.

Once again, I go along with it, not wanting to be rude or draw more attention to things.

"Cheers," Kyla sings, and Ivy joins in.

Shit. Shit. Shit.

I lift my glass and clink it with theirs before faking a drink. The liquid touches my lip, but then I set it down on the table and quickly brush the remnants away.

Ivy's eyes flash over to mine, down to my glass, and back up to me. She definitely notices something is off. I can practically see the wheels spinning out of control in her head.

"Are you ready to get the party started?" Brix shouts.

I almost sag in relief when they turn their attention toward the stage.

The crowd erupts as Madden starts them off on the drums. The beat is heavy before Tysin and Trey join in on their guitars. Brix bounces on his feet, nodding his head in time to the music.

I sing along with them, the surge of adrenaline shooting through me watching Trey again. I can't even imagine what it feels like to play on stage.

Something is different, electric about the smaller hometown venue. Every concert of theirs I've been to has been epic, but something about being at the bar where they first started brings out a different side of them.

They've been eagerly waiting to play their new single, wanting Carolina Beach to be the first to hear it live.

Everyone in the crowd has their phones out, ready to capture it all on video. It won't be long before it spreads like wildfire on social media.

My eyes stay fixed on Trey for most of their set. Strands of his hair fall into his face, and he keeps shaking it away from his eyes.

My thoughts drift back to Ivy, my talk with Madden and the conversations I've had with Trey. I hate knowing I'm keeping this secret from him, and a part of me still fears how he'll handle it when I do.

He's never had a serious relationship. What if this is more than he wanted and he decides it's too much for him? I don't want to do this alone. Even if he wanted to be present in the baby's life, he'll be out on the road, living his rock star life, and I don't know if I'm ready to do this by myself.

My mind is a swirl of worst-case scenarios, and all these thoughts have my heart rate spiking. I press my hand against my chest, trying to calm myself down.

I keep reminding myself he knows I want to get married, settle down, and have a family. This isn't how I saw it all happening, though. I just hope he stands by his word when he said he wanted all those things with me.

It's not fair of me to immediately fear the worst. It's a defense mechanism, a way of preparing me for the worst. It wouldn't be the first time I've been let down by the people I care about, and I'm not going to let a man tear me down by not choosing me again.

Tears prick my eyes at the thought, and a wave of uneasiness rolls through me. I finish what's left of my water and slide down from my barstool. I snatch my cocktail from the table. I have no plans of drinking it. I'm hoping maybe I'll find somewhere to ditch it.

I shoulder through the crowd of people down the long hall, following the sign toward the restrooms. I need to step away from all these people where I can have space to breathe and pull myself out of this sinking feeling I've put myself in.

CHAPTER TWENTY-ONE

LAYKEN

Trey woke me up this morning with breakfast in bed.

I love our mornings where I wake up next to him and I hate how quickly this trip has already flown by. We have a whole day planned. Trey promised to take me down to the boardwalk, and we decided to try out one of the restaurants overlooking the water.

I wish I had more time to go out and explore with him. It feels like I just touched down and I'm already about to pack up and head back to Nashville.

I untwist the towel from on top of my head and let my long hair fall around me. Just as I expected, watching Trey in this very shower, I knew I'd love it too. There are double showerheads and a bench seat. I swear when I sat down to shave, I could've crawled up in a ball right there and fell asleep with the water falling down on me.

Two knocks hit the door and I adjust the towel draped around me before opening it to find a worried Trey standing on the other side.

"What's the matter?" My brows deepen.

He pushes past me into the room, a cool breeze hitting me as he rushes by. He paces back and forth. It's clear whatever is on his mind has him upset.

"Trey, why do you look like a caged animal? What's going on?"

"Do you have any secrets you've been keeping from me? Anything you want to tell me?"

My mouth snaps shut, and I force myself to swallow past the lump forming in my throat. Where is this coming from?

This isn't how I wanted to tell him. I was planning on telling him later today when we were down by the water. There's a part of me that fears maybe he already knows.

How would he though? I haven't told anyone, not even Kate.

Ivy.

"No?" I lie, shaking my head. I hate myself as soon as the word passes my lips.

I shouldn't lie to him, but the way he's acting leads me to believe maybe now isn't the right time. I've been waiting all weekend for the perfect opportunity. From the moment I touched down, we've been racing to their show, then he had practice, and we went out to dinner with Ivy, Kyla, and the guys.

We've hardly had a chance to spend time with just the two of us. I was waiting until today when I knew we'd have space away from everyone.

Maybe he started to notice too.

I doubt it though. It's hard to know how far along I am until I see a doctor, which I plan to do when I get back home. I'm not showing much, which leads me to believe it happened the second time I saw him in Nashville. After doing some research online, it would put me somewhere around ten weeks. My eyes well up every time I think about how the app said the baby is about the size of a strawberry.

Trey stares down at the floor, like he's locked in a daze. He brushes his thumb over his lip, lost in thought.

"Trey, you're freaking me out. What's gotten into you?"

He snaps out of it, his eyes flicking up to meet mine. He takes the two steps separating us and reaches for me, slipping his hands underneath the towel and lifts me onto the edge of the counter.

"Trey?"

"Look at me, Layken. I want you to look me in the eye and tell me there's nothing you've been keeping from me."

I narrow my eyes on him. "What? What is this all about?"

He reaches for the knot holding my towel around me and it falls open, leaving me naked. His eyes move to my hips, and I move to fold my arms to cover me up, but it's no use. He already knows.

He blinks slowly, placing his hand over the front of my stomach. He stares down at the small curve and back up to me, as if trying to find the words.

"Are you pregnant?"

"I, I, Trey, this isn't—"

"I asked you, Layken, and I need you to be honest with me. Are you pregnant?"

"This isn't how I saw this happening or how I wanted to tell you."

"You and me both. You think I want to have Madden blow up my phone *again* to tell me about news spreading, speculating you're pregnant before I have a chance to hear it from you myself? They have pictures of you in a drugstore, holding the pregnancy test in your hand."

I clench my jaw and shake my head. Why do people think it's okay to do invade your privacy like this?

"What is this? Why aren't you saying anything?" he snaps.

"I don't know what to say, okay? I can tell you're pissed, and I told you this isn't how I wanted to tell you. How am I supposed to feel right now?"

"Pissed? You think I'm fuckin' pissed? This is the second time in two weeks I've had my name plastered all over the headlines. Now I have people digging into my past, drudging up my life story, and gossiping about it all over social media. I thought you were one of the few people I could trust. Why would you keep this from me?"

"You think you can't trust *me* because of this?"

"Well, what am I supposed to think? I've never had my life put on blast and now, ever since we've been spending time together, everyone seems to keep my name in their mouth."

"You think that's my fault? I hate to break it to you, Trey, but *you* were the one who decided to lose your fuckin' shit because you saw a man touch me. That's what started all of this. You're in one of the biggest rock bands in the world. You think it doesn't come with a price?"

He steps away, crossing his arms over his chest and grits his teeth.

"I've never given you a reason not to trust me, but you, you've given me several reasons to doubt you. You think I haven't heard what people are saying? You think I don't know about the count-less women you've hooked up with? Hell, how do I know you aren't still?"

"I haven't been with anyone else."

I chuckle, but it's not a genuine laugh. It's cynical and maniacal. Like a jack in the box, ready to jump off this counter and ring his fuckin' neck for thinking I'd ever do anything to hurt him.

"You don't have to wonder about me or who I've been with, Trey. It's only you. It's only ever been you."

He clenches his jaw and tries to step back between my legs, but I slide off the counter and push him away.

He drops his arm to his side, the hurt evident on his face. He's used to getting what he wants, whenever he wants it.

"Yes, you fuckin' asshole, I'm pregnant. Yes, I kept it from you. Not to hurt you, but because I wanted to find the right way and the right time to tell you. I knew you'd be surprised; it was a shock to me too, but someone told me they wanted all the same things I do and they wanted them with me. I guess I'm the idiot who trusted you and thought you were telling the truth."

I wrap the towel around me and stomp into the bedroom where my suitcase is left open on the floor. I rummage through my clothes and toss an outfit onto the bed.

When I woke up this morning, I planned to put on one of my dresses I brought with me. It's one of the few loose-fitting outfits I have here, and I wanted to be comfy when I boarded the plane out of this godforsaken town.

Trey's phone goes off again. I glance over my shoulder to see him slipping it out to check the screen. He clenches his jaw and shakes his head, before pushing it back into his pocket.

When he looks up and his eyes lock on mine, his face softens.

"Care to share what other distrustful things I'm doing now?"

"Layken," he steps toward me, holding his hand out.

"No," I wave my hand to give me space. "Tell me! What is the next bullshit headline Madden is sending you now?"

"There's more to it."

I throw my head back and laugh. "Oh, of course there is. Of course. What are they saying this time?"

He rubs his fingers over his forehead. "There are pictures from a night I went to a strip club. Someone snapped photos of me inside with a woman and as I was leaving. They're trying to claim it was recent, since we've been together."

"Well, are they?"

"What? Fuck no!"

I nod, turning back to my clothes. I pull out my bra and panties from the pile. I debate asking him to give me space to get dressed, but fuck it, there's nothing left to hide from him now.

I drop the towel to the floor and move to put on my underwear when he steps behind me. His arm circles my waist, molding his chest to my back.

"Wait," he whispers into my ear.

"What do you want from me, Trey?"

"You."

I shake my head and unhook his arms, turning to face him.

"You can't use sex to hide from your problems. Fucking me right now isn't going to fix what just happened."

He swallows hard. "I just need to feel close to you right now. I don't want to lose you."

"I can't forget everything you said either. All I keep thinking about is the other women. Did you look at them like you do me? Did you make them feel special? It's all I can think about, okay? I can't just push it away and cover up how I feel with sex. It doesn't work that way for me."

"Fuck, I know. Okay? You think I don't get that? It's what I love about you. You make me crave intimacy in a way I've never felt before. It's different with you. I need to touch you, to feel you beneath me."

He reaches out for me but I take a step away and my legs hit the edge of the bed.

I don't know what it is, but something spurs inside me. I crawl up onto the mattress, my eyes never leaving Trey's as I do.

He darkens his gaze as he studies me, waiting for what I'm about to do next.

He takes a step forward and I shake my head, holding my hand up to stop him.

"I thought you liked to watch?"

He rolls his jaw and nods. I continue again, until I'm in the center of the bed. I recline back on the pillows and spread my legs open for him.

Trey fires off a stream of curse words, giving him full view of my pussy. The Layken he knew at the beginning of the summer would've never had the nerve to do this, but the woman I am today wants to drive him crazy like he does me.

"Let me touch you," he mutters. "Please."

I trail my finger over my chest and down my stomach, flicking my eyes up to his.

"No."

I continue the same path lower, over my mound and down my inner thigh. I've kept the hair short, a small patch above my pussy. I keep going, doing the same to the other side, down my inner thigh and back up. Just like he ordered me to do the first night we were together.

Trey's eyes burn into my skin, soaking in every inch my fingers make.

When I finally give in and brush my finger through my folds, back up to circle my clit, I roll my eyes closed and release a throaty moan.

"Layk, baby, please." He chokes.

"No, Trey," I say, matter-of-factly. "If you like to watch so damn much, then keep your eyes on me. You hear me. Always. On. Me."

He reaches for the button of his jeans and hurries to unzip his pants, shoving them to his knees. His dick is hard and springs from the confines, bobbing against his stomach.

The sight of him wrapping his hand around his cock, brushing his thumb over the bead of precum leaking from the tip, causes my hips to buck before I slide two fingers inside me.

"Fuck, I'm so wet."

He growls. I love knowing I have this effect on him, even if I hate how he has control over me too.

"Let me taste you. I want to bury my face between your legs."

How can I say no when he says something like that?

I don't answer, continuing with my show. I roll my eyes closed and try to tune him out, or else I'll end up giving in to him.

I fuck myself with my fingers, dragging them up to rub over my clit. I keep alternating between the two. The sound of Trey's heavy pants and moans in the background are sweet torture, urging me on.

"Oh God," I moan, lifting my hips when I circle my clit.

"I can see your juices dripping down to your ass. I want to lick it so fuckin' bad."

My whole body comes alive at the sound of his voice and his dirty words.

I roll over onto my stomach, pressing my chest and face into the mattress, lifting my ass in the air.

He growls, giving him a better angle when I enter my fingers inside me. This time it's deeper, my moans muffled by the pillow beneath me.

"Let me taste you, Layken. I can't take it anymore. Please."

"No."

"Dammit," he groans. There's a sound of him spitting followed by the slick sound of slapping, and I picture him fucking his fist.

I adjust my position, dipping my fingers into my pussy, trailing them back to my ass. When I brush the tip over my puckered hole, I moan loudly.

"I can't, baby. Please. Let me touch you." He chokes.

"I thought you liked watching."

"I do, but you're driving me crazy not letting me touch you too."

"Trey," I moan, pushing my finger into my ass.

"Fuck, baby, you're dripping wet. I'm begging you, please."

He's begging me.

"Yes, please. Let me feel your tongue."

He growls, and the mattress moves when he crawls in behind me. His large hands grip my ass cheeks in his. He lands a hard swat before he buries his face between my legs.

His tongue licks and flicks over my clit, up toward my pussy and over my ass. Each one causing nerves in my body to fire, and all I can do is bury my face in my pillow and hold on.

He lands another hard slap before massaging his hand over the area, diving back in to fuck my ass with his tongue.

"Tell me you're mine," he groans.

"Trey," I mutter.

He pushes two fingers inside me, while he continues to tease my ass. I push back against him, desperately needing more.

"Layken, say it."

"No." I rock my hips again.

He doesn't seem to like that answer. He pulls away and flips me on my back until I'm facing him.

He kicks off his pants and leans his body over mine, resting his elbows on either side of my head.

The tip of his dick brushes over my clit, and I wrap my legs around his waist, wanting more.

"Tell me you want me to fuck you."

I grit my teeth.

"Say it."

"Fuck me."

"Tell me you want me to claim every hole in your beautiful fuckin' body."

"I said fuck me, Trey."

"Say it. Tell me you're mine. Every inch of this body is mine."

He leans back, brushing the tip of his dick through my folds. He barely pushes inside me before pulling back out. I grit my teeth, hating how easily I fall back into this with him.

"I'm yours."

He buries himself deep inside me in one hard thrust. I wrap my legs around him and he presses his face into my neck, releasing a deep moan.

"That's fuckin' right, Layken. Mine. All fuckin' mine."

CHAPTER TWENTY-TWO

LAYKEN

We never ended up going down to the beach like he promised. The news ruined the rest of the trip and by the time I made it back to Nashville, I was convinced I needed some time away from Trey.

I texted him after I got home to let him know I made it safely and asked him to give me some space. He was gearing up for his press tour and was flying out to LA. I needed time to figure out my next steps.

It's more than navigating the news of being pregnant and all the changes that come along with it. There's still media speculating on my pregnancy and our relationship. I spotted a couple of paparazzi parked across the street from my house.

As soon as I logged into my social media, I immediately logged myself back off. There were hundreds and hundreds of comments about me, my relationship with Trey, and speculating if the pregnancy rumors were true. My email inbox was full, leaving me with this daunting feeling of all the things I need to do, and I was choosing to solve it by powering down my computer and forgetting it all existed.

There was part of me that resented Trey for leaving me to deal with this alone, but I guess that's what I asked for when I said I wanted space. I learned from an early age not to rely on anyone else to save me, and I sure as hell wasn't going to start now.

I managed to schedule an appointment with an OBGYN. While it should be easy to narrow down the dates, since my periods have been inconsistent my whole life, they suggested we confirm the pregnancy with a blood test before having an ultrasound.

I'm pregnant.

It's not like it's anything I didn't already know. Even though I struggled to read the first test, I ended up taking another at home a few days later, confirming the same thing. I've slowly started to come to terms with it, even if I'm scared out of my mind.

The nurse calls my name and leads me back to the room. The first thing I notice when I walk through the door is how cold and sterile it feels. The white walls, the gray table, with nothing but an ultrasound machine and a giant screen hung up on the wall.

I wish I would've waited until Kate was back. I called her the night I got home and we talked about the rumors. I told her they were true, at least the one about me being pregnant.

I didn't want to pull her attention away for long. She promised me she'd call me as soon as she landed in Nashville, and we'd get together. The doors keep opening for her since getting the styling job for A Rebels Havoc. She's been hired by a couple of celebrities for the upcoming American Music Awards and she had to fly out to NYC for the first round of fittings.

"I'll have you undress and put this gown on. The ultrasound tech will be with you in a few minutes."

I nod. "Thank you."

She flashes me a warm smile, passing by me to walk quietly out of the room.

I release a heavy sigh when the door shuts behind her. Tears prick my eyes as I take off my clothes. As scared as I feel to be here, doing this alone, I'm excited at the same time.

I'm quick about changing my clothes and take a seat on the table with a gown and warm blanket over my lap. It's freezing in here, so I rub my hands over the goose bumps breaking out on my arm trying to bring warmth back to my body.

Someone knocks a moment later and a woman peeks her head in the door. The sight of her smile when she says, "Hello," fills me with a sense of calmness. Something about the soothing sound of her voice when she introduces herself reminds me of my mom, at least the version of her from my younger days, and it's comforting.

"How are you feeling?" Her eyes are bright, her cheeks rosy. She takes a seat in the chair across from me.

"I've had morning sickness since early on, so I'm hesitant to say I'm good, but things seem to be getting better there."

She nods and winks. "It tends to get better the further on into your pregnancy you get. Not always, but often. I guess we can see how far along you are and see if it lines up with things."

She tells me to lie back on the bed and walks me through everything. Any nerves I may have felt through the process were put at ease with the way she comforts me and talks through everything she's doing.

When the image appears on the screen, my heart leaps, and I cover my hand over my mouth.

"Aww," she coos. "You have quite the active one in there, Mama. Look at how much they're squirming around."

Tears form in my eyes at the sight of my baby.

Our baby.

It's hard to wrap your mind around the life growing inside you, but seeing them on the screen, their little head and legs kicking, it brings everything back into perspective again.

I've spent every day since I first took the pregnancy test stressing over the future, what would Trey say, and what will our life be like when the baby gets here. I haven't stopped to remember how lucky I am too.

"I'm going to get a few measurements, just to check how baby is growing. Then I'll print you off some pictures you can have to take home with you. Sound good?"

"Sounds perfect," I hum, staring wide-eyed at the screen.

My heart aches wishing Trey were here to experience this first with me. Guilt twists like a knot in the pit of my stomach, hating that I'm keeping this special moment from him. He has a lot going on, and even though it's hard, this time and space is what we need right now.

After she finishes her measurements and prints off the photos, she tells me I'm just shy of eleven weeks along. I laugh when I tell her I'm surprised I'm not showing more yet.

"You'll get there soon, I'm sure of it." She smiles, rubbing my shoulder before she steps out of the room.

I quickly get dressed and pull on the beanie low on my face with my sunglasses, sneaking out to my car. This moment was one that felt worth celebrating, so on my way home, I stop by the store and pick up some necessities and a few self-care items too, like bubble bath, candles, and an apple pie with ice cream. My stomach growled when I walked by it and didn't even hesitate when adding it to my basket.

I debated stopping by the book section, browsing through their expecting mother's books, before considering how likely it would be someone would see me and recognize me. The last thing I want right now is to draw more attention to the rumors swirling around. I decide to order it online when I get home instead.

By the time I make it back to my place, I'm exhausted and ready for a nap, leaving everything else for later.

It's after six when I wake up and am shocked to find the sun has already started to set. Fall is upon us, making the days short and the nights darker early.

I have two unread messages from Kate and a few from Trey. I skip over his and open Kate's to her sharing she's heading back to Nash tonight. Her flight should be landing in less than an hour and she's coming straight for me.

I fill up the bath tub with lavender scented bubble bath and tie my hair into a clip, leaving a few strands down to frame my face. While the bath fills up, I wash my face and grab my Kindle loading it up with a few new books.

It's exactly what I need right now.

Kate texted me when she landed, and I'm stepping out of the bathroom right as I hear a knock on the door. I check the peephole before unlocking the door and open it to find a grinning Kate on the other side.

She's holding a large box of pizza and what looks suspiciously like a bottle of wine.

"Don't worry, it's grenadine. We're celebrating with some Shirley Temples." She snickers.

I laugh, and she passes by me and heads for the kitchen, setting the box on the bar and pulls out two cocktail glasses.

"We gotta keep it fancy." She winks, mixing it up.

She hands me one before flipping open the pizza box, climbing onto the barstool across from me.

"All right, girlfriend. Spill the beans, starting by telling me I was right." She grins, lifting a slice of pizza to her mouth and takes a heaping bite.

"Like you don't already know?" I smirk, reaching for a piece for myself.

"Well, of course I do, but I want to hear it from your own mouth."

We don't bother with plates, both of us digging in. I stand across from her over the open box and take another large bite. I hum, a burst of flavor and roll my eyes closed and moan.

"Jesus, no wonder you ended up knocked up, woman. You moan like that over a pizza, I can only imagine what you sound like in bed."

I shrug. "Maybe I do, maybe I don't."

I toss the crust into the box and wipe my fingers.

"Be right back." I hold my finger up and quickly walk to my room where I left the ultrasound photos from my appointment.

She's taking the last bite of her slice when I step into the kitchen and hand her the envelope.

"What's this?"

"Open it and see," I hurry her on.

She wipes her hands and carefully opens the envelope, like she's trying to detonate a bomb and isn't quite sure what she'll find inside.

Her eyes light up when she sees the photos, letting them cascade down. Like me, the tears immediately fill the brim of her eyes, and she blinks through them, staring at them all.

"Wow, you can see their little hands and feet already."

I wipe away the tear streaming down my face and nod. "I couldn't believe it either when I saw it on the screen."

"How far along are you?"

"Almost eleven weeks."

Her mouth drops open, her eyes narrowing as if she's trying to calculate in her mind when it would've happened. "Is that the night you lost your virginity?"

I giggle. "The night I spent with him in Nashville."

"Only you would wait until you're twenty-two to lose your virginity and wind up pregnant."

"I guess I went big on that one, huh?"

"With a rock star, no less."

"What's he say about all this?"

"Honestly, we haven't spoken much since I left Carolina Beach."

Her brows bunch together, and she folds the pictures back up, putting them in the envelope away from the pizza.

"What do you mean? You've talked to him about it since the news got out, right? How'd he take it?"

"Not as good as I hoped."

She curls her lip in disgust. "Are you kidding me?"

"I keep telling myself it was more about how he found out. He heard the news with everyone else, with photos of me looking like a hot mess standing in the drugstore holding a pregnancy test."

"He knows how this happens, though, right? It's not like you did this on your own. He was there dickin' around, for crying out loud."

I can't contain my laughter.

"Yeah, he made comments about how he's questioning who he can trust and insinuated these articles hitting the media all began since we've been seeing each other. I don't know if he thinks I'm trying to get attention or what. Honestly, I didn't want to talk about it before I left. When I landed back in Nash, I told him I wanted space."

"Wow. Has he even tried reaching out to you? I'm so fuckin' sorry, but if he thinks you're doing this for clout or to help you financially in anyway, I don't think he's been paying attention to who you are at all."

I shake my head. "How could he think I care about any of those things? I mean, of course I love the band and their music, but I couldn't give a shit less about this life. If anything, being around him and seeing the ugly side of it all gives me my own reservations."

"I'm sorry you're going through all of this, but you're not alone. I'm here for you every step of the way."

She rounds the counter and wraps her arms around my shoulders, pulling me in for a hug.

"How did Rhys take it? I'm sure he's heard the news, right?" she asks when she steps away from me.

I grit my teeth in a fake straight smile.

"Avoiding him too?"

I nod. "I'm avoiding everything right now. I know he'll have questions about Trey, and I can only imagine what he'll say." I shake my head. "I've tried to tell him there will never be anything between us, and I don't want to explain myself to him anymore."

"Right on, sister!" She holds her hand up to high five me.

"She hugs me again, and I tilt my head to rest against hers.

"It'll all work itself out. What matters is you and this baby are healthy and doing well. You're going to make an amazing mom. This kid will be the most loved kid ever."

I sigh. She's right. Even if I don't have everything all figured out, I won't let this baby grow up living the way I did: not feeling chosen by my parents, how I'll eat dinner that night, or if they are loved.

"You'll always have me, too. Auntie Kate has a nice ring to it, don't you think?"

"Best dang auntie ever too!"

She holds her hand up, giving a "rock on" and says, "Damn fuckin' right!"

CHAPTER TWENTY-THREE

TREY

We landed in LA a couple of days after Layken left to head back to Nashville. I've tried messaging her a few times since, but each one has gone unanswered.

I open my messages and scroll back to her last text message and re-read it again.

Layken: Thank you for having me this weekend. None of this came out the way I hoped it would, but I'm sorry for not being the one to tell you first. I want you to know I made it home. Please give me some space over the next week to sort out how I'm feeling.

She wants time to sort out how she's feeling?

A mirage of thoughts swirls endlessly in my mind. All I keep fearing is her walking away from me like my father did, starting another life without me.

I lock my phone and shove it back in my pocket, knowing no matter what I do, it's clear she doesn't want to talk to me.

"You good?" Brix asks, bumping me on the arm.

"Yeah," I reply curtly.

"You don't sound like you're okay. You still haven't heard from her?"

"No, but it'll be all right. It's nothin' you or anyone else needs to be worryin' about."

He nods. "If it's affecting you, it's affecting us all. You let me know when you're ready to talk, though. Whatever happened between you two, I'm sure it'll all be okay."

"Yeah," I mutter. "I don't know, but I hope you're right."

He claps me on the shoulder and nods out the door. "We'll meet you outside in the van."

I stand waiting for my suitcase and cross my arms in front of me, replaying her text on a loop in my mind.

This isn't how she wanted to tell me? Why didn't she call me when she first found out or before she even took the test?

I'm still trying to wrap my head around the thought of being a father, and now she's back in Nashville, and who knows when I'll see her or talk to her again. All I have to go off of is her message, which sounds like she's asking for a week.

Doesn't she understand I can't wait a week?

I can't imagine getting a wink of sleep with how things are between us, and the thought of going through seven nights of this while I'm out on the road feels impossible.

As mad and hurt as I want to be, I keep reminding myself not to be the selfish prick I've been in the past and think about what she's feeling. What pushed her to decide she needs this time away from me.

I crossed a line the last day she was in CB with me, and she was right. I turned to sex to cover up what I was feeling.

All I wanted was to feel close to her again. Sex with her has always been more than the physical act. Now I may have pushed her even further away.

My stomach twists at the thought of her being curled up in her bed at home, questioning things between us, her soft hands holding her stomach with the life we made together growing inside her.

I don't know shit about being a good father. My dad was hardly around. All he cared about was his job, and even when he was home, he was always angry and taking it out on everyone else. Then he ran off and left us for his mistress, playing house with her and her prick of a son.

No matter what happens with Layken, even if we don't work out and she moves on, I'll never let her go through this alone. I'll be there for her in every way I can, and damnit, I hope I can prove to her not to give up on me too.

Who knows, though? Who knows if I can even save what we have now.

What if all hope is gone between us?

If it weren't for the media dragging my name in the headlines, sharing pictures when we weren't together, making up lies and spreading them around—we wouldn't even be in this position.

At least not now anyway.

It's only a matter of time before they found out about our relationship, and who knows what they'd go digging up.

She should've been able to tell me she was pregnant the way she planned, though. We could've spent all day together instead of dealing with the growing tension between us. I fucked up when I told her I didn't trust her and questioned her loyalty to me.

I was upset and hurt and said things I didn't mean at the moment. Now I wish I could take it all back.

We head to the hotel, and I'm ready to drown my sorrows in a pint of whiskey.

"You sure you want to do that?" Kyla asks when I fill the glass with ice and untwist the cap.

"Don't give me this shit tonight, all right?"

She shrugs. "I'm just saying, I don't think it's gonna make you feel any better."

"Ya never know. Maybe it'll take the edge off and help him sleep." Tysin grumbles from behind her, taking a seat on the chair.

He lifts his can of beer in the air, and I raise mine in salute before tossing it back.

"You're not helping you know," she glares at Tysin.

"I think I'm gonna try to call her," I grumble, pouring another glass before downing it. "Even if she doesn't answer, I want to try."

I grab the bottle and the empty glass, carrying them with me to the bedroom, setting them on the dresser.

Tysin is right. I don't want to drink; I just need something to help numb the pain.

I scroll through the pictures I took of her sleeping in my bed this weekend. Her hair is down, laying scattered around the pillow and her legs are curled under her. Her long lashes are feathered across the apples of her cheeks with the light dusting of freckles dotting her face.

She looks like an angel, and it took everything in me not to wake her. I don't know how long I stood there above her, watching her sleep. Long enough to log it into my memory as one of those moments you'll always remember.

Finally, I gave in though, and crawled into bed behind her pulling her warm body against mine. I drifted off into a peaceful sleep, something that's hard to come by these days, and only seems to happen when she's next to me.

I flip back to our messages and click on the call button next to her name. The phone rings a few times before a man answers.

His voice is deep, gruff, and for a second I wonder if I called the wrong number.

I lift the phone back, and sure enough, it's her name on my screen.

"You there?" he asks again.

"Who the fuck is this?" I growl.

He chuckles. "I guess I should ask you the same question," he barks back, "but I know all about you."

"Like hell you do. Where's Layken?"

"She can't come to the phone right now. I drew her a bath and she's trying to relax. You wanna tell me what the hell is going on with you two and why you have her name getting dragged all over the place?"

"My only problem is the fact I'm calling my girlfriend's phone and there's some other man answering. You want to tell me who you are?"

"Don't fuckin' worry about it. You'll find out when Layken decides to tell you. Can't you take a hint? Didn't she tell you she didn't want to talk?"

"Excuse me?"

"You heard me, fucker. She doesn't need you calling her repeatedly when she said to give her space. Now you're dragging her into all this drama. I've seen the bullshit they're spewing about her. If she's your girlfriend, where are you and why is she here with me?"

My nostrils flare. "Who the hell is this?"

He chuckles and the sound grates on my nerves so deep, I'm ready to jump through the phone and ring this fucker's neck. "I'm the person she calls when she needs someone. You hear that? It's me, and I'll always be here for her, doing whatever I have to do to take care of her, to protect her, even if it means scaring off scumbag bastards like you."

I squeeze my eyes shut and press my fingers to the corner of my eyes. I stalk across the room and twist off the cap of whiskey, slamming it down on the counter.

"I don't give a shit what you say or think about me. I'm not hanging up until you let me speak to her."

He responds with another low laugh. "You don't get it do you?"

"What's that?"

"You may have been the one to fuck around and knock her up, but sooner or later you'll go out on the road and will be back to paying for sex from women, and I'll be here. I'll be the one to help her pick up the pieces and raise this child, as if it were my own. You're not the man she ends up with, Trey. It's me. Whether you like it or not. Bye," he sings, and the line disconnects.

I squeeze the phone into my fist and throw it across the room. It slams against the headboard and bounces onto the mattress. If my screen wasn't cracked before, I wouldn't be surprised if that didn't finish the job.

I raise the bottle of whiskey to my mouth and take a heavy swig.

The door slams open, Kyla's worried face peers in with Tysin standing behind her.

"What the hell is going on, and what were you yelling about?"

I finish half of the bottle and pound it down onto the dresser, sagging onto the bed in defeat.

It seems like every damn thing I do manages to push her further and further away from me.

"Are you okay?" Kyla says, stepping into the room. I squeeze my eyes shut and collapse onto the mattress, throwing my arm over my face.

"You can go. I'll be fine."

“You don’t sound fine at all, Trey. What the hell is going on?” Kyla presses.

I shake my head, feeling the effects of the liquor hitting me when I attempt to sit up.

“She’s gonna end up leaving me and I don’t know what to do to stop her. I don’t want to lose her. I can’t lose her. Now she has some guy at her house,” I clench my jaw.

“Some guy? What do you mean?” Tysin interjects.

“I don’t know who he is, claims he’s the one she calls when she needs someone. Why is she calling him and not me? Huh? Why could she possibly think anyone else could want to be with her more than I do?”

Kyla’s face drops, and I want to tell her I don’t need her pity. I wish they’d both leave me the hell alone.

All I want is to finish this bottle of whiskey until I either pass out or it numbs the pain, whichever comes first.

“Trey, man, this has to be some sort of misunderstanding. We’ve all seen you two together. The way she looks at you, there’s no doubt in my mind she loves you. It’s all gonna be okay,” Tysin pipes up. “Give it some time.”

“Time, time. All you keep saying is to give it time. I won’t be okay until I see her,” I huff. “Don’t you get it? She’s carrying my child. Until I talk to her, and see her, I won’t be okay.”

CHAPTER TWENTY-FOUR

TREY

"You dressed?" Ivy knocks.

"Yeah, I'm almost ready."

She pushes the door open and steps inside, shutting it behind her.

"You hear from her yet?" Ivy asks.

I shake my head. "Nope. She's still not answering my calls. All my messages are still unread. I don't know what to do."

"I understand it's hard right now and you want to talk to her, but she asked for time, so I would try to give her space."

"I shouldn't have let her leave the way things were," I drag my hands through my hair and sit down on the edge of the bed, staring at the floor.

She nods. "All you can do is be patient now. She'll come around eventually. The same thing happened when Brix and I had a falling out. I took off running and refused to speak with him for months.

You two are having a baby together. Sooner or later, she'll reach out and you can talk through things. You'll work it out."

I've been going out of my mind since last night. I damn near finished off the entire bottle of whiskey and was left with a massive headache this morning when I woke up. I felt like hell and Kyla was worried I gave myself alcohol poisoning.

She's never seen how much I drank when I was out on the road with Blunt Force Trauma, otherwise she wouldn't be concerned.

Kyla admitted this morning she reached out to Kate and found out it was one of her guy friends in town visiting and reassured me there was nothing to worry about.

It still hasn't helped put my mind at ease in the slightest.

The only thing helping is the fact I've stayed busy with press for our single dropping. I've debated changing my flight from CB to Nashville and heading straight for her instead.

Today is our last day and is packed and we finish with Kimmel, our biggest interview yet. Thankfully, Brix is doing most of the talking, but it doesn't make it any easier trying to put on a happy face when I want to get the fuck outta here.

"What the hell are you two doing?" Brix asks, cracking the door.

"We're busy, go away." Ivy giggles.

Brix shoves the door open. "Getting' busy? Like hell you are," he growls, stalking inside.

"I said we're busy, not gettin' busy. Knock it off." She rolls her eyes and shakes her head.

"Sounds the same to me," he grabs her by the hips and pulls her toward him. She playfully swats at his chest and pushes him away.

"I call her sis, but only one of us means it. Ain't that right, Brix?" I smirk and he narrows his eyes on me.

Brix curls his lip. "She's gonna stay your sis, too. Ain't *that* right, baby?"

"All right, knock it off, both of you. The point of what I was trying to say before is, you and Brix both have a lot in common. You both say and do shit when you're pissed that you wish you could take back later."

He rolls his eyes and shakes his head, crossing his arms over his chest.

"Brix liked to play it off like he was this asshole with a tough exterior, but when it was just the two of us together, he couldn't keep putting on this front. He said and did some things that were hurtful, and it led to us not speaking for a while. He figured out though he couldn't make up for all the hurt by telling me what I wanted to hear. Don't get me wrong, it meant a lot when he wrote a song confessing his feelings, but I needed him to do more than say it. I needed him to prove it."

Brix nods. "She's right. I hurt her a lot when I made that bet with Tysin. I told myself in the beginning what I felt for her didn't mean anything. There was a part of me that didn't want to let her get close, but the thought of losing her forever terrified me. I had to prove to her I wasn't going to hurt her again if I was ever going to be able to fix things."

My phone beeps and I quickly swipe it off my dresser to find a notification come through that Layken is live on her social media.

"How much time we got left?"

Ivy checks her watch. "We gotta leave here in about twenty, so you got some time."

I nod. "I gotta take this,"

She reaches for Brix, slipping her fingers in his and nods toward the door.

"Trey, for what it's worth, you're a good man. I haven't even known you very long, and I can see it. Give her time, give her some space, but I promise she'll see it too."

"Thank you."

I click on the notification and Layken's face appears on my screen.

layken.grant is live! *Get ready with me!*
mel_smith: *u look beautiful*
sammy_2sweet: *where did you get your curling iron?*
treywhitt *joined*

I've never watched a live before. As soon as viewers notice I join, the comments are flooded with messages.

Trey is here.

OMG, Trey is watching.

Hi Trey!!!

I don't care about any of them though. I'm stuck, fixated on her. My heart aches in my chest at the sight of her.

Her makeup is done and she's wearing a burnt orange shirt, complementing her skin and auburn hair. Something about it makes her green eyes and freckles stand out more.

She's wearing lipstick, the kind that makes her lips shiny. I want to lick them and find out if they're as juicy as they look.

She doesn't seem to notice the comments rolling in right away. She's holding one of those hot curling tools in her hand and is too focused on what she's doing while she tells them about the makeup she recently bought.

Eventually, she leans over to scroll through her comments.

"Trey?" she mumbles under her breath, but we can all hear her.

"Yeah, baby, I'm here," I say out loud to only me.

"Wait, did y'all say Trey is here?"

Her lips curl on the edge, and I swear my heart is beating out of control. The sight of her smile when she realizes I'm here watching her fills me with a sense of peace.

As if it's the sign I've needed telling me we'll get through this, and maybe it'll all be okay.

My fingers furiously type out a message and I quickly hit send.

treywhitt: *i'm here baby. U look so fuckin beautiful. i miss u.*

She takes a seat on the chair in front of her vanity and sets the curling iron down on the counter in front of her.

Her eyes light up and I send another, hoping like hell it's mine she's reading.

"I've been listening to your single all day," she smiles, looking back in the mirror to finish curling her hair. "I love it."

Even though there are over five thousand viewers right now, it reminds me of our FaceTime calls, and it's like it's just the two of us again.

Kyla knocks on the door and peeks her head inside.

"We're heading downstairs now. Abel's outside ready to take us to the station."

I nod, muttering a low damnit under my breath. "I'll be down in just a second."

She nods and shuts the door behind her.

treywhitt: *thank u baby. i gotta head to an interview now. i'll talk to u soon.*

"Good luck," she smiles.

I'm half tempted to carry my phone with me through the lobby and to the van, watching her on the drive over, but I give in and close out.

Brix and Ivy are waiting in the room. Ivy's face searches mine, as if checking to see how I'm doing.

"You look like you're feeling better. Everything okay?"

I nod. "Yeah, sis. I'm good."

"Did you get a chance to talk to her finally?"

"Not exactly. She was live though on social media. Apparently, when you start watching, it announces to the world you've joined. It ended up working out though because people commented I was there, and she seemed happy about it."

"I bet she was," she grins, squeezing my arm.

Brix wraps his arm around Ivy's waist and presses a kiss to her cheek. He proposed to her at the end of our tour. I'd be lying if I said watching them didn't make me think about having what they have with Layken.

Being out on the road, crammed in a bus with the guys, Kyla, and Ivy has made me closer to all of them—the girls included. They welcomed me with open arms.

All this shit in the media, though, has me grateful for their friendship. They seem to understand and accept it comes with the territory and never once made me feel like shit, even though Madden gets pissed when I don't give them a heads-up.

Abel is standing outside the front entrance, waiting on us, when we step outside. He opens the door to the large van. Brix and Ivy claim the spot near the back. Tysin, Kyla, and Madden are already seated near the front.

I climb in next to them, and Abel shuts the door behind me.

"You good, man?" Madden asks, clapping me on the shoulder.

I nod. "Better now."

"Good to hear."

"Kyla, any chance I can carve out some time to head back to Nashville?"

She nods. "We have four days off, so it gives you plenty of time if you want to fly straight there from LA tonight."

"I think we could all use some time off to recharge after this week," Madden adds.

Madden and Kyla have been doing a lot for me, putting out fires when it comes to preparing for our single release and dealing with the shit going on in the media.

"I'm just glad you're not letting that shit get to you," Madden quips. "The media and this industry will chew you up and spit you out if you let it. Good friends and loyal people are hard to come by. We got your back, though, brother. You can count on that."

I hold my fist out, and he bumps it and nudges me on the shoulder.

"Let's be honest. It's not like we haven't all got ourselves into shit at some point or another. We can just be grateful Brix cleaned up his image before we signed with the label, or there's no telling what sort of bullshit we'd be dealing with."

"Fuck off, bro," Brix chirps from the back seat.

"He's got a point," Tysin adds. "What he's trying to say is we should all say thank you to Ivy for putting up with your ass and taming the wild child."

"Like you're so innocent and haven't stirred up drama of your own." Kyla raises her brow at him and rolls her eyes. She turns toward me and smirks, shaking her head.

"You're tellin' me. I was asking for trouble going behind the lumberjack's back and hooking up with his sister."

"All right, shut the fuck up. Will ya?" Madden barks, and Kyla giggles.

"Can you help me change my flight?" I ask her, changing the subject.

"You got it." She winks. "Consider it done."

I take a deep breath and sigh. Now all I had to do was get through the next few hours, and I'll be heading back to Nashville.

Back home.

Back to her.

CHAPTER TWENTY-FIVE

LAYKEN

As the days have gone by, the harder it's been for me to remember why I thought distance was what I needed. All the thoughts racing through my mind have left me feeling anxious, and I believed what I needed was time to focus on me and my new reality.

The truth? I've been running.

Running from the fear that there will come a day when Trey won't choose me and our baby. A part of me felt that if I pushed him away, it might reinforce this wall between us.

The nights have only grown longer, and I haven't been able to stop my mind from spinning out of control. It's led to late mornings when I struggle to pull myself out of bed. The fatigue and nausea seem to be back, and it isn't helping my energy either.

I've been all over the place. I'm a walking, talking disaster.

Rhys showed up last night. I've been pushing him away, and he claims he was worried about me, when, in truth, I think he wanted to make one last attempt to win me back.

I didn't have the energy to tell him the truth, so I agreed he could come over tonight on his way out of town.

I've been keeping track of Trey while he and the guys are on their press tour and have been anxiously waiting for his interview tonight. I miss him and want to see him, and going these last few days without talking has been harder than I expected.

My phone vibrates on my coffee table. I pulled out my cozy blanket and pajamas after my bath earlier and have been curled up on the couch ever since. My hair is tied up in a messy bun, and I'm wearing my glasses again. The only person I'm planning on seeing tonight is Rhys, and I stopped caring what I looked like around him a long time ago.

Kate: Three minutes until showtime.

She's been keeping tabs on me all week. A part of me wonders if Trey didn't put her up to it too because she's been even more present than normal while still crazy busy with all her styling events.

The intro credits start rolling, showing the featured guests on tonight's episode. As soon as A Rebels Havoc appears on the screen, my eyes lock on Trey.

He's dressed in a gray Henley and dark denim jeans. His hair is down, and his beard has grown longer over the past few days. He mentioned he was thinking about growing it out more, and, damn, he looks so good. His unbuttoned shirt gives a glimpse of his tan chest and the light smattering of chest hair. My stomach flutters at the sight of him.

Something about lying on the couch where we were, remembering the last time he was here and we were together, has my chest aching, missing him even more.

I fire off a reply to Kate and absentmindedly scroll on social media, waiting for their interview to start. As soon as they start talking about the guys again, I immediately sit up at attention and pull my legs against my chest.

"Our next guests need no introduction but deserve all the credit for taking the world by storm. Their last album went multi-platinum, and their Wreak Some Havoc tour sold out in minutes. Please join me in welcoming A Rebels Havoc."

Tears prick my eyes. Trey told me about how hard it was in the early days when he first joined the band, and he worried about being a good fit. He didn't want to step on anyone's toes, even though he busted his ass to get to where he is today too. He's proud of all they've accomplished to get there and what they've achieved together.

My eyes are glued to the screen. My excitement has adrenaline zipping through me like a shot of liquor, even though I haven't had a sip in months.

"Trey, how has it been for you joining the band?"

He chuckles. "It's been great. These guys are like my brothers. We butt heads at times, like brothers do, but we all want what's best for the band and our music. We're here for each other, no matter what."

"You know, you've made quite a splash for yourself in recent weeks. One could say you've been a rebel." He smirks, and I roll my eyes. "It sounds like there could be some congratulations in order too. I hear you're welcoming your first child?"

"Uhh..." He smiles, nodding. My hand shoots over to grip the armrest. "I am, I am. Thank you. I couldn't be more excited too. I have to say, you know, what has been printed in the media isn't entirely true either. The video didn't do me any favors, but I think I can speak for all the guys when I say we have some very important women in our lives. It was a heat of the moment thing what happened back in Nashville. I was reacting to witnessing someone inappropriately touch someone I love very much, and I guess my temper got the best of me. I couldn't stand there idly and not do anything."

The guys all nod in agreeance with him, but my mind is stuck on what he said.

"Did he just say he loves me?" I mutter out loud.

My phone vibrates, and another text from Kate appears on my screen.

Kate: Did he admit on national television he loves you?

I drop the phone in my lap, my hand flying over my mouth.

"You know, I can't blame you for being upset, either," Kimmel agrees.

"It's certainly not how I wanted things to go that night, but I don't have any regrets." Trey shrugs. "I love that woman, and knowing now she was carrying my child when it happened has me standing firm behind my actions."

I spring from my seat, shooting my hands in the air.

He loves me?

Trey just told me he loves me. On national television for the rest of the world to hear?

Someone pounds on the door, and my hand flies to my chest, taking me off guard. *Jesus, Rhys, you were going to text me when you got here.*

All these paparazzi lately have me nervous to answer my door, especially at night.

I check my phone again, but there's no missed message from Rhys. He wouldn't show up without texting first. He wouldn't shut up about how concerned he was after seeing someone snapping photos of him when he got here.

I glance around the empty room, debating if I should answer. The lights are on, and the TV is turned up, making it obvious someone is home.

A series of knocks continues, and my stomach lurches. I try to quietly tiptoe over to the door, the wood floors creaking beneath my feet. It takes me a second to adjust my vision and realize I'm not dreaming when I see Trey standing on my doorstep.

My eyes dart over to the TV and back to the door, hurrying to unclick the lock and swing the door open.

He's holding a bouquet in one hand with his suitcase at his feet.

"You love me?" I blurt out, and a slow smile spreads across his face.

I point over to the screen where he and the guys are still sitting on stage for their interview. "That's what you said. You told everyone on TV you love me, and you're happy about our baby."

He steps through the doorway, pulling his suitcase along with him and setting it down with the flowers next to the sofa.

"Of course, I am," he says, reaching to pull me into his arms. "Yes, I do love you."

He moves to push the door shut behind him when a voice stops us both in our tracks.

"Layken?"

I move to look past Trey to find Rhys standing on the steps. His eyes are wide as he stares at me and over to Trey, down to where his arms are wrapped around my waist.

Trey turns, and his whole body tenses.

"What the fuck are you doing here?" Trey asks, his voice dropping low. It's cold and void of any emotion.

My eyes bounce back and forth between the two of them like a ping pong.

"Layken, can I talk to you?" Rhys asks, ignoring Trey.

Trey turns to stand in front of me protectively and crosses his arms.

"I don't think so, motherfucker. Whatever you have to say, you can say in front of me."

I pull on Trey's arm, but he doesn't move.

"Trey, it's okay. It's just Rhys. He's my friend. You have nothing to worry about."

"The fuck I don't." He shifts his eyes and glares at me before turning back to Rhys. "It was you the other night on the phone, wasn't it?"

Rhys chuckles and clenches his hand into a fist at his side.

"On the phone? Rhys, what is he talking about?" I interject.

"C'mon, buddy, why don't you tell her? Tell Layken how you answered her phone the other night and tried to warn me to stay away from her."

"You did what?" I screech, moving past Trey.

His arm darts out to stop me, but I push it away.

"Rhys, what is he talking about?"

Rhys stands there, his face hard as stone, not uttering a word. He's two steps below me, and we stand eye to eye. I shove him, getting irritated by the fact he stays silent.

"Last night when I was here, you were in the bath, and you left your phone on the counter in the kitchen. He called, and I saw it was him, and I-I"—he shakes his head—"I answered it."

I turn back to Trey before flicking my gaze over to Rhys. "What did you say to him? Clearly, whatever you said pissed him off."

"Tell her everything," Trey quips. "Every-fuckin'-thing."

Rhys flares his nostrils and clenches his jaw. He steels his spine, turning his gaze back to me.

"I told him I'd always be here for you, to take care of you and protect you. When he goes out on the road again and is back to paying for sex, I'll be here to pick up the pieces and help you raise the child he's walked out on."

"You said what?" I yell. "Rhys, you are my friend, my best fuckin' friend, but you know this is not true. The way you made it sound is like we'll end up together. I've told you this before, and you don't seem to want to get it through your head, but there will never be a you and me."

He clenches his jaw and nods.

"He's not done yet, are you, Rhys? Keep going."

I turn back to him, my mouth open. There's more? What else could he possibly have to tell me?

Trey reaches for my arm, and I step away from Rhys and into his side. Trey closes the space between them, taking a step back in front of me again, standing toe-to-toe with Rhys.

"You think I'm gonna let you come in and take away the woman I love and play house with my fuckin' family? The way your homewrecker of a mother did to my mom?"

My mouth drops open, my mind swirling a million miles a minute.

Joann and Tim? Tim is Trey's father?

"Wait, what?" I push past Trey and stand between them, looking from my best friend over to the man I love.

"Your mom and his dad? She's the one—" I stop, flicking my eyes over to Trey.

His face is hard, but I can see the pain under the surface. Only I know the hurt his father's affair had on him. Watching him abuse his mother, only to leave them for someone else.

"Rhys, you need to go," I say coldly.

He reaches out for me, and I flash him a hard look, one he knows is saying, "Don't you even dare."

What happened between their parents is not Rhys's fault. I know it, and Trey knows it. Rhys knew who Trey was, though. He knew the connection to his dad and the fact I was pregnant with his son. He came over to my house, pretending to care, and then went behind my back to try to push him away from me.

"Can I please talk to you?" Rhys begs.

"I have nothing more to say to you, Rhys. I hate that our friendship got to this place, but what you did? You put me in a position where I was forced to choose. You should've known I would choose Trey. I love him, we're having a baby, and I won't let you come between us."

I slip my arm around Trey, and he holds me close to him, walking with me through the door. Trey turns, giving him one last cold look. Rhys still stands there, stuck frozen in place watching as Trey slams the door in his face.

CHAPTER TWENTY-SIX

TREY

I press my palms against the counter in the bathroom and drop my head between my shoulders, squeezing my eyes shut.

"Trey." Layken knocks on the door. "Are you okay?"

I've been standing here for a while. I pick up on the worry in her voice, so I reach for the lock on the door and open it to find her standing there with her arms folded around her waist.

"Are you all right?" she asks again, and I nod.

"Yeah, baby, I am." I pull her into my arms, pressing her face against my chest, and she sighs.

I soak in the warmth of her body and remind myself she's still here. She chose me. She wants to be with me.

"I've never in my life felt the way I do about anyone the way I do you. I don't want to lose you, Layken; I can't lose you."

She unhooks her arms around me and slips her fingers into mine, leading me over to the couch. I take a seat first and pull her onto my lap, and she rests her arm around my neck.

I slide my hand up her thigh and cover my palm over her stomach.

"You, this baby," I croak. "Our baby. I will do anything for you both. I'll protect you from anyone who tries to hurt you or attempts to tear us apart."

She holds my face in her hand and presses a soft kiss to my lips. It's tender at first. I brush my nose along hers before deepening it.

When I pull back, she sucks in a sharp breath and slowly closes her eyes.

"I'm sorry for pushing you away," she whispers.

"I'm sorry for questioning you and giving you a reason to need space."

"I was overwhelmed with everything going on all at once. Finding out about the pregnancy, the media drama—it all started to get into my head. I haven't been feeling well on top of it, and a part of me is still scared of getting hurt," she says.

"I don't exactly have a track record or reputation that would give you a reason to trust me." My voice deepens, turning gravelly. "It's different with you, though. It's always been different. You bring out this other side of me, and it's not something that's gone away since the very first night."

I stare down at my hand still pressed protectively over her stomach and back up to her.

"A part of me is afraid I'll turn out like my dad. That I'll let you down and hurt you."

"Even if things don't work out between us, Trey, you're nothing like your father."

I shake my head. "How can you say that, though? How do you know?"

She presses her hand against my chest over my heart. "We both know what it's like to have your dad make selfish decisions and leave you behind. You've watched it from a child's shoes; you've seen his temper take over and hurt your mom. You know what it did to her when he left too. You may use sex to fight your own demons, like some turn to alcohol and drugs, but it doesn't make you a bad person. I know without a doubt you'd never hurt me or our child the way you were hurt."

"I promise I'll fuck it up. It's bound to happen, but I'd never hurt you like he did my mom. I'd never turn my anger on you, let another woman get between us, or walk out on you. I don't want to lose you."

She leans in close to me, her warm breath feathering over my lips. I move my hands to grip her hips, pulling her close to me. She straddles my lap and loops her arms around my neck.

"You won't ever lose me. I'm not going anywhere."

I nod, and she kisses me. I brush my tongue over her lower lip, seeking entrance, and she opens her mouth to me. She drags her fingers over the nape of my neck and into my hair, raking them over my scalp.

I release a low hiss and pull back. "One other thing," I say, my voice turning serious again.

"What?" she asks, drawing her brows together.

"Normally, I wouldn't go throwing this on you, but I don't want to do this long-distance thing anymore. I need you and our child with me in CB and out on the road. I want you to come home with me."

Her eyes widen, and she nods. "Where is home? Are you staying in Carolina Beach?"

I nod. "We still have some finishing touches to do on our album, but the label is letting us record our music out of Madden's house. He just finished setting up a whole recording studio. We will still fly out to LA, but we'll mostly be in Carolina Beach for now, and I need you there with me."

"Okay," she says. I can already see the questions swirling around in her mind.

I smirk, and she narrows her eyes.

"What?" She pushes me back against the couch and drags her nails into my hair again, pulling on the strands.

"Be careful," I growl. "I was just thinking how I can see the wheels turning in your head already. We can keep your house here. I like this place. It's cozy, and it'll be good to have a familiar place when we want to return to Nashville. Our moms are here, and Kate is here."

"I wouldn't mind selling it too," she murmurs, leaning her head to the side against her shoulder. "People know where I live, so it's not exactly safe."

My brows furrow. "Did something happen?"

"No, no," she hurries to add. "It's, just, everyone is so close by. I'm starting to feel like I don't have any privacy anymore. People are all up in my business, and it's just not the same living here."

I trace my thumb over the apple of her cheek. She leans her head into my palm and sighs.

"We can find something else here instead. Ivy and Kyla are helping me find you a doctor in the area, and Ivy started sending me houses to check out."

"I like the high-rise and the view. I want to sit out on the balcony staring out at the water with the sun shining on me while I read."

"Whatever you want is fine with me." I kiss her again.

"You've thought of everything, huh?" She grips my chin between her fingers, her eyes turning serious.

"I figured if I wanted you to believe I was serious, I needed to show you I was all in. I don't care where we go. If I have you two and my guitar, I'm good."

"I'm happy anywhere, as long as I'm with you."

I grip her ass in my hands and pull her closer to me. I can't help but think about how I almost lost this and her.

We both go silent again. A strand of hair falls in her face, and I sweep it away. She sighs, her eyes feathering shut. She drags her lip between her teeth, and I want to bite it, then kiss every freckle covering her creamy skin.

What has this woman done to me? The effect she's had on me since our first night together has brought out a different side of me, and I don't want to hide how I feel anymore.

"I'm sorry," I whisper between us.

Her eyes search my face, and her thumb brushes over my lips. "I know you are, and I'm sorry too."

"I'm sorry I broke my promise to you."

Her brows deepen, and she shakes her head, confused on what promise exactly.

"I asked you to promise me that no matter what happens, no matter what gets printed in the media, that you'll talk to me." I sigh.

"I promised you I wouldn't run."

"I guess we both broke our promise."

"We also talked about how neither of us are perfect and we'll make mistakes. Next time, I won't hide anything from you. At least not anything like this."

I pull her close to me again and nip at her shoulder, and she giggles, breaking up the seriousness of the moment.

"You better not keep anything from me."

"Well, I can't ruin good surprises, you know. There will be some things I won't tell you right away."

"Yeah, yeah, yeah. Okay, fine. Nothing big like this."

She smirks. "I love you," she whispers.

I inhale a deep breath and pull her against me, her mouth an inch away from mine. "I love you too. More than I ever thought I possibly could love someone."

I hold her face in my hands, and she crashes a hard kiss down on my lips. I moan against her mouth, her hands dropping between us to grip my belt.

She grinds her pussy down on me, and, dammit, I've missed this. I need to feel her wrapped around me.

She pushes herself back until she's positioned on my knees and quickly unhooks my belt and unzips my pants. Not satisfied with how quickly we're moving, she stands and yanks them down my legs.

"Take your pants off, Layken."

Without hesitation, she shoves her pants and underwear down her legs, and flings her shirt over her head, tossing it across the room to the loveseat.

I smirk when she pushes my chest and climbs on top of me.

"Careful," I growl.

She drags her fingers through my hair, tugging on the strands.

"Or what?" she asks sweetly.

"Or I'll be forced to remind you who calls the shots?"

I slide my hand over her chest, pausing on her heart before continuing to wrap around her throat. Her eyes flutter closed, and she leans her head back, grinding her warm pussy against me.

"Do it," she taunts.

I fist my dick and hiss when she grinds against me, desperate to feel her tight pussy.

She grips my wrist and drags her tongue over my palm, stopping to suck my finger into her mouth. My nostrils flare, and I thrust my hips up against her.

"Layken," I grit out before she releases my finger with a pop.

I stroke my cock between us, and she moves forward with her tits in my face, positioning my tip at her entrance.

She hesitates, barely giving me an inch, and I grip her hips in my hand.

"Quit teasing me."

"Who do you belong to, Trey?"

She's trying to turn the tables and call the shots. If that's what she wants, I have no problem letting her take what she needs from me. Every single ounce of pleasure.

"Only ever you."

She bites down on her lip and rolls her eyes closed as she slides down, and I release a loud throaty moan.

"Dear God, baby. You feel so good, fit so perfectly around me."

I lick my thumb, brushing it over her nipple, and her breathing stutters, her movements growing jerky.

"Does that feel good?" I ask, flicking my tongue over my thumb again, this time rubbing it over her clit.

She moans and bucks against me, leaning back to give me better access.

I thrust my hips in time with hers, my attention on her clit relentless. Her breathing grows heavy and her movements erratic.

"Come with me, Trey," she mutters, her chest heaving. "Come inside me. Let me feel you."

Something about the sound of her voice and the plea on her lips sends my release racing through me like a freight train.

I dig my fingers into her hips to hold onto her and increase the pace of my thrusts. When I'm close, I throw my head back and fire off a string of curse words until we both sag against the couch.

Her arms circle my neck, and I tighten my arms around her waist.

This. Her. She's everything in life that I could want and need.

I'll fight anything or anyone who tries to come between us.

CHAPTER TWENTY-SEVEN

TREY

"Will you relax?" Layken whispers.

"What?" I ask, as her hand darts out to stop my leg from bouncing. I didn't even realize I was doing it, too lost in my thoughts to notice.

"You're making me anxious," she snaps.

She's been a little feisty the past few weeks. To be fair, we have a lot going on. Starting with her packing up and moving to Carolina Beach, then closing on our house. It's all happened in a short period.

It's her hormones talking because a few times when she's gotten sassy with me, she's felt bad later and started crying when she apologized. I won't lie and say it doesn't turn me on a little when she gets an attitude with me.

I slip my fingers in hers and kiss the back of her hand. Her face softens, her eyes glued on my lips.

"I'm sorry, baby."

Her eyes dart around the room to several expectant mothers and couples scattered throughout the waiting room. She sucks in a sharp breath when I trail my lips over the back of her hand.

She doesn't seem to care about all the watchful eyes. She leans over and kisses me, muttering under her breath, "It's okay."

"I'm just excited thinking about seeing our baby."

I turn on my side, pressing my hand to where her stomach swells with our child. Originally, we thought it would be fun to wait and keep it a surprise, but Layken is too much of a planner to go through with it.

Not to mention, I think it was adding extra stress with the move, figuring out what we'll need to get now versus waiting until down the road.

"Layken," the nurse calls, stepping out from behind the door.

She slips the strap of her purse over her head and reaches for my hand. The nurse leads us to our room, and I take a seat on the chair, waiting while Layken goes through weighing in and checking her vitals.

"We'll have you slip your pants down below your waist. They'll have you pull your shirt up for the ultrasound, okay?" She smiles warmly. "They'll be back with you in just a few minutes."

She sets a sheet on the table and steps out the door.

Layken climbs down and wiggles her leggings over her hips under her stomach.

"Don't look at me like that right now." Her voice drops low.

My eyes flick away from her stomach to meet hers.

"Like what?"

"Don't play coy with me."

"Baby, you should see how beautiful you look. You'll be lucky if I don't try to get you pregnant again right after. We'll just move onto the next one. Nothing is sexier than the sight of your stomach growing with our baby inside you."

She steps between my legs and grips my chin between her fingers, kissing me hard.

"You make it hard to scold you when you say things like that."

I rub my hand over her stomach, continuing my path up to cup her boobs.

"These too." I smirk. "I should've mentioned these too. You're fuckin' perfect."

The good ole doc decides that's the right time to join us. Layken swats my hands away and her cheeks turn red, her eyes flashing to mine with a warning look. One that says she's going to make me pay for it later.

"Layken, hi." The man smiles, holding his hand out to shake hers. "I'm Dr. Gallagher. I'll be your new physician."

His eyes linger on Layken before turning his attention to me. He's lucky I don't tell him to get lost.

"Hello, sir. And you are?"

"Trey, her husband," I say, crossing my arms over my chest.

Layken snorts, slapping a hand over her mouth. She tries to hold it in, dropping her hand and pressing her lips together in a firm line.

"We're newly married. Ain't that right, baby?"

She nods, narrowing her eyes on mine. "Yes, this is my handsome *husband*, Trey."

I reach my hand out between them, pulling him in for a firm handshake. He nods, looking back and forth between the two of us.

"Uh-huh, well, it's nice to meet you both. As I said, I'm Dr. Gallagher. I'll be your new physician. We'll do an ultrasound today to see how the baby is doing and how things are progressing."

He continues to ramble on, and all I can think about is how far I'd like to kick him in the ass. He seems to heed the message loud and clear, though.

Layken is mine, and he better keep his hands and eyes in all the respectable places.

The doctor steps out for a few minutes, and the ultrasound tech joins us. She introduces herself as Sierra. I can immediately see the difference in how she puts Layken at ease.

I pull my chair closer to Layken, and she slips her hand into mine. Our eyes stay glued to the screen. It takes a few minutes to figure out what we're looking at, but Sierra walks us through what we're seeing. She outlines the head and body, and before I know it, I'm staring at my child on the screen.

My chest tightens, an unfamiliar feeling taking over me.

I've never loved anyone the way I do Layken. There's something about holding her hand while we see our child for the first time. It's a surreal feeling and completely shifts your whole world on its axis.

Everything I thought I knew about love and my future changed at that moment. I can't wait until I get to hold him or her.

"Would you like to know the gender?" Sierra asks.

Layken looks over at me again, giving us one last chance to change my mind.

I nod. "Yes. Please."

Layken smiles, releasing her grip on my hand to brush away the tear trailing down my cheek.

"My sweet husband," she whispers softly, and I lean in to kiss her.

"We'll be making it official very soon," I murmur against her mouth.

She bites down on her lip and nods. "Good."

We both turn to the screen and wait while she adjusts the wand over her stomach.

"They're quite active in there," Sierra adds, moving it around Layken's stomach to find the right angle.

Each second that passes waiting for her to tell me feels like forever.

"Aah, I thought so." She smiles, turning to Layken. "It looks like you're having a little girl."

I tighten my hand in my fist, holding it over my mouth while I blink through the tears, staring at the screen and taking in every minute.

My heart. Dammit, I swear she holds it in her tiny hand already.

I push myself to stand and wrap my arm around Layken, burying my face into her neck.

"She's gonna be the most perfect little angel, like her mama," I choke out.

Damn, I'm a mess.

Layken holds my face in her hands and kisses me hard. When I pull back, she brushes her thumbs over my face and whispers she loves me.

"I love you too, baby."

Sierra wipes the jelly from Layken's stomach, and we both thank her.

"I have some photos I'm printing off for you. I'll give you two a moment and be back with those for you," she whispers, waving to us before she steps out.

Layken sits up and swings her legs around to the side of the table when I drop to one knee on the floor.

Her mouth drops open, and her eyes go wide.

"Trey?"

"I don't have a ring yet, baby. You can pick one out, anything you want. Everything I have is all yours. It's all for you."

I press my lips against her stomach and lift my eyes to meet hers.

"I promise I'll do this soon. The right way. It'll be big with a beautiful ring. It will be the special moment you deserve."

We both have shared many firsts together, and this is one of those things I don't want to mess up.

"I want you to know and this is my promise to you, one day not too long from now, I'm going to get down on one knee and propose to you. I plan to marry you and get you pregnant with as many kids as you'll give me."

She smiles, wiping the tear away from her eye.

"I promise to give you everything you could ever want or need."

"I already have everything I want with you," she hiccups, and I smile, kissing her hard.

"All I want is our family and to make you my wife. I'd do it right now, but I want it to be perfect. The way you deserve for it to be."

She brushes her hair away from her face, her lip trembling.

"Nothing about our story is conventional, Trey, but it's ours. It's perfect to me, and I wouldn't have it any other way."

"You're perfect for me," I grunt, pushing myself to my feet and kiss her. "Every single inch of you."

The door clicks, and we both turn to find Sierra standing in the doorway holding an envelope. Layken showed me the photos of the first ultrasound, but these are even more special since you can see our daughter growing inside her.

Layken whispers in my ear, "They're staring," when I carry her in my arms out of the doctor's office and out to my SUV.

I don't give a shit what people think, though, and I'm done worrying about what gets printed in the tabloids. They will keep talking and spreading whatever they want.

Might as well give them something to talk about.

Layken keeps her head on my shoulder and her arm circled around mine the entire drive home. I can't keep my hands off her. Her knee, her thigh, every inch of her.

Her eyes are glittered when I put the car in park in our driveway.

"Don't move," I order, climbing out and rounding the front to her side.

She stares down at me, her waist hitting right at my chest. I press my hands against her belly.

"Are you still nervous about being a dad?" she asks, taking me off guard.

I shrug. The truth? I'm fucking terrified.

I don't know the first thing about being a dad, and the examples set in front of both of us were unhealthy. Layken, though, I have no doubt in my mind she'll be an incredible mom.

"Parts of it scare the hell out of me. I'm worried I'll make mistakes and screw my kid up like my dad did with me, then they'll grow up to hate me too."

"Your dad didn't fuck up with you." Her smile falls from her face. "You really think that?"

"I've thought about it a lot, yeah."

She leans down to wrap her arms around my neck and pulls me against her body. I'm careful of her belly between us.

When she leans away, tears are welling up in her eyes again.

"Baby, why are you crying?"

"It just makes me sad to think you feel that way is all," she says.

She tries to force a smile but presses her lips together to cover up the quiver in her lip.

"I have no doubt you'll be an amazing father, Trey," she adds a moment later when her tears have dried up. "I may have been worried early on if you'd want this with me, but only because I knew you didn't want a relationship. Neither of us planned for this, but I've never once doubted if you'd be a good father. I know you'll show her the same love and care you've always shown me."

I clench my jaw and attempt to keep my emotions in check. Seeing her so emotional and hearing her words stir up something in my chest.

I knew my reaction to the news had her hesitating, and it's on me for making her question if I was happy about this. I didn't know how much I needed her to say this until now.

"As long as I have you with me, I know we'll get through anything."

CHAPTER TWENTY-EIGHT

LAYKEN

"Trey, where are you taking me?" I ask, taking a hesitant step forward.

It's quiet, with only the soft sound of footsteps along the wooden planks beneath me.

I reach my hand out blindly for his arm, running my fingers over his skin, only it's not Trey. My body jolts to a stop, and a quiet giggle follows.

"It's Kyla," she whispers. "He asked me to help him. C'mon, we're almost there."

My heart rate slows, and I link our arms together as she helps me down the stairs and instructs me to kick off my sandals. My feet sink into the warm sand before she resumes walking with me.

"We're almost there, just a few more feet," she murmurs.

"Thank you," I say, and she responds by squeezing my hand.

We take a couple more steps before she stops me, holding my shoulders before the silk scarf tied around my head, covering my eyes, loosens.

I slowly blink my eyes open to find Trey standing in front of me on the beach, surrounded by a giant heart made of orange lilies, reminding me of our first date. A heart-stopping grin spreads across his face, his eyes lighting up, reminding me of the very first night we spent together.

Something about the look in his eyes still gets to me, even after all this time.

I press my hand against my belly, where our daughter is growing. We're counting down the last few weeks of my pregnancy. It's hard to believe she'll finally be here in a couple of months.

The last few months living in Carolina Beach have been incredible. Before too long, A Rebels Havoc will be releasing their new music and hitting the road for their next tour.

We've taken advantage of our downtime together because we know as soon as the tour starts and the baby is here, our lives are going to get crazy.

A warm breeze blows in, the smell of sea salt lingering in the air, as I take the steps down the lined path leading to where Trey waits for me.

His eyes drop down to where my hand protectively holds my stomach. When I'm a few feet away, he takes the last remaining steps to meet me, reaching for my hand to pull me into his arms.

"You're beautiful, baby," he whispers, his hands holding the side of my stomach. Anytime we hug like this, he always holds my stomach too.

The sun was starting to set in the distance.

Trey was dressed in a gray T-shirt and denim jeans. He was barefoot, with his leather bracelet tied around his wrist.

This is one of those moments I'll always remember. We didn't get a chance to make it down to the beach the first time I came to visit him last year, but ever since I moved here, he makes it a point to bring me down by the water as much as possible.

"Do you love me?" he asks, his voice breaking when he says the word love.

I move my hands over my stomach, finding his and squeeze his fingers in mine. My brows deepen.

"Of course, I do. More than you could ever imagine."

His eyes start to glisten, but he blinks through it, staring out past me into the distance.

"You know, when I think back to a few years ago when I was playing with Blunt Force Trauma, I never dreamed this is where I'd end up today. Here I am, playing with the guys, we're about to release our next album, and go out on the road again this summer. Then there's you, the best thing to come into my life."

Tears fill the brim of my eyes. My emotions have been like a roller coaster these days, but when Trey opens up to me like this, there's no controlling it.

The bad boy who always believed he'd never fall in love or have a family of his own is proving himself wrong time and time again.

"I wouldn't have found my way back to you if it weren't for joining the band. No matter what happens in our future, what speed bumps or road blocks come in front of us, I'll always be ridin' next to you."

I smile. "Always."

He reaches his hand up, slipping his fingers into my hair, and kisses me. His warm lips and eager tongue brush against my mouth, and I sigh, opening for him.

Tears slip down my face, and he must feel them or hear the shuddered sigh because he pulls back and whispers, "Don't cry, baby," against my lips.

When I open my eyes, he steps back and kneels on the ground. My hand flies to my mouth, and there's no containing my emotions now.

I squeeze my eyes shut, and he chuckles.

"It's okay, baby." His hand brushes over my stomach, giving me a minute to collect myself.

I fold my hands against the side of his face and kiss him.

When I pull back from his mouth, he whispers again, "Marry me."

I nod. "Yes," I mutter, breathlessly. "Yes, yes!"

He chuckles, and I finally see the round diamond ring.

"Trey, it's beautiful." My eyes are wide as he slips it on my finger, my gaze bouncing from the ring over to him.

I wrap my arms around him, and he stands and lifts me into his arms. Only it takes me a second to realize he has no intention of putting me down as he carries me across the sand.

"Where are we going?" I snicker.

"Home." He smirks. "I need to get you home and out of this dress."

Thankfully, we're not far from our house. Trey knew how much I wanted to stay close to the water and made it one of our stipulations when it came to finding a house.

He was ready to buy some land and build our own when the perfect place came on the market. Even better, it was far away from our neighbors and gave us the privacy we wanted.

Trey carries me up the wood stairs leading up to the gate at the back of our property. He sets me down to unlock it but picks me back up to carry me again.

"Trey," I whisper against his ear when he climbs the step to the patio.

"We're almost there, baby," he mutters.

"No, let's stay out here," I say, earning me a low growl.

"We haven't claimed this spot yet."

Our house is a modern black Tudor-style home with wood detailing with floor-to-ceiling windows across the back. We have a large patio with white furniture overlooking our swimming pool.

The temperatures are finally warming, and I'm eager for when we can start using our pool.

Trey carries me over to one of the patio sofas. He lets me stand for a moment before taking a seat in the middle.

I quickly kick off my shoes and pull my dress up around my hips. His eyes lower, watching me. He leans over to run his hand up my inner thigh, pausing when he brushes his finger over the seam of my underwear.

My body trembles, leaving me unsteady on my feet, and I quickly reach out to grip his shoulder to hold me up. He doesn't hesitate, moving his hand farther for my underwear and drags them down my legs.

"Take this off." He nods to my dress.

My breasts have grown a lot over the past few months and are getting more and more tender every day. Something Trey loves, along with giving me the slow lovemaking he wasn't always used to before.

It's just another one of those things he never thought he'd be good at.

I drag the strap of my dress down my arm, followed by the other, pushing the material down my body. Trey sucks in a low hiss when he notices I'm not wearing a bra underneath and leans forward to lightly trace his finger over my nipple before I let the dress drop to the ground.

He picks it up and tosses it on the sofa next to him, leaving me standing in front of him naked.

"Your turn." I smile.

I glance around us at the trees lining the property.

"No one is around, baby. It's just you and me."

I hum, watching him unzip his jeans and push them down his legs, before shrugging his shirt off too.

He wraps his hand around his hard length, pumping himself once, then twice. He leans over and presses a soft kiss against my stomach. He brushes his finger up my inner thigh again, this time flicking the tip over my swollen clit.

I shudder and let out a throaty moan.

"More. Give me more."

He obliges, moving his hand farther to slip inside me, and I spread my legs to give him more room.

"Always so wet for me, baby," he groans. "You ready?"

I nod, but he doesn't stop. His fingers move inside me, his thumb brushing over my clit, and I moan his name.

When I slowly blink my eyes open, his eyes are fixed on where his hand enters me, the other wrapped firmly around his cock. I push his arm back to bend down, sucking the tip of him into my mouth.

"Ah fuck," he grits out, thrusting his hips up greedily seeking more of my mouth. "C'mere, baby."

He grips my hips and pulls me toward him, and I climb on his lap. It's harder to do now with my stomach growing between us, but it won't stop us.

He helps position himself at my entrance, and I slowly slide down him, holding his shoulders as I slam my body down. The sounds coming from Trey intermixed with his heavy breathing urge me on.

He flicks his tongue over my nipple, and I rake my fingers through his hair, tugging on the strands. He clenches his jaw and growls, doing it again.

Each brush of his tongue over my nipple has my body growing more and more desperate for him.

"You look so fuckin' sexy riding my dick, Mrs. Whitt."

I slowly blink my eyes open, and a wide grin stretches across his face, clearly liking the sound of that.

"Say it again," I mutter quickly.

He brushes his finger over my clit, and my moves grow erratic.

"I said 'fuck me, Mrs. Whitt,'" he breathes out. "You like it when I call you Mrs. Whitt? I'll mark it on my skin, baby. My fuckin' wife. You hear me?"

I smile at him through hazy eyes, and he gives me one last flick of his tongue before it's over. My orgasm races through me, and I dig my fingers into his arm to hold on while I yelp and buck against him.

I sag against his chest, burying my face into his neck. My eyes grow heavy when he slips his fingers into my hair, massaging the back of my head, and he presses his mouth against my ear.

"I love you, Layken Whitt."

I can't wait to make it official.

EPILOGUE

TREY

"We don't need another fight breaking out," Abel says, shooting me a warning look.

"Not when we have a visitor in town either," Madden grumbles, flicking his gaze over to the journalist seated at our table at Whiskey Barrel.

Madden and Abel escort us through the packed crowd over to where everyone is seated. I didn't even have to ask, understanding my concern about getting Layken through without anyone bumping her.

"Don't worry, man. I'll make sure nothing or no one gets close to her." He claps me on the shoulder and steps back against the wall, crossing his arms over his chest.

"Thanks, man." I nod.

"I hear congratulations are in order?" Tysin chirps, his eyes bouncing from Layken to me.

My fingers tighten on Layken's, and I lift her hand to my mouth and kiss the knuckle next to her ring.

"I'd say so." I smile. "We're engaged."

We've spent the past three days in a post-engagement bliss. The only time either of us left was when I went to band practice, and Layken decided to get out and move around.

It wasn't going to be long before there were three of us and those moments alone would be hard to come by. Having this time with her made it difficult not to say, "fuck my plans" and call off to stay home with her.

We decided to wait to announce it, although the guys knew it was coming for some time now. Kyla and Ivy stepped in, offering their assistance to help set everything up for me. It took over two hundred dozen lilies to pull it off. They helped arrange them into a heart before Ivy escaped to our house to decorate our house and bedroom with candles and rose petals.

I couldn't have pulled it off without them.

I wanted Layken to know before our daughter was here that I was serious about us. I was all in on forever with her.

"It's all happening pretty quick, don't ya think?" Trey smirks, winking at Layken.

"Listen, only one of us needs to take two years to pull our head out of our ass and realize the woman we love and want to be with is standing right in front of us. I wasn't going to wait that long."

Tysin rolls his eyes and lifts his middle finger, pulling Kyla into his body.

"I guess you could say when I go all in, I'm all the fuck in." I chuckle, and Layken shakes her head.

The rumors started swirling a few weeks ago when she posted a photo of us together on her Instagram. She was wearing the promise ring I got for her, and people immediately started making assumptions.

We didn't care, though. We stopped letting the media control the narrative. I made sure to hire a photographer to capture photos of our engagement. When we got them back yesterday, we shared the news on our own terms.

"I guess that calls for a fuckin' celebration, man. Congratulations to you both!" Tysin shouts.

Tysin and Kyla started their relationship at a slow pace. She was with us every step of the way from our tour to recording our album, and it seems since we've been back in Carolina Beach, things have been steadily progressing between them.

"This calls for a round of shots," Brix adds. "Jayde, can you get us a round and one shot of lemonade for the bride to be?"

Ivy smiles, stepping around the table to hug Layken. Kyla is right behind her. Their eyes nearly bulge out of their sockets when she shows them her ring.

"Holy shit, Trey," Kyla blurts out.

"Wow," Ivy follows. "Trey, you did so good. It's beautiful."

"Thanks, sis." I smile, and they both step in to give me a hug.

Tysin slips his arm around Kyla's waist, dragging her away from me. Brix looks around for Ivy, seeing her tucked under my arm.

"I don't like to share," he growls into her ear, reaching for her hand.

Madden, on the other hand, is lost in his own world. As soon as we got to our table, he's been distracted talking to the journalist, Brielle, from our interview earlier today.

Our record label lined up a special interview with *Limelight* magazine. I think they're trying to smooth over our image after all the drama last year following the fight.

She's only in town for the night, I guess, and it's clear to everyone except her that he's taken a liking to her. Although, Madden keeps trying to play it off like he only wants to get on her good side.

Jayde carries the tray of shots over to our table. We all move out of the way for her. Layken snags her lemonade and smiles.

"Aye, yo, Madden," Brix hollers at him, pulling his attention out of his conversation.

He slowly drags his head away from Brielle to look over at us and smiles. "Sorry, guys."

Madden reaches for two shots, holding one out to Brielle.

"No, it's okay." She waves her hand and smiles before she tucks her blond hair behind her ear.

"C'mon," he jests, "Live a little. I won't tell your boss, I promise." Madden winks.

She presses her lips together, appearing to think about it before she agrees, taking the shot from him.

"A toast," Brix says. "To Layken and Trey. Trey, I can speak for all the guys when I say you're like a brother to us. It's hard to remember what the band was like before you came barreling in. We're happy you two found love. If there's anyone who can calm his chaos, Layken, it's you. To the soon-to-be Mr. and Mrs. Whitt."

"Cheers," everyone says, lifting their hands to clink our glasses together before tossing them back.

The liquid burns my throat, and I squeeze my eyes shut. It's been a hot minute since I've tasted tequila. I forgot the bite it leaves behind.

"Thanks, man. I appreciate it. You have no idea." I clap Brix on the shoulder.

Madden steps around the table and pulls me in for a hug, congratulating me and Layken, followed by Tysin.

"Can you believe this?" Tysin mutters under his breath, watching as Madden slinks around to where Brielle is sitting. "Don't you think we should warn him away from her? I mean, of all the people, he's pursuing the enemy. You'd think he'd be the one to steer clear of a journalist when they come sniffing around."

Brix shakes his head, and I shrug.

"I guess we can't stop him. He's always on the rest of us when we bury our head in some shit. Might as well let him see what it's like for himself."

"No fuckin' kidding." Brix laughs.

Madden whistles to get our attention and nods toward the stage. "We have ten minutes until showtime."

I grip Layken's hips and pull her to me from behind. I run my hands over her stomach. She's still talking to Kyla and Ivy but stops when I press my mouth against her ear.

"I'm gonna go tune my guitar and get ready," I murmur low.

She nods, lacing her fingers through mine, holding our hands against her belly.

"Don't wear yourself out too much, rock star," she says, turning in my arms to wrap hers around my neck. "We still have some celebrating left to do."

I grip her ass and groan. "We can leave here right now. They can play without me. Tysin can handle it. They did it for years."

Her cheeks turn a delicious shade of red, and she shakes her head. "You'll have to wait. I want to watch you on stage. It's like foreplay."

"My girl loves to watch. I'll warm up my fingers for you."

She pushes on my chest and giggles. It's a sound I want to hear forever, that and her moans. Give them both to me every day.

We took the stage not long after. The girls sat close to us, and every time my eyes flicked over to Layken, she'd drag her eyes away from me and down to my hands.

She was right. It was our own torturous form of foreplay, and as soon as we wrapped up our set, I made some excuse about Layken being tired to drag her out of there and get her home.

She curls her finger toward me when we walk through the door, and I follow her, pushing her against the wall.

When I lean down to kiss her, she whispers against my lips, "I'm not wearing anything under my dress."

"Get to the bedroom," I order.

She grins, taking off down the hall to our room. She yelps when I land a swat against her ass.

She shrugs out of her leather jacket, tossing it onto the chair in the corner of our room, then turns back to me.

I let my eyes roam over her body, down to where her stomach swells with our child. She looks so fuckin' beautiful, the sight makes my dick hard.

"We're home and in our bedroom," she whispers, dragging the strap of her dress over her shoulder. "Now tell me what you want me to do, Daddy."

My eyes darken on hers, and she drags her lip between her teeth.

I motion for her to turn and help her out of her dress. She spins around, cupping the weight of her breast in her hands, lifting her eyes to meet mine.

"Get on the bed, Layken," I grit out. "Open your legs. I want to see how wet you are for me."

She smirks and nods.

I guess some things will never change.

Thank you so much for reading TREY!

Still want more Trey and Layken? Don't worry, I'm not done with these two yet.

Turn the page to find out how you can read their bonus epilogue. Don't miss a sneak peek at MADDEN, a frenemies to lovers, rock star/journals romance.

I hope you enjoy!

BONUS SCENE

Dear Reader,

I hope you enjoyed Trey and Layken's story as much as I loved writing it.

I couldn't get enough of their love and wanted to give you a glimpse into their lives, so I wrote you a sexy and heartfelt bonus epilogue exclusively for you. All you have to do is click the link below or scan the QR code with your phone, sign up for my newsletter, and you'll get access.

www.authorbrookeobrien.com/bonus

If you want to stay up to date with my sales and new releases, you can follow me on Bookbub at: www.bookbub.com/profile/brooke-o-brien

Brooke

MADDEN

BOOK THREE

USA TODAY BESTSELLING AUTHOR

BROOKE O'BRIEN

CHAPTER ONE

BRIELLE

I can't fuck this up.

As we pass through the neighborhood, I peer out the window at the stunning homes behind gated entrances with stone pillars and statutes, each with freshly manicured lawns.

We pull up outside of a black wrought-iron gate, and Davis presses the button to the intercom.

"Hello?"

"Yes, it's *Limelight* magazine. We're here for our interview with A Rebels Havoc."

"I'll let you through. Please come to the front door."

The gate opens, and we pass through, down the long gravel road to the circular driveway and park.

Davis whistles when he leans forward to take in the beautiful home.

"Here I thought I've been saving myself for a hot shot financial banker or some successful real estate investor, when I should've been looking for a sexy rock star."

I shake my head. I'm not sure what I expected when we showed up here, but it wasn't this. Black shutters surround two large windows with a balcony on the upper level, a pillared entrance, and black and gray brick below.

I imagine taking in the view of the sunrise each morning with a cup of coffee and the sun glistening on the water.

"You ready to kill this thing?" Davis asks, bringing me back to reality.

He's overly chipper this morning. Something I'm not quite ready for.

I mumble, "Ready as I'll ever be," while mentally trying to hype myself up for what's to come.

It's just the two of us, and it's my first assignment. I can't believe my boss thought to stiff me with this interview on my first week.

"You have plenty of experience in the industry, Brielle. You'll kill it. I have all the faith in you," Sawyer sang, tapping on the doorframe before she disappeared out of my office.

She didn't give me a chance to protest.

Davis adjusts the bag on his shoulder and bumps his arm against mine.

"Let's do this damn thing." He grins.

We take the stone steps up the front walkway to the door. Davis hits the doorbell, and I clutch my bag holding my notebook against my side. I run my hand over my blazer down to my skirt to calm my racing heart.

While I may have years of experience, this job is something new for me entirely. I've never done a sit-down interview with anyone, much less the members of the biggest rock band in the country.

We stand outside, taking in the trellis of vines climbing up the brick exterior, waiting for someone to answer, but no one does.

"Where are they?" Davis peeks into the doorway, looking for any sign of movement.

"What the heck? Don't they know we planned to be here at two o'clock?" I grit out.

I've done my best not to let my distaste for A Rebels Havoc show. I've always thought of them as a bunch of arrogant, womanizing pricks.

"You'd think so," he says, shrugging. "Should I ring it again?"

I glance around, searching for any indication someone is even home.

"We have the correct address, right?"

"I mean, they have private security at the gate, and they did let us in? I'd assume they knew we were here." He huffs.

"No frickin' kidding." With a sigh, I reach across him and punch my finger against the doorbell again.

We wait another moment before we see a figure through the glass door. I can't quite make out the person; all I can see is a fury of purple rushing toward us.

The lock clicks, and the door swings open, and a woman who, from my research, is Kyla greets us. She's dating Tysin, their lead guitarist, and is the sister of their drummer, Madden.

We've been in touch through email over the past week, finalizing the last-minute details for their interview today.

"I'm so sorry to keep you waiting. I'm Kyla, the band's manager. Forgive me; I thought Madden was going to grab the door. It must've been a misunderstanding." She presses her lips together in a forced smile. She folds her hand against her heaving chest, out of breath as if she ran a mile to answer the door.

"The guys should be here any moment. They just wrapped up practice about an hour ago and were getting cleaned up."

She steps back, letting us in.

"Can I get you a drink?" she offers, holding her arm out to lead us inside.

"I wouldn't mind a water," Davis says, smiling.

"I'll have one too," I add.

"Great, I'll grab those for you. We thought we could do the interview over here in the sitting area. Madden displays their awards and mementos from over the years in there."

My heels click on the tile floors as we follow her into a room with a large sofa and two sitting chairs. The stone-blue walls have plaques, pictures, and awards covering nearly every surface.

"This works perfectly. I'll head back out to grab the rest of our equipment, and we'll get everything set up while we wait."

Kyla scurries off, and I turn back to Davis. He shrugs and shakes his head.

"If you want to figure out a setup, I'll get our stuff. You good?"

I nod, waving him off, and he disappears out the door.

Setting my bag down on one of the chairs, I look at all their achievements hanging on the wall.

Over the years, I've covered A Rebels Havoc, so I've heard the rumors swirling around in the media about them. They've had everything from drinking and partying too much to fights and rumored pregnancies splashed all over the headlines.

Their record label knew what they were doing by setting up this interview. They have a new album coming out in a few weeks, and even though there's no such thing as bad press, I'm sure this is their way of trying to smooth over their image.

Despite this being an incredible opportunity for me, I'm not exactly excited about sitting down and talking with them. They seem like nothing but a bunch of punks who only care about drinking and getting laid.

I brush my finger over the frame holding the multiplatinum disc from their breakout album. Not many have accomplished that incredible achievement, so it's cool to see their award in person.

"Fuck, baby, that feels so damn good." A loud throaty groan filters into the quiet space, and my whole body freezes. "Let me see those pretty eyes while you suck my dick."

I gasp, my mouth dropping open before I quietly slap my hand over it to muffle the sound.

Who the hell did I just overhear?

"Fuckkk," he moans. "Take it deep, sweetheart. Mmm, just like that."

My face warms at the sound of his words, heat spreading over my body. His deep voice has me rubbing my legs together.

I can't believe I'm standing here still listening, but I can't manage to pull myself away either.

"Let me hear you, baby," he mutters.

I finally force my feet to move, turning to glance out the large bay window overlooking the driveway. Davis still has the back of the SUV open, shuffling around to collect our equipment.

Kyla will likely be back in here any second. Where are the rest of the guys?

His loud, throaty moan interrupts my thoughts, and I lean against the wall next to a bookshelf, wrapping my arm around my waist and placing my hand on my chest.

She moans quietly, and the sound of her gagging filters through the air.

My chest heaves, my breaths coming out in pants. I can practically feel my heart beating against my palm. I move up, wrapping my fingers around the base of my neck, and lean against the wall.

"I'm close," he mutters. "I'm fuckin' close. Open your throat, baby, and take it all." He grunts, and the sound nearly has me melting on the floor in a puddle.

I'm embarrassed by how turned on I am listening to this go down. Even more, I'm ashamed I didn't walk outside with Davis and give them privacy to finish what they're doing.

I don't think I would've been able to leave if I tried.

I squeeze my eyes closed, imagining he's standing above me, and his arousing words are from my hands and mouth on his body.

It's felt like forever since a man has touched me.

Too long.

If I gave in and slipped my hand into my pants, I'd realize just how desperate I am to be touched again.

I swipe the back of my hand over my forehead where the perspiration dots my brow. I attempt to smooth over my hair, trying and failing to collect myself, when a door swings open. I frantically push off the wall and come face-to-face with a shirtless Madden.

"Who the fuck are you?"

My mouth drops open, and I fumble over my words, not sure how to answer.

"Uh, yes, hi. My name is Brielle."

"What the hell are you doing in my house?"

I steel my spine and narrow my eyes.

What the hell am I doing in his house? What the heck does he think I'm doing?

"I thought we didn't have any hired staff here today?"

I'm tempted to tell him to fuck off. Is this how he talks to guests or people who work for him?

His eyes trail down my body, and the heat behind them causes my brain to misfire. How is it I just overheard him with someone else, and now I'm picturing I was her?

What the hell has gotten into me?

The faint sound of heels clicking on the tile floor moves closer and closer to us. A petite brunette appears, wearing a tight black tunic and a pair of distressed denim jeans.

I resist curling my lip when I notice her smeared lipstick, knowing exactly why.

She stops when she reaches Madden and glances back and forth between us. She sneers, her eyes giving me a once-over before turning to him.

"I'll see you soon?" she asks, running her palm over his chest.

I step back to give them space, hoping this is my out to go search for Davis and avoid this humiliating conversation.

Madden turns back to me and holds up his hand. "Wait, please."

I nod and grit my teeth, glancing away to avoid looking at them. He leans down into her ear and whispers, "Thank you," then hugs her.

"I'll text you soon," he murmurs.

She nods enthusiastically and presses a kiss against his cheek.

"Excuse me," she replies sweetly, moving to pass between us but not before she flashes me a devious grin.

I return hers with a forced smile, stepping back to let her by, and she disappears out the front door.

Madden's demeanor changes when he turns back to me.

"Back to what I was saying," he retorts. His voice drops low, without an ounce of caring. "I wasn't expecting any staff to be here today. In the future, when I have a guest over, I expect you to give me privacy."

I bite my tongue to resist telling him to fuck off.

He has every right to want privacy, except I want to throw in his face how rude it is to invite guests into his home and then treat them like shit.

I chuckle under my breath and shake my head. He takes the step separating us, leaving enough room for me to smell his woodsy cologne mixed with the smell of sweat.

Do not think about how delicious he smells, Brielle.

"Can I ask what's so funny?" He lowers his eyes to my chest.

I'm afraid to even check my own reflection right now because I know the heat flaming my cheeks gives away just how much he affects me.

Whenever I'm nervous or anxious, I break out in what looks like hives. No matter how hard I try, I've never been able to prevent it.

I shake my head and finally glance up, locking eyes with him. It takes everything in me to stay composed.

"I know you were listening to us, and judging by the dazed look in your eye, you liked it. So unless you're waiting for me to drag you into that room for round two, I'll need you to clue me in. Although, I could assure you that you wouldn't find it the least bit funny if I did."

My face falls, and my eyes widen.

Why am I not surprised? Only these guys would finish getting their dick sucked and walk out here minutes later to proposition me.

"I wouldn't let you touch me if you were the last dick on earth," I spit out.

As soon as the words are out of my mouth, I wish I could take them back.

"Um, excuse me, Madden?" A voice interrupts, and we both turn to find Kyla standing in the entryway.

The door opens behind her, and Davis enters, carrying a tripod along with another bag.

My eyes flick back to Kyla, and her face is solemn.

"Can I have a word with you, Madden? Please," she mutters coldly, her eyes wide with a scolding look that says, "You better listen to me right now."

What the hell just happened?

CHAPTER TWO

MADDEN

Fuck, I thought the interview was tomorrow.

"I told you earlier this morning," Kyla snaps.

"I didn't hear you. I swore you said it was tomorrow."

"Yeah, when I reminded you about it *yesterday*," she retorts. "I swear, sometimes you don't pay attention."

I want to fly off the handle with a remark like, "Oh, you mean when you were fuckin' my best friend behind my back?"

I don't, though. Instead, I grit my teeth and pace back and forth in the kitchen, massaging my fingers into my pulsing temples.

Kyla pulls out her phone. "Trey is pulling up now. Brix and Tysin should be here any minute, and you still look like you just got done practicing."

She's right; I need to get cleaned up if we're supposed to do this interview soon.

I'm still recovering from the fact the hot-as-sin woman I hit on is actually here to do a sit-down interview with us.

As if we don't already have enough fuckin' bad press to begin with, now I have to worry about this shit.

"I'm gonna go shower. I'll make it quick."

"Okay. I'll do my best to distract them while we wait, but hurry, will ya? The interview was supposed to start thirty minutes ago."

I clench my jaw and nod, walking past her back into the entryway.

The woman, I think she said her name was Brielle, stands in the living area next to a tall, slender man busy setting up their lighting equipment.

Her big blue eyes flick over to mine, and her face heats when she catches me staring at her. Her hair is sleeked back into a bun and those red lips tempt me once again.

She looks out of place and uncomfortable, reaching to tuck a strand of hair behind her ear. Her eyes flick down to my bare chest before forcing them up to meet mine.

Something about watching the emotions play out on her face, along with her reaction to seeing me earlier, taunts me. She was listening and appeared to be turned on by it.

Then I went and opened my big fuckin' mouth and made the situation worse.

"We'll be ready to start in about five minutes. Ten minutes max," I mutter when I pass by them.

"No problem," the guy replies. "We're just getting set up now."

Brielle peers at me intently. I soften my face and nod as if it's some sort of peace offering, and she returns it by pressing her lips together in a forced smile.

The last thing I need is to start us off on a rocky foot with the stuck-up journalist.

After all the shit in the media over the past year, we hope to shed a different light on who we are with this interview. We're still the same rebels we were early on in our careers, even if the guys have settled down some since falling in love.

Except for me.

I would've thought I'd be the first one to find someone, but the further we got in our career, the harder I've found it to trust people around us.

Loyalty and trust go a long way, but it's crazy what money and fame can do to people. I only want to be surrounded by the people who ride for me, and if they don't, they can get the fuck out of my life.

I jump in the shower and clean myself up, still slick with sweat from our practice session earlier. We're so close to releasing our new album and will be going on tour again this summer.

I can't fuckin' wait to get back out on the road. I miss it so much.

Absolutely nothing is like going out on stage and playing in front of a sold-out crowd.

Playing the drums has always been an outlet for me. My parents never wanted this to turn into my career even though they were supportive and bought me my first set.

They thought it was a hobby I'd eventually outgrow. I still remember my dad's snide comments about getting a real job, refusing to accept this has always been my dream.

Since signing on with our label, he's cut the comments despite wishing I had gone to college and got a degree in business like he did.

I don't give a shit what he thinks anymore. I love what I do, and I'm not in it for the money even though it's definitely one of the perks.

Don't get me wrong, though; this life comes with a lot I wish I didn't have to deal with too.

A black leather jacket and denim jeans with a white T-shirt wait for me in my room. I grit my teeth, knowing Kyla has been getting everything lined up for this interview for a month now.

I slip my leather cuff back on and run some product through my hair and over my beard, trying to look as if I've got my shit together.

I hate these fuckin' interviews. The sooner I get this over with, the quicker I can get the gossiping jackasses out of my house.

Brix and Tysin stand at the end of the hall when I step out of my bedroom. Tysin nods in my direction, and Brix turns, his eyes flaring before he stalks toward me, meeting me halfway.

"Sounds like shit already started off on a bad foot."

I stare at him, deadpanned, and shake my head. "Don't even get me started."

"You don't have to tell me. Kyla already did," he retorts.

I clench my jaw, wishing I had a couple of minutes to give everyone a piece of my mind.

"I'm sorry to interrupt," a soft voice says, and we both turn toward Brielle.

She holds her hand up and dips her head.

"Forgive me; I just wanted to let you know we're ready to get started whenever you are."

Trey sits on one of the barstools behind the sofa, facing two of our chairs. Brielle circles to the other side, and I watch as she runs a hand over her blouse before taking a seat.

She crosses her legs and sits up straight, holding a stack of notecards in her hands.

I know our label cleared this interview and the questions we agreed to go over before they stepped foot in my house. Still, inviting them here doesn't sit right with me, even though the point was for it to feel more personal and intimate.

Too intimate.

I clench my jaw, hating how the sight of her legs captivates me.

Trey must notice and elbows me.

"What?" I grunt as I climb onto the barstool next to him.

"Nothin', just checking for signs of life."

"Shut up," I fire back.

Brix and Tysin take a seat on the sofa in front of us.

When we begin, we talk about how the band got started and what it was like bringing Trey into the mix before moving into our relationships.

Brielle manages to avoid looking at me for most of the discussion.

"Over the years, you've been known to have a way with the ladies. Would you agree?"

Brix and Tysin chuckle and Trey shakes his head.

"Over the years, yeah, I think that would be true. We're all still young and figuring out what we want in life," Brix says.

Tysin nods. "I'll speak for myself in saying I made some mistakes before Kyla came back into my life last year. You learn a lot about who you are and what you want in life when you get out, date around, and meet new people. After a while, though, I realized I was chasing the wrong things. Lord knows it got us into some trouble along the way too," Tysin adds.

"You guys have been talked about a lot in the media as of late," Brielle says, changing the subject. Her eyes move to each of us before landing on mine. "Is there anything you'd like to say about the rumors? Anything you'd like to clear up?"

"We've talked about this in previous interviews. It's starting to feel like the only stories that get attention are the ones painting us in a bad light," Trey shares.

"Before I started seeing Layken, I'll be the first to admit I wasn't going down a good path. I believe now that joining the band and seeing her again out on tour saved my life. I don't think the road I was going down before would've led me to a good place. I'll admit I made mistakes both before we were together and even early on. The stories about going to strip clubs and even the fight I got in back in Nashville were twisted in a way that almost seemed like they were intentionally trying to tear us apart and bring me down."

I nod. It was hard watching what Trey and Layken went through. We've had drama stirred in the media before, stories circulating about Brix stepping out on his relationship with Ivy, and even Kyla and Tysin, when Kyla's engagement to her ex, Canon, was ending.

He's in the media a lot too with his motocross career, so it added an extra layer of interest, focusing all eyes and attention on us.

Those stories were easy to shrug off. The stories about Brix were a load of bullshit. There's no way he'd ever cheat on her. Old photos resurfaced and were made to seem recent when they weren't.

As for Tysin and Kyla, it was bound to happen. News got out about Kyla's engagement ending, and it wasn't long before Tysin and Kyla were spotted together.

They fought against their feelings for years and weren't going to wait any longer. We all knew it was something we'd have to get through.

It was different for Trey and Layken. Every word posted online caused a lot of hurt between them.

"We've started to look at the people we have in our lives, who we trust and allow in our space," I add, and Brielle's eyes connect with mine. "Forgive me for how this may sound, but it's situations like this. Inviting you here, into my home, is like inviting you into my life. When you leave here, you could walk away and write whatever you want based on your opinion of us, and who knows what sort of effects that could have."

Brielle crosses her arms in her lap, her gaze roaming over my face. Something about her posture and her stoic look tells me I may have said the wrong thing.

"I'm here to do a job and do it well. Between all of us, I'm not here to get on your good side to squeeze information out of you only to smear it through headlines later. If I'm being honest, I have no interest in getting close to you at all."

She purses her lips, and my eyes lock on them. My dick hardens in my pants.

She looks like she'd get off on verbally sparring with men, destroying them into a million pieces and living off their remains for days.

Brix clears his throat, and Tysin chuckles. I want to knock their heads together and tell them to shut up.

"What's so funny?" She narrows her eyes on them, and they go silent.

"He's usually the one who manages to sweet-talk women. It's funny to watch him be put in his place for once by someone other than his sister."

"Will you shut the hell up?" I add, and Trey joins in, laughing with them.

The guy working with Brielle, I don't think I ever caught his name, leans down and whispers in her ear. She stares at the floor, as if taking in what he says, and jerks her head into a nod.

"I think that's all the questions we have for you today." She attempts to paste on a sincere smile, but I see through her phony facade.

"We would like to get a few photos of you together for the article, if that's okay?" the man says.

"Yeah, man, no problem." Brix reaches his hand out to shake his, and I hear him introduce himself as Davis.

"Actually, I'm sorry, but is it possible you could come by tomorrow instead? Something came up last minute and we'll need to wrap up." I cross my arms in front of my chest, never taking my eyes off Brielle.

She, on the other hand, looks ready to shoot daggers at me.

"We're only in town for the day. Our flight takes off tomorrow." Her jaw tightens. It's clear I'm getting under her skin.

"Great, we can plan for tomorrow before you take off. It shouldn't be a problem, right?"

Davis glances at me and over to Brielle, then back at me. I hear him mutter under his breath about how they could come over in the morning before their flight leaves.

Brielle snaps her gaze back to me. "Certainly," she replies sweetly.

Brix and Tysin snicker. Meanwhile, Trey stays silent. He's not like them and didn't grow up finding every way possible to dig in under my skin like they enjoy doing.

"We'll get packed up then and out of your way." She turns to grab a clipboard she left sitting on the chair beside her.

The guys file out of the room. I hang back, offering to help Davis.

"I'm gonna take this out to the car," Davis says, looking from me over to Brielle. "Should I meet you outside?"

Brielle nods, but I follow Davis into the entryway. It's not until he steps outside and shuts the door behind him that her voice drops low. Back to the tone she used with me when I first found her eavesdropping earlier.

"Oh, and Madden, make sure you're ready for us tomorrow. I have no interest in a do-over of today either."

ACKNOWLEDGMENTS

To my boys–I love you more than the universe. Thank you for thinking I'm cool and for being proud of mama for writing books, even though it makes me cringe to think about you telling your teachers. We'll just pretend that doesn't happen.

To my AMAZING beta readers – Kristen, Donna, Summer, April, Candyce, and Ana. Thank you for reading Trey and Layken's story before anyone else, for your honest feedback, and helping me make their story better. I'm so grateful for you! <3

Jenny Sims and Rox LeBlanc – Thank you for all your hard work on this project. You both have been so wonderful to work with and learn from. I wouldn't want to do this without you on my team!

To the fantastic bloggers and my Rebel Release Team, thank you for being a part of this one. I'm excited to hear what you think of Trey and Layken. I hope you know how grateful I am for every one of you.

My Rebels Readers – I love being able to connect with all of you in my Reader Group and across social media. Thank you for your love of this series. It's truly changed my life and I'm so thankful for you all!

Anna B. Doe – I can't tell you how much I appreciate your friendship and our chats. Thank you for always keeping it real with me. I always got your back and support you!

April – Thank you so much for being you. We've grown so close over the past few years and I'm thankful to have you and your sense of humor in my life. There's never a dull moment when we're together. I love having you as my book friend and my real friend.

Kristen – Thank you for always being honest with me, no matter what. I can always count on you to keep it real and raw with me. Even when I think every word I've written is shit, you're there to bring me back to earth. I love you!

Kate Jessop and Lyssa Cole – Thank you for your friendship and support, for checking in with me and letting me bounce ideas off you. Your friendship and support mean the world to me.

BOOKS BY BROOKE

A Rebels Havoc Series

Brix
Sins of a Rebel
Tysin
Trey
Madden

Men of Blaze

Personal Foul
Reckless Rebound (Cocky Hero Club)

Tattered Heart Duet

Torn
Tattered

A Heart's Compass Series

Where I Found You
Lost Before You
Until I Found You
Now That I Found You
Where You Belong

Standalones (In order of publication)

Wild Irish

Learn more and purchase your copy at:
www.authorbrookeobrien.com/booksbybrooke

ABOUT BROOKE

USA Today Bestselling author Brooke O'Brien writes steamy and swoon-worthy new adult romances. She's best known for her sports and rock star romances.

Brooke believes a love worth having is worth fighting for, and she brings this into her stories where her characters risk it all for love.

When she isn't writing or falling in love with a new book boyfriend, you can find her spending time with her family, cheering on her favorite sports teams, listening to ASMR, or binge-watching the latest true crime documentary. She loves rockin' a comfy hoodie with leggings and believes the best days include a good nap.

Brooke loves connecting with readers and hopes you'll join her on her social pages or reader group to stay in touch. To follow Brooke and join her newsletter, visit authorbrookeobrien.com/follow.

COPYRIGHT

Edited by Jenny Sims, Editing for Indies.
Proofread by Rox LeBlanc with Rox's Reads
Cover Design by Shanoff Designs
Version: BMO08042023

www.ingramcontent.com/pod-product-compliance
Lightning Source LLC
Chambersburg PA
CBHW060907210726
48293CB00006B/2000
9781954061330